THE PERENNIAL WAR OF PARAMOURS

ROCK KITARO

The Perennial War of Paramours

Written by Rock Kitaro (Rock Tennie)

www.StageInTheSky.com

Copyright 2023

This book is inspired by my very own paramour. She was the muse, the fire, the motivation that sent electricity through my veins whenever I felt like doing nothing, whenever I feel like taking it easy or giving up.

Table of Contents

01. Marcus Angel – Women Really Do Run the World 4

02. Elliot Chan's Story – The Green Cocktail Dress 25

03. Elliot Chan – The Network Executive 44

04. Gladys Vandelay – The Protégé 60

05. Gladys Vandelay - The Initiation 83

06. Jake Buchanan – The Hopeless Commander 104

07. Elliot Chan - Domestication 122

08. Elliot Chan – Assembly 137

09. Gladys Vandelay – A Daughter's Rage 147

10. Anna the Andalusian – The Cult 165

11. Gladys Vandelay - For the Living 188

12. Gladys Vandelay – Redemption 207

13. Gladys Vandelay – The Truth 215

01. Marcus Angel – Women Really Do Run the World

Getting shot's probably not the best way to start the story, but here goes. Streetlights. The glint from her golden earrings. The flash from her muzzle. And then I died. Even as I type this, I still can't believe it. But in the end, what I saw with my own eyes confirmed what I've suspected all along. Women really do run the world.

…

Ever since I first laid eyes on her 12 years ago, Anna Marie's held the title as the most beautiful woman I've ever seen. This includes actresses, singers, and insta-models. None of them could hold a candle to my Anna Marie.

At first glance, it didn't make sense why she was working for a start-up company to begin with. She looked like she belonged on a housewife show, lounging on some beach, or shopping it up. The way she carried herself. Her height, her posture, her physique, it was ridiculous. As if she trained her whole life to win every pageant, Anna was a stunner and she didn't even know it. Or maybe she did and just didn't care.

Back then, Anna was so bubbly and free-spirited, the type of woman who'd get out of my car at a stop light if she spotted a frozen yogurt cart on the corner. I'm not saying I like unpredictable women, but I confess there was something about her that I found superior. She lived for the here and now. She was free. Fearless. I respected it.

Thus, her association with the likes of me was a bit of a mystery in the beginning. Just to be clear, Anna was never officially my girlfriend, but someone who preferred hanging out with me as opposed to everyone else.

Sure, I made her laugh with my observations and blundering blithe. But back then, I was an overweight black guy who was too goofy and animated for his own good. I turned my back on religion and barely had a social life because I didn't drink or smoke. And more importantly, I had no direction in life, no clear or concrete goals. No purpose.

Women like Anna have a way of changing all that. You can't be with someone like her and have absolutely nothing going for you. You just can't. I realized this the first time I pushed her away. My dumbass "caught feelings" and somehow, I had the courage to just come out and tell her I loved her. I told her that to her face.

She smiled and shook her head and told me that it wasn't love but lust. She used a Spanish word to describe it. I was embarrassed and promptly walked away in the middle of the conversation while she was still talking. In hindsight, I do think I should have stayed and played out that discussion. But my heart...I was too weak.

Next came that war, the cold war of awkward tension and lovesick agony. The cliché CW show where the whole season could've ended with just one conversation. For the next few years, Anna and I would toy with each other, each trying to make the other jealous. We'd go the extra mile to outperform each other at work, each trying to rise above the other in terms of station and pay grade.

During those years, I lost over a hundred pounds. I joined a gym, worked on my cardio, and embraced a period of enlightenment, soaking in philosophy on matters that were otherwise foreign to me. Such as psychology, romanticism, politics, and cultural diversity.

Anna evolved as well. She joined a fitness boot camp. Every week it was something new. Skydiving, swimming with sharks, shooting at the gun range. I even heard she took MMA classes, which really burned in my chest, the thought of her rolling around with other dudes. Couldn't watch UFC the same way again.

And, of course, during this time Anna was rarely without a man. One after another, they came and went. Buying her flowers. Picking her up for lunch. I'd sit there in my cubicle and just take it. She'd parade them around, introducing them as if everyone in the office had magically forgotten about the last one. It hurt, but I never let her see it. And it wasn't just that she was going out with other men. It was the kind of men they were.

All of them looked like they played for the NFL. All of them looked like a million bucks, suited and booted, impressive cars, edgy cuts, thick beards or tatted up with that bold "it's all good" charisma. They all had the same bass-heavy voice and barely showed any emotion or facial expressions. They were cool, hip, and exuded an air of confidence. Alphas. The complete opposite of who I was. Call me a hater. Call me a Beta, but I knew. I knew no matter how much I bettered myself I could never be them.

For years I had to listen to Anna brag about her penthouse parties. She appeared in music videos and even modeled designer dresses at the Met Gala. The Met FREAKING Gala! She was living life in the fast lane, so far ahead of me that I couldn't keep up. I want to say that I stopped trying, but that wouldn't be true.

The thing is, I honestly believed Anna was putting on an act, a bold front for her city girls and the socialites she cavorted with. We were in our late twenties. She was a sexy Colombiana who could've had any man she wanted. Of course, she was going to run the town. Of course, she's gonna to get tagged in everyone's social media post.

But deep down I felt I knew "the real" Anna. I was there for her before she donned the skin-tight tube tops and heavy eyeliner. I saw her cry. I heard her regrets. I listened to her speak so passionately about what she wanted in life, why she lived each day to the fullest. I knew about her family, her sister, her upbringing. I knew the real Anna Marie.

Then…three years after I told her I loved her, Anna up and left. I didn't have all the details, but from what I gathered, she found another job on the West Coast. And even though she was never officially my girlfriend, we never kissed or made out or anything like that. When she left...it felt like one of my best friends had just died. I went into work the next day and was like, "now what?"

I know that might sound strange, but the mere presence of her was like a drug that stimulated me. Once she was gone, there was an empty place in my heart. I had withdrawal symptoms that left me somewhat depressed. In the three years that we worked together, I've been attracted to no one else. This woman really was the center of my universe, my drive, the source of all my ambitions. With her being gone, what's the point? Why work so hard? Why this intense focus to keep improving myself?

One day, after a couple months had gone by, I woke up and had that Peter Parker moment when I looked in the mirror and realized…I really am an impressive guy. When you're in the midst of progress, it's difficult to see how far you've come. But I really had transformed, just in time to round my thirties.

My columns now averaged over 30,000 readers. Three of which were circulated nationally and went up for awards. I used to weigh 378 pounds and now I was a solid 215 in a 6'3 frame. I could run. I could fight. My confidence was through the roof and more importantly, I reconnected with our heavenly father, reading the Bible cover to cover. It shifted my priorities and taught me to place my faith in God, not people.

And keeping my eye on the culture, I certainly saw how America changed in the two years following her departure. As a Millennial with some intelligence, I felt responsible for what was happening to my generation. They call us Snowflakes. They said we were lazy and entitled. They said most of us lived in our parent's basements, that the institution of marriage was on the decline.

But there was a silver lining, a beaming ray of light penetrating the dark clouds. That ray of light was "Progressivism." The disgruntled had voices. The special interest groups had assembled. Protests and marches galore. Everyone took to the streets demanding to be heard. And what's more surprising was not only that people were listening, they believed. I believed.

But here's the problem. Here's where I'm more or less bleeding myself as I step out into shark infested waters. What social and mainstream media had been feeding us, what they told us about what was happening in the world, it was all just an illusion. It wasn't real. It was a projected fantasy they were hoping they could make a reality by tricking the masses, by lying to us.

The reason why it worked so well in the beginning, was because people had effectively found a way to silence the opposition. Anyone who disagreed, anyone voicing a view that went against the popular opinion was labeled a racist, a bigot, sexist, or a supremacist. Their careers and reputations were ruined.

As I said…this had gone on for some time. As a minority, and worse still, a minority within a minority, I initially felt like I didn't have a leg to stand on when it came to such squabbles. I decided to make it my goal to expose these tactics and introduce a new theory of soft-core oppression that attacked free speech and essentially, free thought.

Then, last year, a string of sexual misconduct allegations toppled some of the world's foremost figures in entertainment and politics. Good, right? I had no love for the rich and famous, so screw 'em. That was my first thought. That was, until I was approached by a man in a Midtown Manhattan parking garage.

Now, I know what you're thinking. "Oh, that's cliché. And let me guess, he brings you some secret file that proves your theories were right and sparks controversy?"

Nope.

Well…maybe he was going to do all that. But before he could, he fell dead before my feet. I could still smell the blood as it misted across my lips. I couldn't believe it. I must have stood there for some time, just staring, shocked, thinking this can't be real. He was breathing one moment, walking up to me, and the next…

Red and blue lights came out of nowhere. Police cuffed and questioned me at the scene. As baffled as they were, one could only imagine my own mystification that gradually escalated into righteous indignation, a journalistic need to launch my own investigation and get to the bottom of what the fuck just happened.

The man had been shot in the back of the head, but there was no one else in the parking garage save for me. It must have come from a sniper. It was a business district and our parking garage was surrounded by high vantage points. The Chrysler and Empire State Buildings were just a stone's throw away.

I spent the weekend in police interrogation, replaying the scene over and over again. The man said his name was Terry. That's what I told the police. Terry mentioned that he had read some of my columns over the years and respected my intuition. That's what he said.

Now, maybe because it was just past midnight and as a black man in Midtown, I wasn't accustomed to being randomly approached by dudes emerging from the shadows. But what he said after that, left me puzzled. He died before he could explain, but it was enough to plant the seed.

Terry said, "What do you know about a feminist group called the Society?'

As he lay dying, even with half his brains blown out. He whispered, "our turn."

"Our turn."

My boss let me take the week off. I wasn't booked or charged with murder but remained a person of interest. The police paid me a visit every day and my story never changed. I told them the truth as I knew it. But what was the truth? What the hell was the Society? Who the hell was Terry?

I Googled "Feminist Society" and found all sorts of special interest groups. From what I read, the most prominent one involved the LGBTQ community, but not exclusively feminists. It was inclusive of Muslims and minorities, a term rising in popularity called "intersectionality".

I even went so far as to visit the main branch of the New York Public Library. I passed through Central Park and Union Square, asking every hipster and apparent lesbian about it. No one knew. It felt surreal. And it was stuck in my mind, that this man died and his last words were, "our turn."

On a Friday morning, during the police's routine visit to my apartment, again I asked them about the likelihood of a sniper. They said it would have been impossible given the trajectory.

So I said, "what if I wasn't alone in the parking garage?"

Again, they weren't buying it. Despite the fact that I had no gun residue, the fact that I never even held a gun before, the fact that cameras captured me standing in front of Terry while he was shot from behind, they were still convinced I was the killer.

Yep...Law enforcement.

I went back to the crime scene, scoured the parking garage and couldn't find a single clue. The "Society" angle was bugging me. For weeks, I was obsessed with it. I must have published over 20 articles with theories about some underground feminist movement. When I bounced opinions off my colleagues, they all thought I was jaded. There was a bunch of gas-lighting and talk of PTSD, but I couldn't blame them. Maybe I was.

Sleeping was difficult. Even in a half-sedated state, I kept hearing Terry's last words. Our turn. Our turn.

"Our turn. Our turn! OUR TURN!!!"

My eyes opened. It was the middle of the night and I had fallen asleep with the TV on, as per usual. CNN had replays of a party convention in Detroit. What I saw…it sent chills down my spine. Maybe it was because I was still groggy and the rest of my apartment was pitch black, but I could have sworn I saw someone standing in the corner of my living room. I opened my mouth to scream or call out. But what came forth was nothing short of a flat croak.

I swear I'm not crazy. The figure darted across the room like a shadow, wiping by the TV. He opened the front door and left, slamming it with a bang so loud that it sounded like a gunshot. I got up and whipped on all the lights, drenched in sweat.

"It's our turn! Now it is our turn to rise up."

I looked at the TV. The convention. The woman standing at the podium and leading the chant was none other than our first female presidential candidate to ever win the nomination for a major political party. Everyone was cheering for her as if she had already won.

I stood there baffled, cringing with fear and frustration. But it was in that moment that I was struck by an epiphany. I couldn't articulate it just yet. At that point it was just a theory, but something told me that it was in my best interest to attend the next convention and see this presidential candidate up close in person. Hopefully, I could get a chance to speak with her. Maybe she could help me.

…

The next day I had lunch with a colleague. I paid. It was a bribe to get her assignment to cover the upcoming women's convention in Louisville, Kentucky where I knew the candidate was scheduled to speak.

And there…in the midst of my promising some favor I'd never keep, after well over two years, in walked Anna back into my life.

"...oh my god..."

I literally said that out loud as if I was witnessing someone jump in front of a bus. Anna Marie. She was exactly the way I remembered in my dreams, the twinkle in her eye, the sunlight caught in her raven hair. I swear I must have seen doves fly and all of traffic lights stop at once as she crossed the street. It was weird but my mouth watered. She was smiling at me. Heading my way. She was coming to see me. I wasn't dreaming. It was real.

I stood up and waited for her to go first. She didn't. She just smiled as if…because it's not like we were on the best of terms when she left. I even remember sending her this long heartfelt text message wishing her well, and she only responded with 'K'. Now here she was, projecting such adoration.

"Why are you still so weird?" were the first words out of her mouth.

Completely flabbergasted, all I could do was laugh. I introduced my colleague and soon after, Anna and I were strolling down memory lane. It was also down a real hiking trail called Memory Lane, a brick-paved walkway through Central Park where a group of artists gathered to paint.

I asked how she'd been, keeping my questions vague, my guard up. Any attempt to show how much I still loved her would've no doubt put me in the same sunken ship that was now dredged up by her spellbinding visage. She told me she was doing well, making six figures and traveling the world as a brand-marketing consultant.

It was unexpected, how genuinely pleased I was to hear that she was doing well. I used to dream of how our reunion would go and for some reason I always pictured her on a warhorse on the other side of a battlefield. She always said she wanted to get into advertisement. To hear she had accomplished her goals, I was proud of her. Couldn't stop smiling.

"So, what brings you back to New York?"

"Wait, Marcus! I want to hear about you! What have you been up to? What's your latest?"

Do I tell her about the murder? About the PTSD or my obsession in trying to get to the bottom of this supposed Feminist group that may or may not exist?

"I started boxing." I told her. "Yeah. I had my first match a couple of months back. It was for a fund-raiser. I lost but I scored a knock down with a kidney shot. That's all I really wanted. You don't realize it, but you get gassed out pretty early. Three minutes after the first round and felt like I ran a marathon. It was ridiculous."

10

"What about your writing?" She inquired.

"What about it?"

She fumed through the nose. Just like before. It was cutest thing. I could tell she knew more than she was letting on. It wasn't difficult to find out about me. All you needed to do was enter "Marcus Angel" in any search engine. I think she expected me to be as loose-lipped as before, but what the heck. Let's test the waters once more.

"I'm looking into feminism." I told her.

"Feminism? Why? That's not your forte."

"Culture and observation is my forte. And a lot's happened recently that's got me seeking to understand the plight of our fairer sex. To be honest, I still don't even know what Feminism is. There's no concrete definition. A lot of contradictions. Three or four different waves. Some groups say it's about equality, equal pay and opportunity. Others suggest Feminism is exclusively about the betterment of women, specifically in terms of education, acceptance, and more benefits like free healthcare and contraceptives."

"You know it's more than that though," Anna began. "For years, women have been abused, oppressed, and subjected to the tyranny of men. Seen as nothing more than property or objects to cook, clean, and conceive. Not all men think like this, of course, but the men who matter set the course for those who follow. Undue concern for women leads to contempt for them. Maybe. But what's more important than that is instilling a sense of strength in a woman. Not so much, independence. But at the very least, abolishing the fear of said independence. We're not victims as the papers would have you believe. We're survivors. Embattled survivors. There's a difference."

I was blown away. Those were some deep words coming from someone who used to shake her ass in videos that would make Casanova blush. I wasn't above the idea that people could change. But still…She caught me staring. With a playful smirk, she reached over and tapped my cheek to turn me away.

"Why do you do that?" She said. "I used to hate that."

"Do what?"

"Stare at me as the thought bubbles percolate."

"I'm sorry. I'm just impressed. Back then, you seemed so superficial. But perhaps it was my own prejudice. I assumed with that body and that face, and all the dudes that flocked to you…I dunno. I always thought my deep talk used to bore the hell out you."

"It did!" she said, snorting with laughter. "But also, I dunno. I guess a lot of what you said, it kind of sank in. Whether I wanted it to or not. I also hated that. I'd be in the middle of a photoshoot thinking about your stupid theories. You have a way of doing that. Of entering the subconscious and flipping over tables."

"To dig through all the useless stuff and pull out what's important." I added.

"Yes! But there's nothing wrong with a little trivia now and then. What you call, useless. That's something I don't think you ever understood. I know you want to be a Pulitzer Prize writer or whatever but sometimes you get so bogged down on the details that you lose sight of the bigger picture and miss out on what's really important. No woman wants to feel like they're second place to a goal, Marcus. We need to feel like we are the goal."

"Anna, you were. God knows you were. For years!"

"But you gave up on me."

"I told you I loved you! How clear did I need to be? And you laughed and said that it was just lust. Then you brought all these big-ass swole dudes around me when you knew how I felt. You knew!"

"If you loved me, Marcus, you would have fought for me. You would've never let me go."

"I don't want to sound arrogant, Anna, but I'm not like these other dudes out here. I used to weigh 378 pounds. I'm six foot three. I was fucking monster. If any woman tells me no or pretends that they don't want anything to do with me, I back off. Especially now when simply making someone feel uncomfortable is considered sexual harassment in the court of public opinion."

"Yeah, but this isn't the court of public opinion, Marcus! This is me."

"I told you I loved you, Anna! If you think that was easy for me, you're out of your flippin' mind."

"Yeah, well you sure made it look easy."

"That's because I don't mess around. I don't spit game. I'm straight-forward and honest. I know that makes me sound desperate or whatever, but it's who I am. To pretend to be someone I'm not…our relationship would cast off on a ship already full of holes."

"What if I told you, I like monsters…" she said. "You've left an impression on me. I can't…I can't ever shake you. I don't think I want to."

We stopped, face to face in the middle of a scenic park under swaying branches and golden leaves. It was déjà vu. Not the first time we were caught in a standoff, lost in each other's eyes.

"Anna…" I smirked. "I'm not entirely sure if you're trying to sound romantic or soliciting medical advice."

Her smile could melt the polar ice caps. No matter how much I wanted to resist her, she was just too fucking beautiful. Like a coward, I averted my eyes. And no sooner that I did, Anna took hold of me and kissed me with a passionate release like a volcanic eruption. I felt the warm firmness of her body and I'll never forget it. I wrapped her in my arms and didn't let go.

I gave my virginity to this woman. I swore to myself that I'd wait till marriage, but Anna was my kryptonite, the one woman on earth who could break down the walls of my faith. For two months, I spent every night with her. All of my dreams, all my fantasies, all my wishes came true when I was with her. Her eyes, her lips, her smile, her voice. I remember telling her, "I don't mind dying if it's in your arms."

God do those words haunt me.

Interlude

...

Two months after our first night, I was in Louisville, Kentucky for the Women's convention. It was held in a lavish downtown theater. Twas strange, to be honest. As much as the Left bragged about diversity, I stood out like a sore thumb. I was the only black guy in the venue and just one of a few men, carving through a sea of long blonde hair. They were polite enough, but I could sense the caution. It's like being a gorilla at the zoo, they'll watch and marvel at me...but no one wants to get too close.

I found a group of thick beards lounging by the PA system. I asked if it was their first event. You know, small talk, to get them to open up and let 'em know I was a "friendly negro." Every word out of their mouth seemed programmed and rehearsed. I controlled my facial expressions and acted like it was the first time I heard the current events that they were regurgitating from the news.

Then entered the presidential candidate. The lobby erupted. It was louder than a rap concert in Harlem. I thought the chandelier was about to come crashing down the way trinkets rattled. As the huddled mass of blushed cheeks followed the candidate into the auditorium, my eyes settled on a woman in tight jeans. It happened in a split second, and I quickly darted away before anyone could catch me staring.

As I looked away, it was just by chance that I glanced up at the second-floor walkway. A velvet rope blocked the stairway entrance. In that split second, I caught sight of a shadowy figure dressed in black with their hand resting on the banister. The figure moved behind a pillar and into a hallway that was out of view. Damned intuition. I was compelled to follow.

For a man of my height, it was easy to step over the velvet rope while everyone else was still distracted. Borrowing the persona of a security guard, I hurried up the steps but not too fast. Dutifully, as if it was my job to go up and check on something. Approaching a corner, I backed against the wall and peeked around.

Five of the most stunning women I'd ever seen were standing in a circle just as a sixth was joining them. They weren't wearing black robes with hoods as I initially thought. They all looked like businesswomen, dressed in black corporate attire, projecting strong confidence in the boldness of their eyes and the firm posture by which they stood.

I began to slouch, lowering to a crouch, my eyes hooded in suspense. One was black, one was Asian, and the other four were white. It was a team. No doubt about it. They spoke in low discreet whispers with this serious disposition as if they were about to pull off a heist. For all I knew, it could have been someone's security detail. But my intuition was telling me, as always, to be silent and observe.

They started walking my way. My heart skipped a beat, it was so abrupt. I turned to go back the way I came but I saw three more ladies, all dressed in black, heading my way from the staircase. They were about forty paces out and in plain view. They could have seen me. They should have seen me. But they didn't. A pamphlet in their hands kept their attention while I dashed into the nearest room and locked the door behind me.

I found myself now in the middle a ballroom donning the glitz and glamour of the Grand Old South. Wooden floors, burgundy drapes, a grand piano, and paintings of old men in antebellum suits, I wandered amidst it all as the sweat mounted under my collar.

The doorknob rattled. I looked around. There was nowhere I could hide my tall frame except for the piano. I raced for it and slid to my knees like I was leaping over the hood of a car, scurrying to the other side of the piano before tucking into a fetal position between the piano and the wall with my head just peeking around the keys.

The door opened. Clacking heels sounded like drops of hail on the hardwood floors. There were nine of them. They entered and huddled around as if they couldn't wait to get down to business.

"How long is it going to take her?" said one with fiery eyes and a bob cut.

"Soon, Scarlet. First thing's first. What happened at Berkley?" said the ringleader.

The dour mood soured further. Some put their hands on their hips. Others looked away. Breanne. The leader's name was Breanne.

Scarlet had the bob cut with heavy red eye shadow. I could tell she was fearless and wasn't about to back down from a damn thing. Breanne had dark hair with dazzling blue eyes. Her voice was naturally loud, clear, and eloquent. They weren't standing in a perfect circle, but it was clear that they rallied around Breanne.

The black woman, named Celeste, she spoke and said, "According to my contacts, everything went according to plan...but the protests and riots got out of hand. You know how the campuses are these days. It's a powder keg. Once they started setting fires, the police got involved. There was no way we could've gotten to the speaker without being compromised."

"I would've gotten to him," said Scarlet. "If we sent a full-fledged sword in the first fucking place this wouldn't even be a discussion. We gave Celeste a chance with her piece of shit contacts. She blew it. Let me take the first flight out. I'll kill him and be back in time for..."

"Scarlet!" Mandee shushed.

In a flash of caution, Breanne whipped her cold eyes around the room in a scanning sweep. I had no idea what the hell was going on. But in that moment, I felt my phone slipping out of the fabric of my pocket. I took it out and pressed record on the camera.

Here, I recorded all nine women. Four had their backs to me. I had a side profile of Breanne and Celeste. But Scarlet...that harpy was facing my way. It made the hair on the back my neck stand on end.

"We can't have you flying out to California, Scarlet. I need you in New York. Things are going to get worse before they get better." Breanne said.

"What do you mean?" asked another.

Breanne sighed. "Contrary to the polls, more and more it's looking like we're going to lose this one. That orange clown is going to take the White House. We need to start making preparations for our next phase."

"What!?"

"We spent millions on Hollywood!"

"What about the incriminating tape from the bus?"

"What about all that crap we planted with the Russians?"

"Looks like the FBI's sitting on it." Breanne explained. "Look, don't worry. I'll deal with the director myself. In the meantime, we have to face the facts. We've lost this one. I have to explain what happened to the Twelve Chairs. Ladies, all of us are still young. There will be other elections. But for our seniors, they've endured so much for nearly half a century. They've been waiting their entire lives for this moment, their entire lives to see a woman in the White House and we blew it. We pandered to the wrong groups. Millennials are idiots. And Hollywood's so blinded by money that they could care less about any cause or conviction."

"As expected," Celeste quipped.

Breanne squinted. "Excuse me?"

"I told you that pandering to the minorities and special interest groups was a waste of time. Political correctness, social justice, it's just a fad. I was against it from the start. We underestimated the silent majority. Whether we believe it or not, it does exist. You don't oust people from power. You use them!"

Breanne's lips tightened. "I don't disagree with you, Celeste, but you're crying over spilled milk. We cut our losses and continue to move forward. Get rid of all loose ends. I mean it. Nothing's guaranteed. That's why we have contingencies. And you'll do well to keep that ego of yours in check."

Celeste turned away.

Scarlet was emotional, the frustration apparent. "We have to make this right! We owe it to the Society to make up for our failure."

"Speak for yourself, Scarlet. I did not fail!" Celeste snapped.

"Enough!"

Just as Breanne was raising her voice, Scarlet moved to shove Celeste against the wall with a knife to her throat. Celeste was trying to push away but Scarlet was leaning in with all her strength like a defensive tackle. It was scary intense. I thought Scarlet was going to slit her throat the way they thrashed about. Celeste didn't scream or beg her to stop. Everyone just stood around watching like it was a gang initiation.

"You're starting to try my last nerve." Scarlet growled.

Celeste smirked and spit in her face. Their struggle intensified before Breanne finally nodded for the others to casually walk over and separate the two.

Then the door opened. One of the men I was talking to earlier had entered with a bewildered expression. Breanne threw a judgmental glance at the other women before approaching the man.

"Oh! I'm sorry. I thought I heard a commotion and figured I'd just check…HUP!"

Before the man could finish Breanne yanked him into the room sliced her bracelet across his neck. It was unreal. I watched as a painful grimace stretched across the man's face. He dropped to his knees and plopped chest down on the floor as blood drained from his neck.

As calm as she appeared, I knew Breanne was furious. She stood in place for no less than ten seconds, staring at the body before she slammed the door shut and locked it.

"Code 78. Do it please." She instructed.

Just like that, Celeste immediately shed her contention with Scarlet and whipped out her phone. The other women rolled up their sleeves as they huddled around the man's body, checking his pockets, collecting his fingerprints, and snapping photos from every angle. Meanwhile, I was petrified, my heart beating like a kick drum.

"Yes, is this the stage manager?" Celeste said in a country accent. "Listen here. I planted a bomb under the stage. If you whores think you can come in my county and indoctrinate our wholesome women with your immoral, wicked, and ungodly ways, you got another thing coming. You sum' of bitches got three minutes to evacuate the building. If anyone dies, the blood on yer' hands."

With that, Celeste and two others left. Already, I could hear the panic from the lobby with the opening and closing of the doors. Then, three more women entered. These newcomers were in casual clothes as if they had been part of the audience. They brought heavy-duty trash bags and a caddy with cleaning supplies. There was no emotion. It was like routine. The man was still alive and bleeding out. I saw his feet twitching.

Scarlet and Breanne had the man's wallet. They exchanged a look of disappointment and stepped away from the group, coming closer my way.

"That was Terry's brother. Fucking loose ends! I knew we should have dealt with him too. We need to burn down this venue. At the very least, this ballroom." Scarlet suggested.

Breanne nodded, sighed, and whispered, "I'm only barely containing my rage right now. These mistakes are adding up. They're hurting us. They're hurting me."

"Then enough with the games." Scarlet said in fiery whispers. "Enough with the manipulation. Enough with the incentives of wealth and power. I say we move to instill fear in these motherfuckers. The Society is not to be trifled with. A sword once drawn must taste blood before returned to its sheath. The wheel will never be broken."

Breanne looked as if she was strongly considering Scarlet's words. The women dragged Terry's brother away from the door and onto the outstretched trash bags. They emptied bottles of cleaner on him, one after the other. I couldn't stop staring. The ammonia was intoxicating.

"And if you ask me, I say we start with the Andalusian."

"Scarlet, don't…"

"She's still technically an outsider. She still hasn't finished her initiation. It's been two years!"

"She's one of our best operatives. If it wasn't for her…"

"I get it! But the girls are talking. It's not fair that we had to kill our men, while hers is still alive and kickin'. You know what kind of message that sends."

"She'll do it," Breanne asserted.

"And if she doesn't?"

"Then I'll kill him myself."

My palms were damp with sweat. The phone slipped from my hands and hit the floor with a hard clack. Just as my eyes widened with horror, Scarlet stomped at the piano bench, slamming it against my wrist and the wall. I shouted in excruciating pain. The jig was up.

I never knew what they meant by "adrenaline kicking in," but I shit you not, pure adrenaline had kicked in. I just went into autopilot. I can't explain it. The throbbing pain in my wrists acted as an ignition switch by which my motor skills fired on all cylinders.

One hand picked up the phone while the other shoved the piano bench back towards Scarlet. I saw a glimpse of Breanne's soul-piercing eyes from up close and I swear it was like staring into the face of a lion, the furl of her nostrils, the rage shaking the bangs of her long black hair. She ran at me with a quickness and I damn near dislocated my knee trying to jolt up to a full stand.

Breanne threw two punches. I dodged the first, but her right cross hit me like a baseball bat. Thankfully I stayed upright with wobbly momentum carrying me closer to the door. I eventually took off in a full sprint, stopping just for a second to see if I had grabbed my phone. It was sheer dumb luck. I had stopped just in time to avoid a dagger Scarlet had just flung at me. It struck the wall before my eyes, so I thought, "screw the phone" and raced for the exit.

I barged out the door. Two ladies were on the ground. Apparently, they were guarding the door when I came barging out. Scarlet and Breanne were charging like the special teams from a kickoff and Celeste was dashing up the stairs to my left.

In an act of sheer desperation, I leaped over the second floor banister. My foot caught the railing and I plummeted into the lobby, crashing through a foldable table full of bottled waters and white linens. Everyone was in full evacuation mode. And oddly enough, I didn't feel a thing. I rolled to my feet and kept moving.

Sharp zips passed by my ears like angry gnats when suddenly people started to topple over. Screams screeched and I saw the blood splattered over white shirts and horrified faces. I knew. I didn't have to look. Someone was shooting at me. I just kept moving towards the front doors until finally I was out in the middle of downtown Louisville.

The police had showed up and formed a perimeter, but by then, I was couple of blocks away. I got in my rental and just sat there drenched in sweat, my body sweltering even though it was freezing outside. The state of disbelief was monumental. It felt like an elaborate prank as if they knew I entered the ballroom, as if they knew I was hiding, and they killed that guy just to fuck with me.

I started the car and drove just a few blocks down the street where my hotel was, still downtown. It was a historic hotel, complete with a grand atrium, bellhops, and concierges at every turn. I was so traumatized that I didn't want to turn my back to any woman. I distinctly remember a team of female basketball players lounging by the bar in their jumpsuits. One of them waved at me with a wink and a smile and I must have just stared at her as if she had three heads.

I've never been so nervous in my life. My head was throbbing. The pain from Breanne's punch and falling through a table gradually settled in. I couldn't hear anything. Not the running water from the fountain. Not the ambiance music. Not the scores from the TV set. Nothing.

I remember hunching over in the elevator lobby as I waited for the doors to open. I thought I was about to have a heart attack or a stroke. There was this dense fog clouding my vision, a side effect of the migraine, I thought.

It wasn't until I got in my hotel room and sat down at the table that I calmed down and had a moment to process. I had just witnessed a murder. My prints were everywhere. I had to report it to the authorities.

I reached into my pocket and there it was. My cell phone.

…

It was no prank. When Terry's brother entered the room, Breanne slit his throat with some razor on her bracelet. I covered my mouth in horror as I watched the recording, seeing Terry's sick and twisted expression.

"Shit man…" I whispered over a clenched fist. Keeping oxygen in my lungs was somewhat of a task. That, and fighting off the urge to puke my guts out all over the carpet.

The Society…

"Who the hell are you people!?" I whispered.

BAM BAM

My eyes darted to the two hard slapping knocks coming from the door and for some reason I looked at the window too, as if someone was about to come crashing in by repelling from the roof. I didn't have to answer it. I came to Louisville by myself. Maybe it was the hotel staff? Or one of the female basketball players coming to try her luck? More than likely, it was the police. So, I hid my phone in a slot by the AC unit before heading for the door.

I remember looking through the peephole and nothing could have prepared me for the stupid panic attack that scathed across my chest. It was Anna. My Anna. Anna Marie. The Anna Marie who strutted back into my world just three months earlier.

She knew I was going to be in Louisville, but I never told her which hotel. Now here she was standing outside my very door, dressed in professional black corporate attire, same as those cold-blooded bitches who murdered Terry's brother. I stood there, petrified as if my brain was still in the process of rebooting.

Before I knew it, Anna kicked the door in, and it smashed into my face.

I staggered back, gripping my nose as she entered with this grim disposition.

"We need to talk," she said.

I look at the nightstand and rushed for the landline. She charged over and tackled me against the bed. My head hit the nightstand and we tangled up. I double-hooked her arms to swing her off of me, but she did the same and swung me away from the phone. While I had superior upper body strength, Anna was a dancer. She used those powerful hind legs to pick me up and propel me backwards into the bathroom.

We went crashing through the doors like two bears fighting over territory. She kept mumbling something, but I was genuinely frightened for my life. I tried to use the sink to pull myself up, but she pulled me back down. The side of my head hit the edge of the toilet.

"STOP!" she shouted as if she wasn't the one whoopin *my* ass.

I didn't stop. I didn't want to die, not in a bathroom in the middle of Kentucky. I confess, I was fighting her with the same maximum effort I would've towards a man. Not that it did any good. I was throwing jabs and uppercuts that she parried and slapped away as if she was playing with a toddler. She threw haymakers and elbows that connected and rattled my frame. She was properly trained, and I was outmatched. But I couldn't give up. I didn't want to die.

I swung for her face, giving it all I got. She caught my arm, pinned it against the sink counter, popping it out of place like snapping a branch from a tree. I must have screamed so loud. The intense fiery pain burst from my arm like boiling acid within.

She put me in a headlock and after grappling for some time, I finally took the shower curtains and wrapped it around her head. Hooking her with my good arm and a last burst of strength, I forced her out of the bathroom and slung her across the bed.

She went rolling. I went running.

I heard her shouting my name as I dashed down the hallway. I ran for the stairwell at the end of the hall and just as I came within twenty paces of it, two ladies in black pantsuits exited the stairwell doors. They whipped out guns but before they were able to take aim, two shots crackled out. The ladies fell and I turned around to see it was Anna with a Glock in her hands, chasing me like a leopard hunting down wounded prey.

I gimped into the stairwell and used my belt to latch the door handle to the knob of a nearby gas pipe. As soon as I did, Anna banged against the door. I never thought I'd be so terrified of that beautiful face. I limped down the stairs, floor by floor. Each step I took sent shooting pain from my shoulder down to my spine.

Entering the lobby, confusion hit. It seemed more packed than earlier and it was getting late. The basketball team was still there by the bar. They were all staring at me. The two female receptionists were staring at me. The female concierges, the female bartenders, the females with male companions in the lounge…everyone stopped and stared at me.

The elevator chimed.

At once, almost all fifty women in this hotel lobby took action. The entire basketball team charged at me like a herd of bulls. The receptionists had shotguns. The concierges pulled knives from their hair and the lady escorts with male companions were flipping over couches and chairs to come at me.

I'm not lying. I know all this sounds crazy. But as soon as that elevator chimed, it was like a dam had burst and over fifty ferocious faces flooded me at once.

I ran as fast as I could for the front entrance, but it hurt so bad. I was out of breath. My legs felt like they were weighed down.

A shotgun blast tore into a support column directly in my path. I spun as an eruption of rocks and wood sprayed and scraped across my face. One of the basketball players shoulder-checked me and I went crashing through a window, falling at least six feet onto the sidewalk outside.

Bystanders gawked as I was writhed on a bed of broken glass and cold cement. I looked down past my boots to see women pouring out of the hotel. I cringed, clinging to the God given inclination to survive, prompting me to bypass common sense and stagger into busy traffic.

In the middle of downtown Louisville, I hobbled across a six-lane street as cars blurred by, the wind drift, tugging me along like a leaf caught in a current. Horns blared and brakes squealed. It was hopeless but I kept going, one step at a time, bleeding, and clutching to my dislocated arm.

Then, just as I was one lane away from the other side, I turned with one eye open. The women from the hotel were staying put. They had formed a line, standing abreast in front of the hotel as if…dare I say, they were merely commissioned to bear witness to my execution.

A black SUV with tinted windows hit me dead on. I felt my shins and knees shatter like graham crackers. My organs exploded within. I was launched fifteen feet before skidding into a gutter.

Half-submerged in filth, piss, and rainwater…I watched as the woman of my dreams approached and stood over me with the city lights behind her. Anna Marie aimed her gun and fired twice. Once in the chest, once in the neck. My mouth gaped open as my head went limp and slumped over.

Then, she walked back to the SUV entered with Scarlet behind the wheel and Breanne in the passenger side. Don't ask how I was able to observe this. Just know that I did. The SUV accelerated. Scarlet intentionally drove up on the curb and the right front tire came inches from grazing me. She missed my head but crushed my arm that was already dislocated.

That's the last I remember. I survived, clearly. But how, why, and how long I've been out, it's all still a mystery to me. The only thing painfully clear is that the love of my life tried to kill me. The love of my life.

And as soon as I get out of this place, I'm going to find her. This isn't over.

- The Perennial War of Paramours -

02. Elliot Chan's Story – The Green Cocktail Dress

"When I count to ten, I want you to open your eyes. Tell me what you see. One. Two. Three. Four. Five. Six. Seven. Eight. Nine. Ten. Elliot, open your eyes. Tell me what you see."

"It's dark. Like nighttime. There's a light to my left. The TV's on. Everything's grainy like the Zapruder film but I see the semblance of an American flag. I'm sitting low on the floor. I don't like this."

"It's okay, Elliot. It's okay. Don't be afraid. This is why we're here. Confront this. You are not alone."

I was sitting back with my eyes closed but my mind open. My palms were sweaty. I didn't want to see it, but she was right. It would never end if I didn't go through with it.

"Tell me what you see," she prodded.

"I see a fat man sitting down in a loveseat. He's in a white shirt, black pants, big belly. He's bleeding. He's bleeding out. He's twitching. The handle of a knife is sticking out of his chest and I'm just sitting here watching. What is this?"

"Keep watching," she said.

"I'm not doing anything! I'm just sitting here. It's the same as before! Nothing's changed."

"Keep watching!"

"Wait…" I gasped. "Someone just walked by. A green dress. High heels glistening from the light. I smell her, her scent. Looks like she just came back from a cocktail party or something.

"She's walking towards the man. She's standing there. The man, he's…he's struggling to look up at her. I hear him. He's wheezing. What's he saying? OH! She just grabbed the knife! She's shoving it deeper into his chest. Dude! What the hell is this?! He fell back! She literally just shoved the knife so hard he fell out of his chair. She's screaming. She's screaming as she's stabbing the hell out of him! I can't do this!"

"Keep going."

"This is messed up!"

"Keep going!"

"No!"

"You've come so far, Elliot! See it through. You're the only one who can!"

"There's nothing… She stopped. She's getting up, standing over the dude's body. Man, there's blood everywhere. It's pooling around her heels. Oh my god, she's walking my way. I see the knife. It's drenched. I can't make out her face. Not enough light from the TV. Long dark hair. Still clenching the knife. It's completely drenched."

"Don't be afraid."

I don't remember if it was Dr. Wilkerson or the killer who told me that, but at that point, I was out of breath.

"Go on, Elliot."

"She drops the knife." I continue. "It hits the floor. She's walking away. I turn to watch her go but I can't see her anymore. I just hear the heels popping in the distance."

"And the knife?" Dr. Wilkerson asked.

"I don't pick it up. I don't do anything. I just sit there. Like a dumbass."

Finally, I opened my eyes to the ceiling. Dr. Wilkerson's nodding, seemingly proud. Of course, I didn't particularly feel accomplished. I wasn't fulfilled and I for damn sure wasn't satisfied.

"How do you feel?" She asked.

"Not good, doc. Not good at all."

"Before we entertain the possibility that this actually happened, is there any chance you saw this before? On TV or in a movie?"

"Ma'am, I saw Scarface and Goodfellas when I was six. This doesn't even compare."

"Where are you going? You have thirty minutes left in the session."

"Doc, I really appreciate everything you've done. Truly, today was a breakthrough. I'll follow up next week. I promise."

I was halfway out the door when she tugged on my sleeve and said with caring, compassionate eyes, "You really do need to talk about what you saw."

"Ma'am, I just did."

…

This all began because of a reoccurring nightmare that decided to hit not long after I entered film school. I understood the neighborhood of Chelsea tended to have that effect on impressionable artists, but this was different. New York was supposed to be a place where I could shed off the past and make a fresh start. But no matter where I went. The unanswered questions lingered like a chronic illness. There's no vaccine for what I had.

I was walking past the hipster boutiques when I felt a vibration in my pocket. It was Marvin, my dad, giving me a call.

"Yo!"

"Hey, son, how'd it go?"

I sighed before changing directions on a course for Washington Square. It's a park in the Village known for its rip-off of the Arc de Triumph.

"Dad…I have something to ask and I think it's about time."

He's groaned. I got the feeling he knew exactly where this conversation was going.

"Dad…who are my real parents?"

After a long pause, he said, "Elliot, I think it's time for you come home for a visit."

"Yep. Was thinking the same."

…

Killeen, a flat sun-blasted city in the middle of Texas where it rained very little and everything was painted the color of sand. It's here that I spent most of my childhood.

Marvin Burroughs was a retired drill sergeant from Fort Hood, having served in the Gulf War. His wife, Sandra, was a city administrator. They're good people. I couldn't have hoped for better adoptive parents.

There's just one thing. They're white and it was more than apparent that I'm East Asian. I would've said Japanese or Korean, but the truth was I had no clue. The questions, the unanswered truths. It really was like a chronic cold. It'd hit me with this unshakeable depression for days before I built the immunity to shrug it off. But it never completely went away. The questions would keep come back. The sudden onset of reoccurring nightmares was just a tipping point.

They greeted me with warm hugs and kisses, asked about campus life and if I've met someone yet. It was always the same. I told them I was progressing but in order to have someone love me I must love myself. How could I love myself if I didn't know "myself"?

I literally ask them that. Then the mood sobered, and we got to the crux of the visit. Marvin went to his storage closet, pushing aside old uniforms to pull out a wooden trunk. That trunk…I remember dad being territorial about it growing up. I always assumed it was where he kept his guns. And I wasn't wrong but there was more.

I was on the edge of my seat as he brought the trunk out into the living room. Sharon held my hand. I sensed trepidation and so badly I wanted to tell her that nothing would change how I felt about them, but I wasn't sure how true that would've been.

So, let me stop here to explain something real quick...

Growing up the only Asian at a school in the middle of Texas was probably about as stressful as being the only Christian in ISIS. It was diverse on the military bases because we had all kinds of ethnicities transferring in and out every year. But Marvin retired when I was in fifth grade and we were forced to relocate to the civilian life of Killeen.

Everyone made fun of my slanted eyes and how short and scrawny I was. In Texas, it wasn't about how cute you were. The anime, kawaii phase hadn't kicked in just yet. The girls were like lions. They only went for the biggest and the strongest. I was called everything from Jackie Chan to Bruce Lee and eventually they started calling me a Power Ranger because I learned karate to defend myself.

Marvin did his best to inject some masculinity in me. He took me out on hunts and encouraged me to study kung-fu flicks since I had a passion for Hong Kong cinema. But being different was abysmal. I sucked at math, I couldn't draw, and my interest in anime was only so-so. I was called gay so many times that I was starting to think I actually was.

28

Marvin opened the chest with a cloud of dust percolating in the sunrays from the windows. He looked at me, expecting me to dive in but I didn't. Not at first. There was a box of bullets stacked on one side. Then I saw documents. Adoption papers. My heart was about to burst.

As soon as I reached in, something caught my attention. It was a dated newspaper with the headlines, "Baby Found Covered in Blood". The browning newspaper felt hard and brittle like it was about to crumble in my fingers. A picture of a baby crying on the sidewalk was on the front cover.

"Is this me?"

Sharon covered her mouth as the tears started to flow. That answered my question.

According to the article, the baby was found a block away from a mansion that burned down in an upscale suburb outside Dallas. Firefighters found it. Paramedics were already on the scene. The coroner pulled a man's body from the rubble. Everything was burned to the ground. Pictures, any trace of culture or evidence that I would've loved to get my hands on went up in smoke that night.

Apparently, Marvin and Sharon were visiting their own family in the area when they saw the article and felt compelled by their Christian duty to take me in.

Reading that article was heavy. My eyes glossed over with tears as the paper slipped from my hands. I didn't know what to say.

"You alright, son?" Marvin asked.

"Was the deceased my father?"

"We believe so."

"Do you know if he had any stab wounds?"

Marvin looked puzzled. "I don't know. The body was badly burned beyond recognition. I doubt they were able to determine his exact cause of death. The house was registered to a Richard and Michelle Chan. So, we named you Elliot Chan. We believe the deceased was Richard. No word on your mother."

"What does that mean?! I mean, where is she?"

Marvin shook his head. "Don't know. We're not even sure if Michelle is her real name. You have to understand, when the Chinese immigrated to the Americas, it wasn't uncommon to have their names changed to sound more Western."

"So basically, what you're telling me is that my real father's dead and there's no way to find out about my real mother?"

"Not sure what to tell you, son."

"Alright. Well, who was this Richard guy? What did he do? He must've been rich to be living in this big mansion, right?"

"I um…" Sharon said as she moved so close that we touched knees. She rummaged through the storage trunk, searching for something.

"I actually did some digging about him. He worked as a translator for the Peace Corp. He traveled the world, going into war torn countries to promote peace, and third-world development. His parents, your grandparents were activists in China. They were actually part of the Tibetan Uprising in 1959. They're still considered dissidents by the government. I think that's kinda groovy. Something to be proud of."

She handed me a copy of Richard's passport photo. He was a bit rounder in the face, but it was him, the man in my nightmares. Yet, oddly enough, I smiled.

"You're right, mom. That is groovy. I just wish I knew more about my biological mother. There's something I'm not telling you. I want to tell you but it's crazy. It sounds crazy."

"Well, it can't be more absurd than finding a baby covered in blood, just crying on the sidewalk." Sharon pointed out.

"Yeah, I suppose. Um, I finally took you up on your advice and spoke to a therapist."

"About the nightmares?" Sharon asked.

"Yes. She put me in this half meditational state to relive the nightmare and see it all the way through. But still, to think I was just a baby. How is it possible that I remember all that?"

"What did you see, son?" Marvin asked.

"I saw Richard bleeding out in a chair. I think I was in the house before it burned down. I think…God…I think it was his wife, my mother who killed him."

"Oh my goodness! That's terrible." Sharon gawked.

"Yeah, you ain't just whistling Dixie." I sighed, raising up to stand. "All of this is pretty heavy, man. I mean…armed with this knowledge, what do I do?"

"Are you still having the nightmares?" Sharon asked.

"No."

"Then I say problem solved. You have to put the past behind you. That's my recommendation. Now then! I'm going to go get dinner started." She said before giving me another hug.

She kissed me and told me how proud she was for overcoming the obstacle. The thing was, I didn't fully overcome the obstacle. For crap's sake, I just told them that I thought my mother killed my father. And what, I'm supposed to just leave it at that?

She went off into the kitchen and I didn't stop her. I slowly turned to my dad and let my low brows do the talking. He understood. Marvin motioned for me to approach. He was discreet and it almost made me chuckle. Like when he used to let me have candy before dinner when mom said no.

"You understand what I'm saying, right? Like, I'm not crazy for wanting to get to the bottom of this, am I?"

"El, serving in the military, you see all kinds of shit. None of it good. And even when you return from the front lines it still haunts you. For you to see what you saw at so young an age…God have mercy."

Marvin stretched his neck to peek into the kitchen. Mom was hard at work boiling spaghetti and preparing sauce from scratch.

"You want to talk about crazy, after Sharon and I finalized the adoption process, something happened. I was attacked. On base. You know how Fort Hood is. Coming after a drill sergeant, you're asking for a world of hurt. But there were four of them. All dressed in black fatigues. And Elliot, they were women.

"I've fought the Taliban. I've dealt with insurgents in Yemen and even learned Savate from French Special Forces. I got my ass handed to me that night. And to be honest, they didn't need all four to do it. I couldn't touch 'em. It was the worst beating of my life."

"You know that sounds ridiculous, right? Four women out of nowhere just up and kicked the shit out of you? Does mom know?"

"Told her it was a training accident. An IED backfired."

"IED? Are you serious? Like, there's medical documentation to prove all this?"

"Oh yeah. Ruptured spleen. Cracked ribs. The whole nine yards."

I can't imagine how bewildered my expression was.

"Listen, son. Whoever these women were, they weren't military. They had better training. There was an aggression unlike anything I ever seen. Beat me to an inch of my life until someone told them to stop."

"Someone told them to stop?"

"I was curled up against the Jeep when she came. Another woman. Wearing high heels and a green dress."

"Green dress?! Are you sure? How do you know if you were beat up?"

"Son, she was beautiful. When you think you're about to die, there are few quintessential things you'd remember. Things like that. The four kicking my ass feared her. Stood at attention for her. The woman in the green dress stood over me. Said something in broken English but I was able to make it out. It was simple. She said, 'he dies, you die.' Elliot, I think that was your mother."

…

I flew back to New York a new man. I still had questions but at least I had clues, a map, a direction to go in. I attended classes, maintained grades, and filmed content for a website to make ends meet, but all my free time was devoted to the mystery of my mother.

If Marvin was right, then my biological mother sounds like a flipping force of nature. It's messed up that she killed my father but oddly enough, I was kinda over that. I just wanted to find out who she was, why she abandoned me. If she knew Marvin and Sharon had custody of me, had she been keeping tabs on me all these years?

As crazy as it sounds, I started doing research on secret military groups. I looked up the Black Ops from the CIA, Delta Forces from JSOC, the KGB, MI6, even China's Ministry of State Security. The world was full of paramilitary groups and privatized organizations, more or less straddling the fence of what's considered legal since everyone's always skirting protocols established by the Geneva Convention.

The strangest thing was Marvin getting manhandled by a bunch of women who he claimed were better fighters. Was it possible that there exists an exclusive all-female team of elite soldiers? I looked into it.

In Libya, there were the "Revolutionary Nuns" who were famous for being the tough-as- nails bodyguards assigned to protect Muammar Gaddafi. Out of Russia there was a battalion known for their beauty and bravery in airborne insertions. Russia also had a secret group working with the Spetsnaz to conduct spy missions across the globe.

The Middle East had a bunch of all-female combat units, but not with enough resources to be a global scale. I found out about a Chinese group of female-led Special Forces through Youtube. And one can't forget the gorgeous ladies of the Israeli Defense.

And yet...I wasn't impressed. Something about these groups lacked a certain sophistication, a certain authority of domineering and overpowering the way dad conveyed. High heels and a green cocktail dress. I couldn't help but smile thinking about it. With each passing day, the legend of my mother grew in my own mind. I felt like the son of a Greek goddess. Sounds silly, but I felt special.

Interlude

...

Three years a later, I was a senior finishing my last semester of college. The world had changed. Can't say for better or worse. It was an election year. Everyone was so excited to have the first female president. I didn't consider myself political, or rather, I tried not to be. But it was everywhere. You couldn't escape it. You couldn't be neutral. Not in New York City. Everywhere I went, the subway, the coffee shops, the park, there were demonstrations, rallies, and protests out the yin-yang.

It was in your face. I couldn't just go about my day. They forced me to care or else I'd run the risk of being called intolerant or a bigot. So...I pretended to be a Liberal just to fit in with my classmates. I wore effeminate clothes, demanded women got paid the same as men, produced short films mocking the NRA, and even lashed out at everyone shouting "All Lives Matter" at the BLM rallies.

Truth was...I didn't care. I was just playing the game to win. Marvin and Sharon sacrificed a lot, too much to get me into film school and I owed it to them to see it through to completion.

Spring break, two months before I was set graduate and the thought of it almost brought me to tears. Not because I'd have to say goodbye to campus life and the friends who only knew who I pretended to be. But because it felt like I wasted so much time, weekends, vacations, all in the futile pursuit of my mother. This was time I could have spent going to parties, getting laid, finding that special someone, networking for a future career.

I had my whole life ahead of me, sure. But when a chapter of your life is drawing to a close...there's this dread, this fear that overtakes you. It's like you're running out of time. Maybe it's irrational, maybe it's not. But in the back of my mind, I began to wonder if I'd go on spending the rest of my life searching for something I'd never find. In that sense, I'd always be alone. And I was tired of being alone.

It was that Friday on Spring Break, in the library where I spent most of my free time reading all kinds of books about Feminism and secret societies like the Illuminati. It was then that I came across an editorial piece written by a journalist named Marcus Angel. It was called, "Women Really Do Run the World."

I clicked on it. This guy...First off, by no means would I describe myself as a Men's Rights Activist or someone who empathizes with the plight of men. I just wanted to find my mother. Didn't give two shits about the battle of the sexes, I really didn't. But this article. It piqued my interest.

Marcus theorized that there was this underground society of Feminists who were hell-bent on taking over the country. He asserted that they had infiltrated nearly every facet of society that dictated culture and policy. According to Marcus, the earliest forms came from the suffragettes. But before that, there was the Temperance Movement following the Civil War. He believed that these movements were early prototypes that grew into the highly advanced society of Feminists that now ruled the world.

According to him, this organization orchestrated the overthrow of some of the most influential men in the world. CEOs, politicians, actors, studio heads, generals, kings, and presidents. They've conquered them all by means of seduction, blackmail, data manipulation, public opinion, and even instigated wars.

Seemed far-fetched and it was a gutsy move, writing this article. I spent the rest of the weekend researching his claims about the suffragettes and the Temperance league and at last, I was impressed. Allow me to explain.

In the wake of the Civil War, alcohol consumption reached an all-time high. Vets struggled to find work. European immigrants came off the boat taking all the jobs. So, the old Union boys found solace in the bottle. And when they were all liquored up, they'd come home and take out their frustrations on their loved ones. We're talking bare-knuckle abuse on a nightly basis. Women lived in perpetual fear in a world where the law did very little to protect them. So, women took action to protect themselves.

Thus, came the genesis of the Women's Christian Temperance League. Now these ladies were truly bad-ass. It began in 1873, but within twenty years, their membership ballooned up to 200,000. Their earliest members would go from saloon to saloon chest-bumping with bigger, scarier dudes, demanding they dumped their alcohol.

They were chased out of town on numerous occasions, sure, but they kept coming back. I heard one saloonkeeper even aimed a cannon at the group and a woman just jumped and sat on the cannon, still screaming for him to get rid of his spirits. Fucking hilarious.

In 1868, Elizabeth Cady Stanton said this at a convention in Washington:

"Manhood suffrage,' or a man's government, is civil, religious, and social disorganization. The male element is a destructive force, stern, selfish, aggrandizing, loving war, violence, conquest, acquisition, breeding in the material and moral world alike discord, disorder, disease, and death."

Strong words. I began to think Marcus was right. Women are more powerful than the "fairer sex" seemed to suggest. It was women of the Temperance movement that led to Prohibition in the 1920s. And it was women that repealed it, led by Pauline Sabin in 1929.

By the end of Spring Break, my brain was fried. After deliberation, I decided to look up this Marcus Angel. He was based here in New York so it shouldn't have been too difficult to arrange a sit down. But, as with all my pursuits…

I went to his office in the Flatiron District. As soon as I entered, I could sense despair. Everyone got defensive as soon as I dropped his name. His editor came out of an office, glaring at me like I wrote a hit piece about them.

"Hey, look. If Marcus isn't in, I can come back later?" I told them.

"Who're you with, kid?"

"Nobody! I'm just film student about to graduate."

"How do you know Marcus?"

He was interrogating me in the middle of the bullpen with ten sets of eyes on me.

"I read his latest article about…" I felt awkward saying it out loud. "...women really do run the world."

"What the hell are you talking about? Marcus hasn't published anything in over a month?" the editor told me.

"It's on your website. The title is literally 'Women Really Do Run the World.' I'm not lying."

"What kind of sick joke is this?" a writer snapped from the nearest cubicle. "There is no article!"

She showed me Marcus's webpage. It was gone.

"Well then someone deleted it. I promise you it was there."

"You need to go," said the editor.

"Wait! Just let me talk to him! Five minutes! That's all I need!"

"Marcus is dead. Hit by a vehicle outside his hotel in Louisville."

I had a stupid look on my face as he shoved me out the door. Couldn't believe it. Not again. Another dead end! Wasn't sure how many more setbacks my heart could take. No! Screw that! Pick yourself up! This isn't the end. Something isn't right. So, use your brain and figure it the fuck out! That was my mindset.

Before the stroke of midnight, I acknowledged that screaming voice, the impulse deep in the pit of my stomach telling me what I should do next. I raced home and packed my bags.

Whilst packing, my parents called. I put it on speaker and told my dad everything.

"Well, son. You do what you got to do."

I stopped and gave him my undivided attention. Something in his voice...

"You know, whatever happens you'll always be my parents, right? I'll always love both of you. No matter what."

"I know, El. You're a good son. Sharon and I are proud of the man you've become. You got a good head on your shoulders. And you've had to survive in this world that's constantly turning its back on you. But I'm not worried. Because the Lord looks out for his flock."

"Amen..." I said in an emotional whisper.

He cleared his throat. "Anyways. How long are you gonna be gone?"

"Not long. I can attend some of my classes online, but I'll be back by Friday. Oh! Why'd you call, dad? You called *me* but the second I answered, I just dominated the conversation with all my garbage. Hahaha! What's going on?"

"It can wait. It can wait. You said you'll be back by Friday, right? We'll talk about it then."

"You sure?"

"Yes. It's no problem at all."

"Alright. Thanks Dad. For everything."

…

Downtown Louisville.

I stood where Marcus died. Across the street was the majestic hotel. It was strange. A window was boarded up. There was a "pardon our construction" sign on the wall. It was cordoned off by yellow police tape, but I could still see employees coming and going. So, clearly, they were open for business. Wasn't sure what to expect.

For a Tuesday night, downtown was certainly busy, sprawling with pedestrians and commuters still driving as if it was rush hour. Shouldn't be too hard for me to slip in under the police tape and act like I belonged at the hotel. And just as I was about to step out onto the street…

"Let's go for a walk."

A man came and patted my arm. It was hard, like a dull slap, enough to scare the shit out of me. I almost slipped off the sidewalk, so of course I was pissed when I turned and whipped my eyes on this guy.

He was already a stone's throw away. Tall. White. Nestled up in a thick black jacket and dad jeans. I could tell by looking, he was military. It's the way he walked. His gait was fast but not in a hurry. He didn't look back to see if I was following, but he checked everyone else around him.

We walked two windy blocks from the hotel by which I stayed ten paces behind him. By the time we crossed the third intersection, my patience was up. I was about to unload questions when he abruptly turned to the side entrance of a corporate complex. Buildings toward over us, and I couldn't see the nearest street sign from where I stood.

"In here. Trust me."

Trust me, he said.

The lights came on, orb lights on black iron lampposts with that 1920s Art Deco feel. It was breathtaking. Hundreds of empty office windows looked down on us as we stood in the middle of the second-floor atrium. It was weird. Like someone had just pressed pause on time and everything around us.

"You can call me, Jake. That's all you need to know about me for now."

"Alright. Well…Why'd you bring me here, Jake?"

This guy…he was a soldier, alright. But as soon I asked him the question, a myriad of expressions flashed he leaned over the walkway railing.

"You're in danger, kid. I know you don't trust me, and I don't know you. But I know you've been snooping around about Marcus Angel. If we know. They know."

"Alright...Who's *they*?"

"I think you know."

"Seriously, bro? You brought me all the way out here to play the pronoun game? Who's *they*? Just tell me, man!"

"You read the post Marcus wrote before he was killed. Well, he was right. For over a hundred years, we've known. But thanks to Marcus we have proof. Video evidence he recorded the night he was murdered."

"So, he really was murdered."

"You don't sound too surprised." Jake pointed out.

"In truth, I don't know what to believe. For the past four years it seems I've been trapped in my own sci-fi thriller. Just an hour ago I was staring at a hotel about to investigate. Now here I am, in a vacant building with some shady, washed up soldier talking conspiracy theories."

"You're the 'bloody baby,' aren't you?"

My heart skipped. "How do you know about that? Who the hell are you?"

Jake stood up and squared his shoulders. He scanned me with cautious eyes. I could tell he was dying to spill the beans, but why so reluctant?

"What I'm about to say, you can never repeat," He began. "You have to understand, I'm taking a shot in the dark just by saying as much as I have. I'm taking a shot, because I want you to join us.

"Elliot, if you've been reading about the Illuminati and Freemasons, then it shouldn't be too hard to believe that this world is full of secret groups who have managed to stay hidden. I belong to such a group. A brotherhood. We're called the Paramours. Naturally, our counterpart is a sisterhood of deadly Feminist bent on world domination. We refer to them as the Society.

"We are the loved ones lost, the bleeding hearts, the dead romantics. Everyone one of us has either survived the Society or was ruined by the Society. But despite the destruction, damage, and pain inflicted by these women, it's undeniable how much we still love them. We believe that in order to become a member of the Society, every woman has to kill the man they love the most in this world. It's part of their initiation. That's why your mother killed your father."

His words…each syllable was sledgehammer to my heart. I could barely move, paralyzed and caught in a web of what-in-the-actual-fuck.

"Elliot, as sure as I'm standing here before you, you can bet your ass that the Society is on to you. You're on the right path. You've caught their scent and you're getting too close. That's why I decided to bring you in, should you choose to join us. That's all I can say for now."

"Sir…" I said with a tremble in my voice. "Do you know who my mother is?"

"I'm sorry, I don't. The Society is a global organization. To date, we have tabs on about twenty Feminists in China whom we suspect are members. But odds are, there can be hundreds more. They're everywhere. Like the CIA, the Society uses civilians from all walks of life as pawns on a chessboard. She could be anyone."

"Alright." I said, wiping a tear from my face. "What do I do?"

"Join us, Elliot. I guarantee you'll have a better chance of finding your mother and you might stay alive long enough to meet her. We'll train you. Not strictly an assault unit, but we serve to correct the course."

"The best defense is a good offense..." I said.

"We've gone down that road." He chuckled harshly. "Believe me. We can't win. Men may be bigger and stronger but the thing that separates us from the women is our tendency to forgive and forget. They do not. They will not. Even if it looks like they've embraced you, I guaran-damn-tee you they're waiting for the right moment to strike back."

"But my mother's a member. And I think she's high-ranking. She wouldn't let them kill me. I know she wouldn't."

He groaned, stretching out his back. Probably thought I was being naïve, and he may have been right. But if my mother wanted me dead, she would have killed me when I was a baby. On this, I was willing to bet my top dollar.

40

"Son…if you think for one second that the other women in the society, who have had to kill the ones they cherished the most in this world. If you think they're just gonna sit back and let a nosy little brat like you ruin everything they've worked so hard to accomplish, you're sorely mistaken. I don't care if your mother is the top dog, the Society's full of egos and hot-tempered women who will always do what they think is necessary. Trust me. I saw the video Marcus recorded the night he was killed. These women are fierce. Lions. Intelligent and ruthless, they will eat you alive. And if you don't think your mother would toss you over the bridge if it means protecting her status or the greater Sisterhood, you're an idiot."

He gave me a business card, phone number written on the back.

"Memorize it and give it back to me."

My heart rate was pulsing. I wasn't even sure if I had finished memorizing it before he snatched the card back and nudged me along.

"We gotta go."

He led me out a different way from whence we came.

"When you get back to New York. Get rid of your smartphone, tablet, any device you used for research. Everything has a digital trail that can be traced back to you. Even speaking key phrases over the phone will alert the Society. Right now, you're a threat. Had you gone into that hotel you wouldn't have come out alive."

He shoved me out a side door and didn't come with. I looked back. The door was closed and that was it. I was back out in the middle of downtown Louisville. Jittery and paranoid out of my mind.

That night, I laid in my hotel looking up at the ceiling, replaying everything over and over again. Everything sounded so insane. If not for the reoccurring nightmares, I wouldn't have believed Jake for a second. And despite it all, I couldn't shake this overwhelming sense of admiration. I knew she killed my father, but that didn't bother me. She was still my mother. And Jake was wrong. She wouldn't kill me. She just wouldn't.

Who cares if they want to dominate the world? Let 'em! The Paramours sounded like a bunch of pussies anyway. Correcting the course…Psh! Bunch of Beta simps.

…

The thing about being naïve…Up to this point, everything I've written was to capture how I felt in the moment. But if you've read this far, then I'm sure you're starting to detect an undercurrent of tragic regret. I really was so stupid.

When I got back to New York…you have to understand, it was just after Spring Break. I was about to graduate. I had my whole life ahead of me. The reoccurring nightmares had stopped, and I was on a career path towards succeeding right here in the heart of the TV industry.

Thus, I was finally ready to put the whole "mommy issues" behind me. I believed everything Jake had told me, but I just didn't care. I didn't care about women ruling the world or the fact that she had killed my father. In the back of my mind, I wanted to believe my mother was always looking after me.

Then… I'll never forget it. I had just gotten out of the taxi in front of my apartment building when this loud, deafening, explosion ripped through a unit on the 5th floor. It was around 6pm so the streets were packed. Almost everyone had ducked in unison as shattered glass rained down.

I had a feeling, but it wasn't until I shouldered through the crowd that I knew. It was my apartment that blew up.

"My roommates!" I shuddered to think.

I imagined myself running in to see if they were alright. In truth, I just stood there like a deer caught in the headlights as the fire and billowy smoke streamed up the building.

Sirens, fire trucks, and paramedics came. I was still standing in the same spot with my roller suitcase down by my side. Dusk had turned to night. Streetlights came on. Hours had gone by and I was still standing in the midst of panic, the swarm of activity.

The EMTs wheeled out two bodies, one after the other. My heart was pounding as I thought about my roommates and whether they suffered.

"Yo, El! What the hell happened?!"

I turned to see my roommates shouting at me. They had just gotten off the subway and came running. They were asking quickfire questions, but it was like a cacophony of sounds and flashbacks flooded my senses.

Saying nothing, I ran across the street and charged for that ambulance where they brought the two bodies. The police stopped me. I shoved one out of the way before another wrestled me down and that's when I lost it. I knew it. Before it was even confirmed, this powerful eruption in me...I was screaming, fighting to get up. More cops got involved. And I…I don't remember anything else about that night.

...

—

42

"Hi, Elliot!!! Hahaha! So, your father and I wanted to surprise you with an early graduation gift, but the thing is, we can't find the key to your apartment. I know you said you hid it somewhere for your roommates. But hahaha! Marvin's looking all over the place. Oh! Found it! He said he found it. Dang it! Whelp. Looks like the surprised is ruined. But I think you'll like what we brought you. I hope you have a safe flight back! We just landed. New York is huge!!! We can't wait to see you tonight. Love you!"

That was left on my voice mail.

The two bodies were that of Marvin and Sharon Burroughs, the Christians who were kind enough to adopt a Chinese baby that was found covered in blood on the sidewalk. They were kind to me and never owed me a damn thing. They were my parents. My real parents.

...

The marshal claimed the fire was the result of a gas explosion. And, shamed to say, I couldn't help but notice the fire marshal was a woman. She was explaining what happened to a bunch of us tenants, but I had a feeling she was talking only to me.

Recovered from the fire was Marvin's suitcase. Inside was my graduation gift, a manila envelope with my name on it miraculously undamaged by the fire. I was in the main branch of the New York library when I decided to open it.

Sitting away from everyone else in the archives section, I took a deep breath and reached inside. The envelope contained one item, an 8x10inch portrait of a woman named Jaida Fong. At the bottom, in handwritten ink were the words, "your mother."

I remember crumbling up the picture with my bare hands. The fury was indescribable. I didn't wipe my tears. I didn't give a shit if people walked by. I was just so angry, snarling with rage. The injustice...

This woman was not my mother. My mother died in an explosion that may have been meant for me. That night I gave Jake a call and the rest is history. I joined the Paramours.

...The Perennial War of Paramours...

03. Elliot Chan – The Network Executive

Training to become a Paramour was about what one would expect from any covert Special Forces training. Combat training. Firearms instruction. Exit and infiltration tactics. War paint. The whole nine yards. It took over the course of three years by which, you had to maintain the appearances of an everyday civilian by progressing in your respective fields.

For me, that was in the television industry. I got an entry job at MBC straight out of college and began working my way up as a production assistant.

The Paramours had outposts all around the world, but our headquarters was based in England. It was an old estate in the English county of Derbyshire along the River Derwent. Officially, the name of the Tudor mansion its surrounding lands was the Leigh Estate. But the Paramours affectionately called it, Hollow Rock.

The first time I saw the place, it was breathtaking. Like a whole new world. The beauty of its green luscious splendor. Most of the actual training facilities were underground and hidden from aerial coverage, such as the firing range and armory.

Hollow Rock was vast, open, remote, and peaceful with singing birds and the trickle of the creeks. Everything had this quaint, old countryside feel to it. Like a step back in time. It was just what I needed to accelerate the healing process of having just witnessed the violent murder of my parents.

"To correct the course" was the mission of the Paramours. While it was mostly men here, I saw plenty of women, daughters, sisters, and mothers who lost their loved ones to the Society. We're not an offensive unit. We observe. Protect. Defend. Rebuild. And on the rarest occasions, just ever so often, we prevent. It's that "prevention" part that's dangerous because the Society doesn't give a f***. Anyone perceived to be a threat gets taken out. Anyone. Man or woman.

Goes without saying, there was often an air of melancholy through the halls of Hollow Rock because the Paramours formed bonds over the years through their crucibles. A lot of Paramours died in the field. Self-sacrificing. Martyrs. Whatever you want to call them.

I reconnected with "Jake" at Hollow Rock, the man who first told me about the Paramours and the Society. His real name was Col. Jacob Buchanan, having served in the Gulf War and had engagements in Bosnia and Kosovo.

During the years of training, Jake became my closest friend and confidant, a mentor I'm most grateful for. I remember one of our conversations during that first week of boot camp. We were walking along the river when I asked him something that's been on my mind since I joined.

"Here's my problem with the Paramours." I began. "It's sort of like a comic book, right? The hero saves the day, but they don't kill the villain. So, the villains keep coming back. They keep doing the same shit. I don't get that! To know that this secret society exists but no one's doing anything to expose them to the public? We don't even turn them into the authorities, so they just keep on murdering and ruining innocent lives. Does no one feel guilty about all that? Doesn't anyone feel responsible?"

Jake stared out over the river with his crew cut and cold blue eyes.

"Elliot, do you know what a Paramour is? By definition, do you know what a paramour is?"

A question with a question...friggin love those.

"It's like the person you love the most." I grumbled.

"It's an illicit lover, El. A secret lover to a married person. In that sense, I think Lord Byron aptly named us when he founded the brotherhood. Granted, not all of us were married or have ever been married. The key word there is love. You never met your mom. But you love her, don't you?"

"I don't know. I guess."

He scoffed, shaking his head. "It's like this, when you're here, we train you, we give you the tools and trust you to assist your brothers out in the field. If you kill, if you choose to kill, you're no longer a Paramour. You're not one of us. Not in your heart. But once you're put in the position, once you come to that fork in the road where you have that choice and you choose not to kill, right then and there, you'll know what it means to be one of us."

"I get what you're saying. You can't kill because you love them. Sure, whatever. But what if someone else kills them for you? What if one of your comrades kills them because you can't bring yourself to do it yourself? But you know! You know without a shred out of doubt that this bitch needs to die. Like, put down for good! Why can't that happen?"

He started chuckling.

I threw up my hands. "You get what I'm saying, right? This is ridiculous! When does it end?"

"The same way it always ends."

"Well!? Let's hear it, colonel!"

"You stick around long enough, you'll find out."

"That's bullshit." I said before storming off.

Anyways…

Marcus Angel was also here at Hollow Rock. I couldn't believe it. The man who's writing started me down this rabbit hole. When I first came to England, he was still in a coma and to be honest, it didn't look good. Shot multiple times. Broken ribs and a fractured skull. This man's been through hell. He was on life support, costing the organization five grand a day but they had no intention of giving up on him. It was endearing, their level of compassion. Of course, I wouldn't find out until later how much everyone was depending on him to regain consciousness.

The Paramours didn't just give me my military training. They were all about refinement, the stuff of gentlemen. The education, the in-depth history taught to me was more than I ever knew existed. I learned six different languages and took acting classes to control my emotions and express the right ones to elicit any response I wanted. The Paramours focused on stealth, intelligence, and subterfuge. Perception was everything and I was conditioned to think five moves ahead.

After three years of training, the Paramours started taking me out in the field. At first, it was just to observe and shadow more experienced members. My non-descript Asian appearance was extremely helpful. It didn't matter what country I was in, there was something about me that whispered, "nothing special" or "he's harmless."

Then came the first mission where I had a more pertinent role. It was the summer of 2018. The leading Paramour was a revolutionary named Arsen Masol. My unit was posing as documentary filmmakers and I was the cameraman. Arsen's mission was to provide the authorities with proof that deputies within the Verkhovna Rada (Ukraine's parliament) were being blackmailed and coerced to stay in the European Union.

What did any of that have to do with the Paramours? Had no idea. And honestly, I didn't need to know. It was Arsen's mission. He had his reasons and we were simply there to support him. I never doubted for a second that when the time came, my newfound comrades would assist me in my personal mission as well.

That's the thing about us Paramours…we're intensely loyal. When you're in hostile lands or working in countries where things like "due process" and "probable cause" are laughed at like bar jokes, everyone's afraid. The threat of death or imprisonment is a rational fear. But we weren't alone. Our comrades were with us. They had our backs.

We've been shot at. We've been wounded. We've been caught. We've been killed. But no one has ever revealed our existence to the outside world. Even the Society didn't know about us to the best of our knowledge. The Paramours who were declared dead in the real world could never leave Hollow Rock. That included men like Marcus Angel. Should he ever reappear, he'd jeopardize us all.

After five years of running with the Paramours, it was my turn to step up to the plate. It was a difficult decision that I knew would change my life forever. Once I crossed the threshold, there was no turning back. From here on out, I'd have to spend the rest of my life looking over my shoulder. The Society wouldn't stop until I was killed. That was the risk I was willing to take to confront my mother…a high-ranking member of the Society named Jaida Fong.

If you were to ask me why I chose to do this, I couldn't pinpoint a solid answer. So badly, I wanted her to pay for what she did to my adoptive parents. I wanted to look into her eyes and unload all the pain and suffering she and her stupid little club inflicted not just on me, but the hundreds of brothers and sisters I've come to respect at Hollow Rock.

Jaida Fong. My mother. She was a real piece of work.

Jaida Fong was the youngest of five children and the only daughter of a Chinese billionaire. That's right. While I had to scrap for groceries and hustle just to afford a fifth-floor apartment, my grandfather was a transportation magnate who could've bought up half of Soho.

Goes without saying, no expense was spared on Jaida's education. From Vancouver to Columbia University, Jaida was a treated like a princess who demanded the best of everything. Now I had to think for a moment. What the hell was she doing with some random peace worker in Dallas, Texas? It didn't add up. Not for a normal person.

But if you're a rebel whose sole purpose in life seemed to be getting back at those who doubted you, I guess there's some logic in that.

You see, Jaida was expected to join the family business, to be some CFO or account executive. Instead, she ended up falling for a lowly Peace Corp volunteer and got pregnant. I'm guessing the rest of the family wasn't happy about that. Soon after I was born, she completed her initiation to the Society by killing the man she loved the most in the world. Richard Chan, my biological father. Not me…her biological son.

Since then, Jaida has risen through the ranks to become a prominent figure in the entertainment industry. It's just by coincidence that I'd enter the same field. Starting out as a creative director and eventually working her way up to executive producer, Jaida launched an empire of creating hit TV shows to reach the masses. She didn't need her father's wealth. She built her own. I'd even go so far as to say she didn't need to be a high-ranking member of the Society to taste power, but truth is, everything was connected.

What do I mean? Well, it's not like every premise she pitched was loved and well-received by the studio heads. They were coerced, blackmailed, and extorted into approving her pilots and storylines. The Society was in on it.

Why would the Society care what Americans were watching? Influence! It goes back to my time in film school. I used to argue with classmates that anyone could change the culture through the media. My classmates disagreed. They claimed people weren't so easily manipulated. So, I asked, "how do you explain advertisement or propaganda?"

My point was: If you wanted to, anyone could create a new reality if they make it look appealing enough to the masses. Not to pick on hip hop, but the saying goes "hip hop is the art of making bad things look cool." Hollywood has the power to influence goals, to sell the American Dream, to change what you think the American Dream is or should be. They have the power to dictate what is or isn't acceptable. And that's exactly what my mother did.

For instance, in 2009, she created one of the most celebrated TV shows about a high school drama club where every episode had some musical dance number. It focused on the more "marginalized" social groups, fostering acceptance and inclusion for homosexuals, transgenders...pretty much anyone who struggled with their race and identity.

Sounds harmless, right? But what if people, specifically teenagers and the impressionable youth, started believing that real life should be like this fictional one? As if, people should change to be like these fictional characters and if you don't, then there's something wrong with you.

In 2010, Jaida created a sitcom about a group of awkward sciency nerds. It was a cute show in which you could hear the laugh track before the characters even finished their punchlines. It garnered huge success with an average of 15 million viewers per episode. People actually liked it. Who am I to judge, right?

I just found it odd that almost every one of these male geeks had the hottest girlfriends. It's almost like they were pushing the idea that sexy women actually desire weak effeminate men. Or if they don't, they should.

Here, you'd probably say, "Well, no Elliot. You're just being narrow-minded. Maybe it's not every hot girl. But some do. And maybe this show just focuses on the hot girls who do."

Maybe...One last point and that's the rise of the "strong female protagonist". There's been an explosion of open sexuality, as I'm sure you've noticed. It's in your face, you can't avoid it. Back in 2012, Jaida Fong was the executive producer for a trilogy of films starring a strong female character where the outcome of her entire dystopian world hinged on her every decision.

Since then, scores of movies, books, and TV shows have come out with heroines who, oddly enough, acted like traditionally masculine men in a hot woman's body. Meanwhile their male counterparts were weak, timid, and depended on them to solve all the problems and save the world.

Here's the thing. At first, I was cool with the trend of empowered women. But as the years went by, I saw the detrimental effect it had on my generation. It convinced ladies to embrace the idea that they "don't need no men," diminishing the motivation for men to want to step up and lead. The corporate competitive alphas of yesteryear were demonized as toxic males, shamed into a corner to sit down and shut up while women took over the reins. Well played...

As President AABC Productions, Jaida Fong was the chief architect in all of this. Her minions included best-selling novelists, show-runners, and a whole stable of celebrities who used social media to hypocritically judge others with words like "bigot" and "white privilege," ruining the careers of anyone who disagreed and driving some to suicide.

All this...I knew all of this going in on the day that I finally met my mother.

Interlude

...

I remember the night as if it happened yesterday. My heart was racing. I was one of twenty staff writers sitting around a glass conference room on the 38th floor of a Manhattan skyscraper with an impressive view of the Empire State Building. This was the AABC's semi-annual pitch meeting to determine which shows our network would produce for the next season.

Yes, after working my way up from production assistant to stage manager, I was finally a show writer. Everyone around the table looked like friends. Actually, they all looked like clones of each other just different races and genders. For an industry that preached diversity, I found it strange that everyone talked, dressed, and behaved the same way with the same ideologies, hobbies, and fandoms. It was college all over again.

The meeting began at 6pm with an executive running the show. The agenda was to go like this: One by one, we'd progress around the table and pitch our ideas for TV shows. We'd discuss if it was viable, if there was an audience for it, and if our clients, the advertising companies would find it lucrative enough to market it.

Then…at approximately 6:13pm, the glass doors opened. In walked five individuals. The network heads. One of them was wearing a satin green cocktail dress with high heels that clacked like marbles slapping the hard floor.

"Oh my God," I whispered as the heat rushed up from my chest.

It was her. She looked like she hadn't aged a day in her life. Average height, not too short, not too tall. Contrary to the fierce Amazon I thoughts she'd be, Jaida seemed humble and sweet. Her smile was so bright and optimistic. She nodded and glanced around the room as if *she* was the one honored by *our* presence.

I confess…my eyes watered up and, in that moment, I almost forgot I was on a mission. Nothing about this woman seemed dangerous, sinister, or violent. She was beautiful. She was my mother.

As night fell, the city lights glimmered. One by one, we pitched our ideas. There were nine ahead of me and each person ate up about half an hour. Everyone thought they had the next big idea when really, they were just pitching remakes, spin-offs, or cashing in on some trend that already had an established fan base. There was nothing original. No courage in their creativity. But everyone laughed and applauded as if it was all so groundbreaking and new.

I observed Jaida like a science project. I studied her every twitch, the way she breathed, how she fiddled with her fingers, how she tugged the neckline of her dress, how she sipped from her daiquiri. I noted the inflection of her voice and the way she reacted to stupid suggestions with a soft smirk. She was good at feigning surprise. And as much as everyone was puckering up to kiss her ass, she never let on that she was used to it.

After the fourth pitch, Jaida stressed that we needed to be mindful of the current political climate. She openly asserted that the president of the United States and his horde of white nationalists were determined to regain control of this country and overturn everything progressives worked hard to accomplish over the years. Thus, this new season of programming needed to be inspirational. It needed to be entertaining, but persuasive and engaging, providing the marginalized with a voice that would educate the majority.

Around nine o'clock, dinner was brought in. We took a break and ate together, the executives with us lowly grunts. Jaida conversed with the more charismatic (outspoken) writers about their background and aspirations. I wondered if she even knew I was there. Or if she had recognized me. In the first three hours, she probably glanced at me maybe once.

Also…Jaida wasn't the only member of the Society present. One of her assistants came in during dinner to bring her a note. I recognized this assistant. She was young, black, gorgeous, and had the aura of someone who was more important than the courier role she pretended to play.

I wouldn't find out till later that this woman's name is Celeste, a formidable enforcer. The first time I saw her was back in Berkeley. She was dressed in all black along with the rest of Antifa during the protest of an Alt-Right speaker. Celeste was the one who threw the first punch that initiated an all-out brawl in the middle of the street. She was incredible. By herself, she must have laid out at least four or five dudes.

Everyone thought she was a guy because she had a hood on and definitely displayed unrivaled aggression, but I was on a rooftop conducting surveillance. When the police came, throwing tear gas to disperse the crowd, I watched as Celeste casually walked behind a row of bushes, took off her hood and strutted off as if she was just an innocent student caught in the madness.

And if Celeste was here, I knew there had to be more. That's alright. I anticipated it. As everyone ate from their trays of take-out sushi, I scanned the office outside our conference room. It was way past closing hours but there were at least seven ladies still sitting in their cubicles. Two locked eyes with me and I had to play it off as if I was just shy and awkward.

The anxiety was killing me. My intestines could not screw any tighter. Several times I caught myself just staring at my pen for well over a minute without blinking. As the long hand on my watch moved ever so slowly, my worst fears began to bubble up. What if it got too late? At any moment, I expected Jaida to be like, "Whelp. It's getting late. Why don't the rest of you guys type up your treatments and send them in to us in an e-mail."

I've waited my entire life for this moment. And hearing these bastards pitch the same shit over and over again was more than I could stand.

At last, it was exactly 11:07pm when it was my turn to speak. All eyes on me. Jaida and the network heads were exhausted and worn out, but they seemed intrigued with me. Everyone else was so full of brio and excitement when their name was called. But when they said my name, it was like a spell was cast, freezing me in a catatonic state. My mouth slacked opened to speak, but words didn't come.

"It's okay," she said. "After Jessica hit us with the exploding nutsack joke, I think we can handle anything."

Those were the first words my mom ever said to me. I wasn't looking at her. Not at first. My hands rose up as if I was carrying a priceless vase. And then I began.

"Sometimes taking life seriously, the privilege of starting from the bottom and working your way up, it makes success that much more satisfying. Anyone can ride a helicopter to the top of a mountain. But to climb it yourself and reach the peak, that accomplishment, that reward is a gift that no one could ever give you. Only you can achieve this for yourself. Just you."

Silence. One could hear a pin drop in the room. I continued.

"Ladies and gentlemen, what I have for you is an eight-part miniseries. It's a mystery thirty years in the making. And it all starts deep in the heart of Texas."

I looked to Jaida. I wanted to watch as the realization washed over her. I wanted to savor it.

"A child, a baby is left sitting on the cold tile floor. Directly in front of him is a man, the handle of a knife sticking out of his chest. He's gurgling. He's choking. He's gasping for air. He's bleeding out. Then, all the sudden, a woman in a cocktail dress and high heels comes into view.

———

52

"She throws her weight on him, forcing him out of the chair, stabbing him over and over again. This child, this baby, this toddler sees everything. He remembers EVERYTHING! The last thing he sees in this traumatizing scene is the woman, callous and cold, coming to stand over him with the bloody knife. She doesn't kill him. Instead, she drops the knife at the child's feet and walks out of his life."

Everyone's staring at me like I've lost my mind. I know. There's nothing tasteful or entertaining about this story. One by one they start firing off questions about what the baby does, who the woman is, or where's the conflict in the story. They ask why she killed the man. Why she dropped the knife? Why didn't she take the baby out of the room first?

These are questions are typical of those who live in a small world, a world only comprised of those who lived and acted just like them. These people, my peers could never understand anyone who's ever walked a different path, though they so desperately wish they could. And since they can't understand, they refuse to believe you. They tell you it's unrealistic.

They say no woman would ever do that. They say my story doesn't make sense. I don't blame them. They're right. It doesn't make sense to the rational mind. And suddenly…I saw the real Jaida Fong.

She wasn't smiling anymore. With her legs crossed, she sat back with this inquisitive look. Not anger or disappointment. She didn't seem scared or nervous, but more so, curious. It was so hard to tell whether she understood the implications or not. For a moment, I began to doubt she was really my mother.

It got to the point where the room started debating the story without me, when finally, Jaida asked, "What inspired you to write this story?"

Everyone stopped and awaited my answer.

"Ma'am, I'm from Texas. A military couple out of Fort Hood adopted me. They told me this urban legend about a bloody baby who was found not far from a mansion that burned down in Dallas. For some reason the story always stuck with me. You know? In fact, one could say I've been waiting my entire life to tell it to you."

"To me?" She asked.

"To you."

She smirked.

"Would everyone give us the room?" she said. "In fact, let's call it a night and pick this up around ten o'clock in the morning. How's that sound?"

It's not like they were going to say no. As everyone packed up, I stayed put. As did she.

When the last one left the room, Jaida got up, her heels clacking on the hard polished floor. She pulled out the chair next to me and sat down. Her fragrance was intoxicating. She seemed so young, like she could have been my older sister. Her expressions were hard to read. But so badly, I wanted to believe that she was impressed with the man I've become.

With her legs crossed and one elbow on the table, she examined. I said nothing, but my heart and stomach were making all kinds of noises.

"Are you the baby?" she asked.

I glanced out the room. All seven ladies were still at their cubicles. All of them, watching me like owls on a branch.

"Jaida…"

"It's Mrs. Fong. If you, please."

"Yeah, I'm gonna go ahead call you Jaida. I don't give a shit."

She snickered. "Oh dear… Okay. Go on."

"Why'd you kill 'em? Why?"

She squinted, batting her long, dark lashes.

"Don't worry," I told her. "I'm not wearing a wire."

"Oh, I'm not worried. Not for my sake. Let's see. Where do I begin? China is a complicated place for a woman of my making. That's a delicate way of saying I hate it. To my father, I was nothing more but a bargaining chip. He never loved me. He never saw me as a child or daughter. My education, the pampering, the royal treatment was all to mold me. To make me a suitable wife to whomever he saw fit. I had no say in the matter. Or so he thought.

"On top of all that, China implemented the Family Planning Policy. I'm sure you've heard of it. Families could only have one child per household. The government's idiotic plan to curb the burgeoning population.

"Herein lies the rub. Men carried on the family name. So, men were the desirables. Women…Millions of innocent little girls died. Families killed off daughter after daughter until they were able to conceive a son.

"My family didn't have to go through such an ordeal because we were ridiculously rich. But I'll never forget a visit to Leshan in the Sichuan province. I was fifteen, traveling with my class, all of us privileged and oblivious to the world outside our diamond encrusted bubbles. We were on a boat, rowing up the Min River to see the Giant Buddha. And there, floating at the surface like discarded trash were dozens of dead little girls. When I told my father about it…he laughed."

I saw the fire in Jaida's eyes, glossed over like she was about to cry.

"When I met Richard, he was so very different from the scrooge corporate worms I grew up with. He really believed he could make a difference with the Peace Corp. He was convincing. Or rather, I let myself be convinced. I fell in love. And I got pregnant. When my father found out, he cut me out of his inheritance and disowned me. What little money I did have was used to buy that humble little mansion in Dallas.

"So, you ask why? Why I killed him? I don't know. I suppose a life of simple domesticity just didn't suit me. I have no regrets. Everything I've done was for the betterment of our society. I wouldn't have been able to accomplish anything if I was stuck playing some middle-class tiger mom, going to PTA meetings, picking you up from soccer practice, working some dead-end job. Ugh! Fuck that. FUCK THAT!"

She stood up and paced around. Every time she turned her back, I glanced outside the room. I was in danger. The ladies kept switching cubicles, moving closer to us.

"So, what do you want? Hmm?" She asked. "You think you're entitled to what I have? You think I owe you something for missed birthdays? What?"

I stood up and shook myself loose, letting out a deep breath like a whale that had been holding it in for so long, "You know it's interesting. I asked you why you killed 'em. I wasn't talking about Richard Chan. I was talking about Marvin and Sharon. My real parents. The ones who did what you were too selfish to do."

She tried to slap me, but I grabbed her wrist mid-swing and turned her around, bringing her close. I was about to whisper something badass in her ear, but Jaida was stronger than she looked. She elbowed me in the chest, stomped on my foot, and in that brief flash of me being hunched over, she shoved my face into the edge of the table.

I rolled to the floor, spitting blood from a chipped tooth. In the corner of my eye, I saw the ladies coming over from their cubicles. Jaida raised her hand to stop them.

"Yeah, you're my son alright." She said as she straightened herself out. "But it's ten years too soon for you to ever! Think! About! Beating! Me!"

She landed a kick with each exclamation. And suddenly I started laughing. You know, like a lunatic.

"Yeah, you're my mother alright!" I chuckled. "It's just too bad you hit like a fucking girl!"

Before she could kick again, I double-hooked my arms around her legs and with all my strength, I picked this bitch up and ran to shove her through the glass walls of the conference room. At once, all seven ladies drew Glocks and aimed at me.

Suddenly, the power went out. A blackout. The ladies opened fire but hit nothing. The emergency lights came on just in time for them to see me booking it down the open hallways. The floors were slick. Stopping on a dime was impossible. I had to damn near hook my arm around a pillar to turn corners.

"Stop. Go to the elevator."

It was Jake. He was speaking through my earpiece. The Paramours were here. They had my back. It was the Paramours who cut the power. It was the Paramours who gave me the tech advanced contact lenses that allowed me to see in the dark. Everything was going according to plan.

"The doors should open manually," Jake said. "It's your best bet. A package is on the roof. Just like we rehearsed."

In Jake, I trust. I could hear the hard clacking of footsteps closing in, and I'm sure I would have heard the same if I opened the stairwell. Jaida was a high-ranking member after all. I doubted they'd leave her protection to seven cronies who were so stupid they'd open fire in a dark room, taking the absurd risk of shooting Jaida.

I reached the elevator door and pried my fingers through the crease to get them open. There was no lift, just an open shaft all the way at the bottom floor. But the plan wasn't to use the lift. I pulled out rubber gloves with thick padding made from the same stuff used to make tires. I jumped, caught the cable wire, and started climbing.

Calm and steady wins the race. I didn't fear death. Should I slip and plummet, it was well worth it just to confront my mother. I was halfway to the top floor when suddenly I smelled something sweet. I looked down in horror expecting to see someone climbing up after me. Then to my left. There, on the second cable was Celeste with her corporate white collared shirt and that whimsical smile.

"Hey, boo!" She said casually before kicking, digging her sharp-ass heels into my hip. It felt like a fucking knife. As I hunched over, hanging on for dear life. She grabbed me by the back of my neck and curled me closer. She was trying to strangle me with some length of rope, but I wrestled free and elbowed her in her face.

"Motherfuck…No you did not just hit my goddamn face!"

I swear. The bass in her voice put the fear of God in me. She latched onto the same cable I was climbing and grabbed me by the ankle. She started pulling me down and I'm telling you, her strength was no joke. I'm not sure what kind of training they had, but it was ungodly. My hand was starting to slip out of my super-grip tire gloves. I had no choice but to stomp her as hard as I could in the face

She whimpered and began to plummet. I looked down and somehow, her leg managed to wrap around the cable fifty feet down. She dangled like a toy on a pull-string before willing herself back to an upright position. By then, I was at the top and kicking open the air vent to get out onto the roof.

The biting wind and starry sky was a sight for sore eyes. There was a helicopter on the helipad but that wasn't my ticket out. I ran down a set of steps and saw two female snipers passed out from tranquilizer darts, no doubt fired by the snipers from my team.

Around the corner, there was a "Break in Case of Emergency" case where a fire hose was rolled up. I broke the glass and clawed out the hose. Behind it, was a package that looked like a backpack. With the tug of the ring, wings for a hang-glider fanned out. A simple breeze pulled with such force. As if my adrenaline wasn't already pumping full throttle.

"Elliot!"

I looked over. My mother was standing atop the steps on the helipad. Power came back, lighting us up in dramatic fashion. It was awesome. She was smiling. So was I.

"I don't know who you're working for, but you should know that I'm going to find you!"

I remember scoffing. She was in the TV business, but that was the best line she could come up with? Then, Celeste came bursting through the doors, so I delivered my retort with one foot off the ledge.

"Yeah, but I found you first. So, I win!"

Gunshots whispered in the wind. Probably Celeste. She was pissed. I really hope I never run into that one again.

But my mother. She really is so amazing. I know this sounds silly, but...I really don't mind dying if she's the one who kills me. That would be the greatest. Hmm...I guess I really am a Paramour.

04. Gladys Vandelay – The Protégé

Now there was once a certain senator who was known to frequent the clubs and popular spots around Uptown Toronto. His name was Jared J. Chrysler, a despicable bully who had a penchant for strong-arming his proposals through city hall.

Sen. Chrysler was not a good man. Not a good man at all.

As it was, I knew Sen. Chrysler before I met him. His dossier came replete with sexual assaults, everything from rape, torture, and murder. He was once caught on camera literally stripping the clothes off a reporter in an elevator. He was high on coke.

His name dominated headlines after he declared in Parliament that women had no place in politics. He never apologized. Never chalked it up to some gaffe or a slip of the tongue. Instead, Chrysler had the gumption to stand by his words. And despite widespread protests, solidarity from the academia damn-near screaming for his resignation...this unsavory fellow managed to stay in office.

The icing on the cake was that Chrysler had dealings with the Bratva. He aided in human trafficking and had the nerve to call for stricter immigration laws when one of his mistresses threatened to go public. Of course, this mistress disappeared soon after. Everyone knew he dabbled in narcotics. And every so often, he'd had to get rid of his limos because no matter what, they couldn't get the stench of marijuana out of the seats.

That his execution didn't come sooner, I think, emboldened his god complex. At the same time, it made him an easier target for those who weren't so bound by silly things like laws or ethics. I think that's why they chose me.

"The first kill is always the hardest," they say. But honestly, there was no fear. No anxiety. I wasn't reluctant nor did I hesitate or have any second thoughts. I didn't feel anything, other than the smooth friction of my knife sliding across his neck. I killed the man. But the ladies killed his legacy.

That's how we worked. A death shrouded in mystery would only inflate his infamy. Couldn't have that. So, his hotel room was staged to look like a break-in. His business partner, just as corrupt as he, was our patsy. There were recordings of the partner hiring a hitman years ago. The coward called it off, but we still had the tapes. Damning evidence, really.

You must understand, I wasn't a full-fledged member of the Society yet. I wanted to be, more than anything. These ladies, these women...They're extraordinary. Every one of them has this overwhelming presence by which you couldn't help but wonder if they came fresh from commanding legions on the battlefield. Perhaps by becoming one of them, I thought I could soak in but an ounce of their charisma, their raw unstoppable power.

Sorry. I suppose even now, I find it hard to denigrate them. They trained me. Believed in me. I wouldn't be who I am if it wasn't for them.

…

In New York City some years ago, I was but a budding flower, just graduated from Elysium with a 4.0 grade average. Having grown up in the halls of Papa's corporate offices, I was exposed to the high stakes of million-dollar hedge funds. Despite all that, I was groomed to be a classical composer. That's the path my parents chose for me.

My mother and our nannies came from Surrey, hence the accent I inherited. I began playing the piano when I was about five or six, and to date, I've mastered all of Chopin's compositions. However, Erik Satie was my idol. It's all about the timing in his works and the one thing I appreciated the most was the risk by trying something new and, dare I say, awkward. "Gymnopedie" is my favorite. I must have rehearsed it a thousand times. Even in complete silence, I can hear it in my head.

To much is given, much is expected. That is, unless you have six older brothers and three older sisters, all more outspoken and impressive than yourself. Goes without saying, my own candle paled in comparison.

They dominated everything. Dinner conversations, galas, parties and pageants. At some point, I suppose I just got lost somewhere in the back and didn't mind. I had no talent for oratory and the moment eyes fell on me, I'd freeze up with the most terrifying heart palpitations.

Don't get me wrong, I love my family. My brothers were so cool. Strong and handsome. And my sisters…Well, I suppose it's a bit ironic now that I think about it. Clarice, Emily, and Victoria. My heart weeps as I say this, but every time I was alone in the same room with them, I was afraid. They picked on me for being so short and thin. I had asthma and they'd mock me relentlessly for the wheezing, the "overdramatic" desperation I'd exhibit to draw breath.

Papa made them take me everywhere and I could tell they resented it. It's a horrid feeling, to have so much in common with expensive luggage. It's because of Papa that they included me, but I understood why. He didn't want me to feel alone. Papa was always looking out for me. He was perhaps the one ray of light that kept me warm in an otherwise cold and abysmal childhood.

It was because of Papa that I had the strength to smile. When I was little, I used to stare at him like he was the ceiling of the Sistine Chapel. The hope that most people have towards Christ is how I felt towards him. He came to every one of my recitals. Words couldn't express how elated my father was. He'd cry. Such emotion. I felt the love. I didn't have to question it or wonder whether it was real. I knew how much my father loved me by how open and affectionate he was. It was in his arms that I'd run. It was in his coat that I found salvation.

Felix Domina Vandelay II. That was his name, a titan on Wall Street with investments around the world. We were descendants of King Wilhelm Vandelay of Godland who surrendered the throne to the Swedish Empire. Our family was paid handsomely and has dominated the shipping industry ever since, back before the English stole New York from the Dutch.

Papa loved history and I took after him. My siblings didn't seem to care one way or the other, but I did. Money was something everyone could get, more or less, but our heritage, our pedigree, to come from royal blood was something my father regarded with pride. He installed our family crest in the corporate emblem. I'll never forget the smile on his face when he took me to see it. Just me. No one else wanted to come.

And that's how it went. The Vandelay name became synonymous with both opulence and, surprisingly enough, generosity. A lot of what I know about capitalism and economics came from what my father taught me. He'd let me sit in on the big important meetings, trusting with good measure that I'd behave and silently observe. And I did. It was interesting. I enjoyed listening to them talk, more so than watching Saturday morning cartoons or coloring in books. The tension, the frayed nerves, the adrenaline of risking so much on stocks or some new venture, as CEO, Papa was the mediator to temper all tempers.

One time, Papa introduced me to the president of an airline company. It was just a joke, but Papa said I was his only daughter. I know this sounds bad, but I often fantasized about being his only child. I imagined a world without brothers or sisters or even my mother. Just Papa and me. I would've been so happy. It would've been the perfect world. But as it was, my brothers and sisters existed. In particular, Clarice, the eldest sister, born six years before myself.

Clarice was in a lot of ways the ringleader of so many cliques that tormented me from one boarding school to another. You could blame it on her youth, sure. But I never understood it. I heard stories about bullies being jealous of their targets or wanting something their victims had. But Clarice was taller, popular, drop-dead gorgeous and intelligent enough to know when to acquiesce for the sake of appearances. She never abused me physically. Just stole or broke anything that belonged to me. She called my recitals boring and, sometimes, I could hear her and her friends laughing from the balconies as I played.

When the Society approached me, it was during a very dark chapter in my life. And it was all Clarice's fault. My music teacher of eight years had just lost his wife to leukemia. I was his favorite pupil, so I wanted to be there for him, to commiserate with him, to let him know that he wasn't alone. But my family had this tradition of taking the yacht across the Mediterranean every Easter. I begged mother to let me stay behind and support him but Clarice…She put it in my mother's head that my teacher fancied me beyond what was appropriate.

We had just ported in Barcelona when I learned that my teacher jumped from his 25th-floor apartment. I had just turned fifteen.

Racked with guilt and grief, I stopped eating. I refused school and stopped playing music. One afternoon, I returned home to find my bedroom nearly stacked to the ceiling with rows of my favorite flowers, white hydrangeas. It was classic Papa to go to such extremes. Out of respect for him, I returned to school and forced myself to eat again.

By then, something in me had changed. A darkness began to shroud the sliver of light my father once provided. Everyone could see it and finally, they stopped tormenting me. I no longer smiled. I lost the ability to laugh or giggle. I stopped coming to Papa's offices, and every time I entered a room where I knew Clarice was present, I'd keep my gaze to the floor.

I really hated that bitch. When I cried alone, it wasn't because I was sad. It was the pain of restraint, holding back the overwhelming rage in my heart. Every time I'd hear her laugh, or talk, or so much as clear her throat, I'd be struck by this incredible urge to stab her with the sharpest thing I could find. It was bad. I knew something was wrong with me. But who could I talk to? Who could possibly understand?

Three weeks after the maestro's passing, I found myself sitting alone in an herbal teashop down in the Village. It rained that evening. I'd hone in an out of the raindrops on the window. Red and yellow lights blurred in straight lines that zipped up and down the wet city streets.

Two hipsters approached and offered to buy me a drink. They appeared college students, and well-intended, but I dismissed them.

Then...she sat down. A velvety black coat that still had beads of rain. Long dark hair. Shimmering blue eyes. Without saying anything, she just smiled, and I was instantly caught in her spell. She extended a handkerchief to wipe my tears and I still remember my mascara bleeding into the cloth.

"May I help you?" I asked.

She sighed and looked around the room before settling on me.

"Your guilt is unwarranted. You are trapped, my dear. Like a bird, a caged canary. I am here to set you free."

It was surreal. Everything I needed to hear came from those words. She followed up with nothing else, but casually scooted her chair out and grazed past my shoulder as she made her way for the exit.

"Are you coming?"

I turned around. She was waiting for me, her and three others, all wearing the same dark velvety coat, but different styles of shoes and earrings. There were two black SUVs parked on the curb behind them.

I didn't get up at once. The notion was absurd, and I think she saw it in my eyes.

"I can only unlock the cage. It's up to you to spread your wings and fly." She told me.

"Who are you?" I asked in a shaky tone.

"I'm Breanne. This is Scarlett. She's Mandee. And that one, we call her the Andalusian."

Breanne, Scarlett, Mandee, and the Andalusian. These were the first Swords of St. Catherine I had the pleasure to meet. And if all Swords were as impressive as they, with all due respect, there isn't a force on earth powerful enough to stop them.

I ran away from New York City that night. Sadly, no one noticed. Not even Papa, who was away on business.

...

Far away on the other side of the continent. In British Columbia, not too far from Vancouver, that's where I absconded. It was in the middle of April, but the snow-capped mountains still looked like Christmas. Bright lights glittered from torches and iron-wrought lamps. It was like a dream.

I had no idea what to expect. I barely knew Breanne or her associates. Even during the ten-hour flight, Breanne was reserved in her responses, answering my questions with "everything will be explained" and somehow, that didn't bother me. It didn't tickle my trepidation or rouse suspicion. She'd just watched me with fascination, like a figure in a snow globe.

The villa was more or less a massive luxurious compound complete with two towers on both the east and west wings. Its driveway was lined with some of the most expensive cars I've ever seen, even for me. There was a helicopter and a boat on the glassy lake out back. Everyone seemed busy, coming and going with a strong sense of urgency as if their individual tasks seemed so dire, so pertinent.

And of course, it didn't take me long to realize what the staff and visitors all had in common. They were all women. Young and old, but all of them, strong. You could feel it. From the tall to the smallest, everyone emanated this aura of being in charge.

The interior was magnificent, sleek and modern. A tamed fire burned within a central fireplace. All the counters had sharp edges, and everything was an accentuation of black or white surfaces. There weren't many photos. I didn't see symbolism or any indication that would lead me to believe this was some kind of organization, just a lot of lamps, tables, and comfortable places to sit. Everything looked clean and new.

I saw a group of women emerging from a hallway, all wearing white fencing uniforms, exasperated with sweat and carrying rapiers. I saw another group not much older than me assembling rifles in the living room as they watched live news on the giant flat-screens. They knew what they were doing. All of them wore different styles of white collared shirts tucked into their black skirts or pants. And for the first time in a long time, I smiled.

"Have you ever fired a gun?"

I looked over my shoulder. Breanne was without her coat and looked even more stunning than before. Her black dress showed off an athletic physique with a golden pin clasped over her left shoulder. She was staring down at her smartphone and there was an assistant standing by. Scarlet, Mandee, and the Andalusian were gone.

"Have you ever fired a gun?" She repeated.

"No."

"Come along."

"Come along" seemed to be her catchphrase for a while. The first thing she did, wasn't giving me a tour of the facilities, it was escorting me to an elevator that took us underground. Even before the doors opened, I could hear the pops that would eventually become music to my ears. The doors opened up to this extensive shooting gallery and a fully stocked armory.

They were toys, an entire library of deadly instruments and their accessories. Racks of shotguns, AR-15s, fully and semi-automatics, bolt-action rifles, Berettas, pistols, precision models, tactical and military grade hardware…I was salivating. Everything was black. I could feel the texture of the grips without even touching them. I could smell the oil and gunpowder. It was amazing. I was starstruck.

For some reason I was drawn to the Sig Sauer P238. It was one of the smaller, compact pistols at the end of a row of handguns. I was just about to slide my fingers over the handle when someone startled me with, "I wouldn't."

It was the Andalusian, watching me with an amused smirk.

"Actually, could you?" Breanne asked her. "Something's come up."

"Of course," the Andalusian nodded.

"We'll see you at dinner." Breanne told me before hurrying off with her assistant.

"Try the Gen4 Glock 19. The Sig Sauer only holds six rounds. You'll want something with less recoil since you have small wrists. The nineteen is perfect."

Taking the Andalusian's advice, I picked it up. It was the first time I ever held a gun. After approaching an open lane, she loaded it with a magazine of 9mm rounds. A paper sheet human target was wheeled back to twenty-five yards.

"Keep your finger off the trigger until you're ready to fire. Mind the muzzle. When you're ready, turn the safety off and square up your sights. You'll feel a force popping the gun back as you fire. That's your recoil but it shouldn't be too bad. Fire once and relax. Breathe before you pull the trigger again."

The Andalusian was nurturing in her tone. She handed me a set of earmuffs and encouraged me to wear these yellow protective goggles. Then, she simply extended her hand, motioning me to approach the booth before she took a couple steps back.

In that first shot…a loud, powerful discharge was released in so many ways. And much to my own surprise, I hit the target in the dead center of its chest. Right on the "x". I don't blame you if you don't believe me. I couldn't believe it myself, but it was dead on. Even the Andalusian was taken aback. I wished Papa was there to see it.

She encouraged me to fire again. I didn't hit the "x" again, but I was close. Over and over again I fired until all fifteen rounds were out. Of the fifteen, I hit the "x" three more times and the groupings showed I wasn't far off with the others.

"Is that good?" I asked.

"It's not bad. You got an eye for accuracy. But I won't call you a Mary Sue just yet. We'll see how well you do on the obstacle course."

"I'm sorry, obstacle course?!"

"Mm-hmm. Scarlet holds the record but that's because I stopped timing my passes."

I chuckled, "I'm assuming, by passes, you mean your attempts at it?"

"That's right," she said as she removed the gun from my jittery hands.

"Why do they call you the Andalusian?"

"Call me Anna. My name is Anna Marie."

"I'm Gladys."

"That's a pretty name."

"Thank you," I curtsied.

It was Anna who gave me a tour of the facilities. This place had an indoor pool, a massage parlor, a state-of-the-art communications center, and a computer bullpen set up to look like the inside of a corporate office. The top floors had hallways like a hotel, which it was. There was a commons area on the third floor where a group of women were discussing current events with mimosas.

A fully staffed kitchen worked to prepare dinner. I noticed the roof and several balconies had sentry guards, gorgeous women with long hair and scoped rifles scanning for activity. We were out on the frosty 2nd floor terrace overlooking the lake when I finally asked what I should have asked two hours ago.

"What is this place?"

"Better question: why'd you come?" she countered.

At that age, I wasn't exactly prone to self-reflection. Anna's question stumped me.

"It's okay. Sorry." She said. "I don't mean to pry, it's just...you don't strike me as...well. It's just strange."

"Why are you here?" I asked her.

She took a moment and said, "Because I believe in what we're doing. I'm willing to sacrifice everything to accomplish our mission. It's not just for myself. It's for women of all races, creed, and class."

Staring out at the mirror surfaced lake, Anna continued with, "Once, there was this woman who was raped by a football player, a superstar. She reported it to the police, but they were reluctant to press charges. The league had an army of lawyers who destroyed the woman's reputation and painted her out to be some kind of gold-digger. On top of that, the football player was married. His wife threatened to file a defamation suit against the woman if she went public.

"Then, we stepped in. We obtained a copy of him knocking out his wife in the lobby of a casino. We had it played everywhere. I'm sure you've seen it. He lost his job, his career, and two years ago he was convicted of first-degree battery. While in prison he was killed during a fight. The killer was one of our pawns. We have pawns everywhere."

I wasn't sure what to think, whether she was serious or whether the story was true...but again, I was compelled to ask, "what is this place?"

A loud melody reverberated around the estate. It was the dinner bell. Anna took in a deep breath and suddenly smiled with this twinkle of optimism in her brown eyes. Rubbing my shoulders, she said I was about hear all the answers to my question.

It was in the dining room, a massive hall with a long black-stone table positioned over a white almost fur-like rug. There were sixty seats, sixty plates, sixty settings. The hanging crystal lights were cool but difficult to describe.

After washing my hands and primping myself next to Anna, we entered the dining room together. Almost immediately wave of anxiety rushed over me. Breanne was at the head of the table with the sharp-eyed Scarlet to her right.

Everyone else was a new face, all beautiful, unique, and intriguing. They saw me but no one said hello. They just smiled politely and engaged in their own conversations. We found a pair of seats just five away from Breanne and instinctively I almost bowed before sitting. Her blue eyes shined like diamonds. It's hard to hard to pull away from them.

Before the food and beverages were brought in, Breanne stood up. At once, there was silence. All conversations ceased.

"Thank you all for being here. I know many of you have waited days, some of you weeks since I brought you here to our lovely Château de Cliff. But at last, the time has come for formal introductions.

"First and foremost, it is incumbent upon me to make it clear that you are not one of us. Not yet. We will train you. Mold you. Instill in you with the capability to call yourself a Sword and if you are ready and prove yourselves capable, then we will draw you from your sheaths. It is then that you will have the eternal honor to call yourself a Sword. We are the Swords of St. Catherine. Plainly put. We are the ones to keep the world moving forward."

Immediately seven women of the sixty stood up and placed their right hands over their hearts, extending two fingers to touch the left edge of their clavicle. I and a few others thought we were supposed to stand as well, but Anna sat me back down.

The seven women, who included Anna, Mandee and Scarlet, recited an affirmation in unison with Breanne. "The wheel will never be broken. We till the earth. We grow the seeds. We've come to collect on all man's deeds. To the martyr. Till the end."

"I am Breanne Cunningham. I am the head this estate and, in a sense, your benefactor, your sponsor. I am responsible for everything you do from here on out. If, after our training you prove yourselves to be more than dainty flowers with pretty faces, you will become one of us in a private ceremony held in her presence. Those of you who fail to make the cut will be released and set free to live your lives as you see fit. But know this. We will watch you. You will be scrutinized and followed till we are satisfied that you are no longer a threat.

"You have an opportunity here to become something greater than anything you've ever seen in the movies or on TV. This isn't a fairy tale. We are not here to have fun. At present, know that you are Protégés. Once you become full-fledged members, you will henceforth be known as Swords. Our mission, our goals, our history, what we intend to accomplish, none of this information will be made privy until you become full-fledged Swords. Understand?"

Perhaps, seeing I did not, Breanne clarified with a smile, "We are a secret organization. We intend to keep it a secret. If you are here, it's because we are choosing to trust you with what little information I've just provided. If you betray us, if you utter any of this to anyone outside of our little club, we will kill you. I'm not joking. This isn't a bluff. As sure as we have brought you here, we will take you out. Having said this. If anyone thinks they've bitten off more than they can chew, there's the door. I advise that you leave now."

No one moved at first, but six girls eventually stood up. I could tell they were scared. So was I. They were escorted from the dining room. Their chairs and table settings were taken away.

I should have left right then and there, but I didn't. It was all too intriguing. And there was something about the way Breanne looked at me. It's as if she could sense a potential. No one else ever saw me as something more, as something important, or capable of great things.

And so, I stayed. I became a Protégé. We didn't sign some contract or take a blood oath. We gave them our word and that was enough. Before then, I honestly felt so alone and helpless. But after that night, I had entire army of Amazons at my beck and call. After that night, I was fearless.

Interlude

...

The next morning, I flew back to New York. I still had to go to school and maintain appearances. But it was different. I was different. The classrooms I once fretted, now seemed so juvenile and beneath me. I was no longer bothered by Clarice's irritating laughter or the feeling of being discarded by the rest of my siblings. They had their country clubs, their shopping sprees, their brunch and fashion weeks. I had my secret. And of course, I had Papa.

I couldn't wait to see him. I was bursting to tell him of my adventures, having fired a gun, and meeting these extraordinary women. But I didn't. I kept my word. All I could tell him was that there was a six-week program for aspiring musicians in Seattle. I asked if I could attend over the summer and, simply relieved to see me smiling again, Papa said yes.

That summer was the most brutally intense period of my life. I wasn't exactly the active, outdoorsy type. Even after I fired the gun for the first time, I could still feel the rattling in my wrists for days. The training was ridiculous. I was the youngest, the smallest out of my class, but I was still expected to keep up with the rest.

We trained on the grounds of Chateau de Cliff under a strict diet of steamed chicken breast, select vegetables, and a blended variety of protein shakes and cleansers. I had to wear a vest that weighed forty pounds as I trudged up and down those forest hills around Whistler Mountain.

My asthma made it difficult to breathe and I passed out on the first day. No one came and got me. I woke up in the middle of the night, lost and alone. When I got back to the chateau, they immediately threw me into the pool and made me swim in increments of twenty minutes. When I could no longer lift my arms, two women carried me from the pool to the showers. They washed me and clothed me in a clean robe.

From there, I was escorted to the theater where a group of protégés were watching a marathon of the most violently choreographed martial arts movies I've ever seen. The chairs were recliners. We plopped our throbbing, sore bodies down in these seats and rehydrated with cold bottles of water.

I was too tired to notice at first, but the movies were played at a low volume. I wouldn't find out till later, but this was a technique to implant instincts in us. We watched everything from kung-fu flicks to war epics. The plots were useless, but it was the action we soaked in. We fell asleep to it. Then, we'd wake up and repeat. We did this every day for the first week and thankfully, I was able to finish the mountain course by my third outing.

The second week, Crossfit trainers were brought in. These women were sculpted goddesses. They could run, lift, climb, and throw better than any man I'd ever seen. They instilled in us the mentality that as long as we applied ourselves, as long as we were determined, nothing was impossible.

They taught us how to do deadlifts, the proper way to perform squats and pull-ups. I was actually good with the pull-ups and the ring-dips. I could climb the rope pretty fast. The kettle bells were a problem. So were the medicine balls and the box jumps. But still. We started out light and worked our way up. The fact that we were all women, enduring the same hell, I think it brought us closer together as comrades.

After the Crossfit training, we were still expected to run with the heavy vests and swim every day. All of it was to build our endurance and stamina, to teach us how to commit and follow through with each exercise, preparing us to follow through with each mission.

On Friday during the second week, I bonded with some of the other protégés around a campfire in the woods. I learned some of their backstories, their aspirations. Some of them had some pretty harrowing tales of sexual misconduct, rape, and child abuse. Some even survived attempts on their lives by deranged stalkers and possessive boyfriends. It was clear they absolutely hated injustice and used their anger to get through some of the training.

When they asked what was driving me, I was a little embarrassed to tell them. I could have mentioned Clarice and how she accused my favorite teacher of sexually harassing me. I could have mentioned that my teacher committed suicide or that I never got any respect from my peers. But compared to the others, I didn't have some superhero type revenge story compelling me to work hard.

"It's just rage." I told them as if I was talking about a sore throat. "It's this burning rage that I have deep inside. I'm sorry. I don't know. I can't explain it."

"Rage?" a girl scoffed. "No way. You barely raise your voice. I've never seen you get angry about anything. Haha! You're so polite. What do you know about rage?"

"I know a thing or two." Came an outside voice.

Scarlet paid us a visit. She came from the bushes and immediately everyone stood up to salute. It was strange seeing her out in the woods dressed in formal business attire with her bob cut and heavy red eye shadow. Every time I saw Scarlet it sent shivers down my spine. She wasn't that much taller than me, but I knew she was dangerous. Even as she approached, stepping in the dirt with those thousand-dollar heels, she was twirling a switchblade with a grin.

"Em-hmm. And what the fuck is you doin?" said another approaching voice.

Scarlet groaned as turned and saw that she was followed. It was another full-fledge Sword, my first time seeing this one. Her name was Celeste, one of the few African Americans I saw in the society and perhaps the only one, other than Anna and Breanne, who had no fear of Scarlet.

"Why don't you go back inside! Hovering over my shoulder is only gonna get on my fuckin' nerves."

"Leave 'em alone, Scarlet. We're all friends here." Celeste said, almost amused.

Scarlet smirked, "Well this one claims she has rage. I want to help."

Celeste looked me up and down. She said we were friends, but I didn't that impression.

"Gladys, right?" Celeste asked.

"Yes ma'am."

"Aren't you the one who got lost her first day out?"

"In the middle of the night. And I found my way back. Alone."

Celeste grinned. "Everyone has rage, sweetheart."

"Everyone breathes too," Scarlet said. "But I have weak lungs, so I don't breathe as well as the rest of you bitches. The same goes with rage. Just because everyone has it, doesn't mean we all have it the same way. Some have it more than others. Isn't that right, bright eyes?"

I nodded.

Celeste shrugged, "Very well. If she has rage, she has rage. Let's go, Scarlet. You can torment them later."

Scarlet retracted her switchblade and tossed it to me. "A gift. Friend to a friend. Do your best, ladies!"

Once they were gone, we all shuddered with relief. I couldn't figure out the dynamics. Were we friends? I studied the switchblade and felt glad. There's nothing wrong with having the scariest person in the house on your side. Or so I thought.

In the third week, we still kept up with our Crossfit, but before we ran the mountain, we were introduced to combat training for the first time. Everyone was given the option to choose their own style of fighting. We'd eventually have to learn more, but our first was to be our principle, the specialty that we had to master above all others.

Initially, I chose boxing. Because honestly, I thought it would be the easiest to absorb and take in. But Anna showed up that afternoon. She was dressed in a two-piece fitness suit that put the rest of us to shame. She really was built like a magnificent Andalusian horse in so many ways. I could tell she was strong and fast with legs that could bend steel.

"You can do boxing too. But I want you to learn tai chi." She told me.

I wasn't about to tell her no. There wasn't a Tai Chi master present, so I had to run the mountain until the master's flight arrived two days later. Her name was Wing Qiu, my Sifu.

At first, I wasn't sure if Anna was trying to give me break or insult me by assigning Tai Chi. Because the first day of practice was relatively easy. It was a lot of stretching and breathing techniques. Just what my body needed. But by the fourth day, we started these wrist-to-wrist exercises called chi-sau drills. From there, the intensity escalated.

By the fourth week of summer, I was worn out and exhausted but saw results when I looked in the mirror. I was never fat or terribly skinny. But suddenly I had biceps. I could see a six-pack coming through. My quads were thicker. My calves were rock solid. I felt…Yeah, I felt sexy.

The entire summer consisted of strengthening the body. By the time I had to return home for school, I was conditioned and memorized a lot of the exercises so I could practice them on my own.

I was also given a list of titles to read as homework. On my sixteenth birthday, I cracked open a collection of Emma Goldman's essays about anarchy. I also pored through Virginia Woolf, Simone de Beauvoir, and who could forget Eve Ensler's "Vagina Monologues".

It was very much an enlightening period in my life. I stopped going to my father's offices and rebelled against the family in their traditional excursions around the world. Every time they left me at home alone, I'd venture off to Chateau de Cliff. I'd continue my training and ask for more books to read. I was becoming more of a regular, more so than all the other protégés. Wasn't trying to garner favor. There was simply no place else I'd rather be.

…

On Christmas Day, Papa was stranded by a blizzard ravaging Chicago. The idea of spending my favorite holiday with the rest of my family was utterly dreadful, so again, I embarked to Canada.

Chateau de Cliff was practically empty when I arrived. Most of the staff was allowed time off. I remember walking down the long 3rd floor corridor with the high ceilings when I heard the soft chime of someone sobbing. It wasn't continuous, like someone who wanted to be heard, like a cry for help. I stopped and focused to see if I could hear it again. All was quiet. Then, I heard the tap of glass hitting something hard. It came from Anna's room.

Ever so cautiously, I turned the handle and cracked open the door. "Oh my god," I whispered. Anna Marie was always the leader, the intrepid ignition that lit a fire in the rest of us. Never before had I seen her so distraught, so sad. I was compelled to enter.

Her room was much larger than my own. It had its own fireplace and an entire wall made of glass that provided a breathtaking view of the mountains. Anna had the drapes closed so the afternoon appeared as night.

She was curled with her back against the corner of her bed and nightstand. A half-empty bottle of rosé was by her side as she stared daggers into the wine glass held up by her careless grip. Even from twelve paces off, I could see the fire flaring in her eyes.

"Anna? What's wrong?"

She shook her head, "Please, just go."

"I can't do that. I see you're in pain. How can I enjoy this Christmas when one I truly admire…Please, let me help you? I promise it'll stay between us. I promise."

She said nothing for nearly five minutes. I sat on the floor in front of her and wrapped around my legs. Up till this point, I honestly didn't know much about her. I revealed a lot about my own upbringing, but I remember walking away from those conversations as if I'd just finished talking to myself. She'd only respond with, "dang" or "that's messed up."

I glanced at the door with thoughts about leaving when suddenly she said, "If you tell anyone. I'll never forgive you."

"I swear it! On pain of death, it'll never leave my lips."

In the depths of her dagger-like stare, I could tell she had every intention of holding me to my word. Then, she began.

"Memories...I'm beginning to think that's the reason why no one really wants to live forever. No sane person. I can't get the memories of him out of my head. He haunts me with his smile. He haunts me with his laughter. He haunts me with his love. I didn't ask for it. But he… He was the only one who ever knew the real me and I killed him. There was something in his eyes when I shot him. It's like...it's like he was speaking to me through that look. But for the life of me, I can't figure out what he was trying to say. Asshole!"

"Who was he?" I asked.

"Just a man."

"What was his name?"

"Doesn't matter."

"Anna, I'd like to know."

Anna finished her wine and set the glass on the nightstand with a hard knock. She stared at it in a half-drunken stupor, the pink wine gradually pooling to the bottom. The lamp's golden glow washed over the right side of her face as her head tilted and her gaze gravitated to the light.

"Angel," she said. "Marcus Angel. My Angel. Breanne, Celeste, the others. Even you. Everyone knows a side of me, the side I allow you to see, the only side I want you to see. But Marcus, he saw through the bullshit, the games, the masks, the lies. He knew I was a monster, but he loved me anyway."

"You think you're a monster? Anna, why do you think you're a monster?"

She rolled her eyes. "We're all monsters, Gladys. All of us."

"No, we're not! I'm sorry, but I believe you do yourself a disservice with such degradation. I don't like that. The fact that you think so low of yourself shows that you're not bad. It shows that you're humble. The real monsters would never give in to self-reflection. Real monsters don't cry. Perhaps your man saw you cry. Perhaps...Perhaps that's why he believed, as I do, that there's more to you than meets the eye. And considering you're the most amazing person I've ever met, that's saying something."

"You think I'm amazing?" she said with a condescending smirk.

"Yes! Do you not?! You said you don't time your passes on the obstacle course, but you did in the beginning. I saw them. I saw the tapes of you in the combat trials. You took out five Marines using what looked like some kind of kickboxing?"

"Krav maga."

"Krav maga! That's amazing, Anna! Truly, it is! I know we all have to start sparring with the other Swords sooner or later, but out of all of them, I wouldn't want to face you."

Anna sighed as she pulled herself up and straightened out her blouse. "When you grow up, learn to read between the lines. We'll talk again."

"That's not fair!" I glowered. "I may only be sixteen, but you have no idea what I've been through. I understand completely."

"Well clearly you don't understand words. Because *completely* implies there's nothing else to understand. You haven't even asked why I killed him. Don't you think that's important?"

"I'm sorry. I'll go."

"Wait," she smirked. "I didn't ask for your help, Gladys, but I appreciate what you're trying to do. I don't want to insult you by assuming what you do or don't know. On the same token, you need to understand that it's incredibly frustrating when people assume they've figured you out based on what little breadcrumbs you've given them."

"Anna…I"

"Forget it. Scarlet said something about rage? I can see it. You should be careful with that."

"Or else what?" I teased.

"You'll turn into Scarlet."

"Well, we can't have that can we?"

"Let's go." Anna said as she brushed past my shoulder.

We grabbed a couple of laser-sighted MP-15s from the armory and went to the tactical shooting course. It was an abandoned mining town from the 1870s on the other side of the mountain pass. Bundled in our white coats, we jogged north to get there. Everything was covered in ice and daylight faded. But with a cheerful smile, Anna flipped a switch to turn on the floodlights and activated the timed targets.

In below freezing conditions, she and I combed through this mining town, building by building, from the saloons to cabins, as ballistic targets emerged in random intervals at random locations. It was so fun! Assessing threats, taking down stationary targets, and fending off ambushes from drones while avoiding paintball attacks from random sentry guns that popped out of nowhere. We were a good team.

I couldn't remember the last time I laughed so hard. I remember jumping through a saloon window when I saw a sentry gun and glass shards got stuck in my hair. I got popped three times in my ass. The rubber pellets felt like I was getting spanked by a red-hot poker. Anna was keeling over with laughter as I limped to get away. My thighs were cramping up and I kept slipping in the snow. It was ridiculous. It was fun.

Anna had it ten times worse, being that I was smaller and quicker. I remember seeing her roll across the table. She thought she was about to roll off and hit the floor for cover, but she rolled directly into a flat wall because the table was part of a booth. She was riddled with paintball pellets. Seeing her squirm while spitting with laughter was definitely a sight to behold.

We limped back to the villa around a quarter past nine. Our undergarments were drenched with sweat. Our white coats, spotted as if we crashed through a rainbow, and my rifle was broken on the account of my swinging it like an ax.

We sat by the fireplace of the golden library that night, watching reruns of "Home Alone" and drinking from mugs of hot cocoa and marshmallows. Her idea, not mine.

"Anna, how long do we have to be protégés before we become Swords?"

Her brows raised. I knew it was sudden, but the question had lingered for some time. Lowering the volume, she turned to me with an arm over a headrest.

"What's the rush?" She asked.

I nestled further into my blanket and batted my lashes. "Well…I'd be devastated if I wasn't accepted. Meeting all of you and coming here is the best thing that's ever happened to me. I never want to leave."

—

Her lips were slurping from the mug. I couldn't tell from her grin whether she was taking me seriously.

"Gladys, have you ever killed anyone? Scratch that. I know you haven't. But have you ever thought about it? Like, if you were put in the position and given an assignment, do you think you'd be able to do it? To bring yourself to end the life of another human being?"

"Absolutely." I said without a shred doubt in my mind. That was the truth. I couldn't explain why I was so certain...or eager for that matter. But I wasn't blind to the fact that every Sword in the Society was a certified killer.

"Why?!" she asked.

"Because some people need to die. Honestly."

"Gladys, please tell me you're just saying that."

"No. I mean it."

"And you feel you're the best qualified to determine who and when?"

"Yes, I do."

Anna just stared at me.

"Gladys, who do you think you are?"

It was more than just a question. There were implications, a veiled accusation and it scathed in my chest. I didn't know what to say. For the first time I really did start to wonder, "Who *do* I think I am?"

"It's okay, Gladys. I don't mean to judge. And please don't take this the wrong way, but there really is a lot you just don't understand. Not yet. And there's nothing wrong with admitting that.

"In fact, it was Marcus who had the balls to encourage me to do the same. There's a lot I don't understand. The world is huge, there's so much, so many philosophies, customs, cultures, ethics, art, beauty. We are but two individuals in a world filled with billions. Being a part of our group is a commitment. You'll have to do things you might not agree with. You'll have to make sacrifices that'll test your commitment. Don't be so eager to jump in headfirst if you don't even know what you're jumping into."

"Whatever it takes. This is what I want." I whispered.

"Why?" She whispered back. "You don't even know what the hell *this* is. That's what I'm trying to tell you."

"You don't think I'll be able to handle it."

"Gladys…"

"No. That's what you're trying to say. Isn't it? I'm the best shot in my class. I can carry more than twice my own weight and I've only failed to complete a training course but once! I've read all the books they've given me. I've done everything they asked! So, what don't you think I'll be able handle? Please! Just tell me."

"I'll tell you what," she said. "I have a mission coming up. It's an official one. This scumbag senator out of Toronto. Now this is a man in serious need of some killing. I'll talk to Breanne and ask to bring you along."

I gasped so loud, propping up on my knees like a puppy ready to go for a walk. Anna chuckled, "If she agrees to bring you, I'll insist that you're the one who kills him. From there, it'll be up to you. If you succeed, you'll increase your chances of becoming one of us. You chicken out, the game's over. You'll only get one shot. We don't tolerate failure."

"Don't worry. Consider it done."

…

I did do it. At a fund-raiser held at an elegant hotel. My fingers were numb from playing a number of Mozart's sonatas. But when Chrysler requested a private audience with me, a sixteen-year-old who could easily pass for a twelve-year-old, my resolve was cemented. If I got caught and had to spend the rest of my life in jail for having killed that stupid bastard, it would have been worth it.

Alone in his suite, I remember sitting on his lap as he told me some story about his childhood. He kept scrubbing his thick mustache against my cheek. His breath was a like a burning exhaust of scotch that made my stomach curl into knots. And when I could take no more, I got up and casually walked around to the back of the couch, keeping my fingertips on the shoulders of his coat. Then, like a python my arms coiled around his forehead. I leaned him back to expose his neck and swiftly wiped a dagger across his throat. There was a world of satisfaction in seeing the blood spray all over his coffee table.

My first kill. So easy it's scary.

Spring Break marked the end of my first year in training with the Society. Of the fifty from my class, only eight of us remained. Most of the class performed poorly in the tactical course. They struggled to master their assigned form of martial arts through an obvious lack of commitment. But the nail in the coffin were the combat trials. We had to spar with official Swords, which included Scarlet, Celeste, Mandee, and even Anna.

There wasn't a single day where they took it easy on us. Ruthless. We were given the option to double-team or employ some ambush tactic like using decoys while someone attacked from the rear. But every day, we lost. To call it traumatic was putting it lightly. We were allowed to wear face guards to avoid having to explain black-eyes and busted lips to friends and family. But I had my elbow dislocated. Massive welts found places on my back and thighs. And for two days, I urinated blood after receiving a heel kick from Anna directly to my midsection.

Those combat trials had girls falling like flies. They'd go home and never come back. It was insane, really. In order to pass the combat trials, one had to survive a full minute of full contact sparring one-on-one with a Sword. It took me three months before I chose none other than Celeste.

I won't lie. I didn't think I could last fifteen seconds against Anna, and I saw how Scarlet deliberately tried to inflict permanent bodily injury on her opponents. Celeste was just as tough and fearsome as anyone else, but I also gathered she was more of a talker than a brawler. And as any fighter would say, "thinking" is the biggest enemy in a fight.

Celeste had mastered an Indonesian style of martial arts called Silat. She had the zero-fat body of a track-and-field sprinter. And even before we started, her hazel eyes conveyed that she felt sorry for me. I'm sure she saw the fury in my own blue eyes, but it didn't faze her the slightest.

Using tai chi, I engaged her. It was tough. Tai Chi employs the stratagem of using an opponent's momentum against them. But Celeste's attacks were short and powerful. There was hardly a moment where she fully extended any limb that I could latch onto. Uppercuts to the ribs, elbows to the face, and kicks to the legs came in quick successions.

My only option was stay small. In a wide-legged stance, I moved in with palm thrusts to her chest, chops to her neck, and strikes to the back of her knee. Out of the two dozen attempts, I probably landed three or four blows. Nevertheless, I lasted the full minute without dropping to my knees.

When the bell rang, I received an applause from the thirty in attendance. It was cool to see Anna smiling so proudly. I wished Papa was there. Because God knows I was scared out of my mind. But the rage overpowered the fear and I simply plunged ahead. This is the commitment they preached. You don't stop. You follow through. Celeste shook my hand and even Scarlet gave me a reluctant nod.

At last, the combat trials were over. I'd still occasionally spar with them but not as hard as in the trials. I even took up boxing, which was what I wanted in the first place. And while I thought my initiation was nearly complete, I'd soon discover the worst was yet to come.

Upon graduating high school, I had a heart-to-heart talk with Papa about where I wanted to attend college. It was one of the most difficult conversations I ever had. Here, he expressed how disappointed he'd been since I've stopped coming on family trips. He said he understood that being a teenager meant giving me space and letting me grow, but he truly missed me. So, when I told him that I wanted to study abroad, it moved him to tears.

It really did break my heart to grieve him so. But I had to go. To soften the blow, I told him I wanted to enroll in the London School of Economics. That perhaps one day I'd follow in his footsteps as a savant in finance. He promised the door was always opened and that the boardroom chair by his side would always have my name on it. With a tearful goodbye, I embraced him and left home.

Training in British Columbia was only the beginning. The real trials lay waiting in the Middle East.

05. Gladys Vandelay - The Initiation

In the U.S., I heard there was a march on D.C., a Women's March where prominent figures of influence and fame gathered in solidarity. It was a rallying call to address human rights and equality for all. Of their grievances, I heard they called for things like reproductive rights, gender equality, healthcare reform, equal pay, and an overall acceptance towards the preference of a woman to do and be whatever she wanted.

I'm not sure if this movement was promulgated by the Swords of St. Catherine or not. Either way, I couldn't help but feel conflicted in so many ways. In the United States, women have so much control, so much power, so much influence. We can say what we want. Do what we want. There are obstacles, sure, but the trials and tribulations make us ten times stronger.

And if the women of America are ten times stronger than men on the basis of that logic, then I can tell you from the bottom of my heart…the women fighting in the Middle East are on a whole other level.

In many of these countries, women are still treated like cattle, like currency, like a bartering chip between families. I've seen women stoned for exposing too much skin. I've seen teenagers beheaded simply for reporting they were raped. I've seen entire villages beating a woman for walking without a man's supervision or daring to take off her hijab in the scorching sun.

In parts of Saudi Arabia, there's a practice called Wahhabism by which groups of clergymen literally patrol the streets like wolves to surround and attack anyone they deem violators of their sacred laws. They were given carte blanche to determine for themselves what's consider blasphemy or treason. Women are their main targets.

Here, women need the permission of men to marry, divorce, educate themselves, seek employment, or even open a bank account. That's just to name a few. And God forbid any woman was caught driving, though I heard they recently 'laxed on that law. The punishments ranged from mutilation, stoning, acid to the face, and on occasion, crucifixion.

...

Medina was my first stop when I came to the Middle East, one of the "holiest" places in Saudi Arabia. An underground activist tutored me on the customs, me and the three other Protégés I came with. My blue eyes and blonde hair would have been an eyesore. Thus, it was to my advantage to wear the abaya and niqab, black robes that would conceal every inch of me. Additionally, I darkened my face with foundation and used brown eye contacts.

Initially, the plan was to spend five days in Medina before smuggling ourselves north into Jordan. But one of the Proteges, Shelly, she saw a group of men raping a student in the alley outside our apartment building. Shelly attacked. The ensuing battle was loud, bloody, and attracted the Wolves of Wahhabi. That's when I intervened with my trusty Dragunov. The bodies we left in the streets roiled the public for months.

We were long gone by time the police raided shops and homes with impunity, but I learned very quickly that all actions had unintended consequences. The public demanded justice and the government gave it to them. The student who was raped was publicly beheaded. Her entire family was stoned in the middle of the town square.

When I heard about that, my heart blazed with rage. As much as I was pissed at Shelly for getting involved, it made me sick to my stomach that an innocent student could be killed for simply being a victim. And if you'd ask the locals, they'd tell you that she wasn't innocent, that she shouldn't have been walking alone, or that she was wearing clothing that invited such an attack. Animals. That's how I judged them. Only animals are numb to compassion, acting on their baser instinct like mindless fucks chomping at the bait. Vile putrid savages!

It was the first of many dilemmas I'd encounter in the Middle East. Injustice was an everyday occurrence and we had to discern, we had to pick and choose our battles. Some, we intervened. And some, we simply had to endure the screams, the heart-wrenching cries for help. We couldn't risk exposing the organization, compromising our allies, and sabotaging the myriad of missions that were already in motion.

After a three-month odyssey, us four Protégés reached a desert village about fifteen miles south of Raqqa in Syria. Here, we joined a group of guerillas who came from all over the world. It was a resistance group in retaliation to ISIS after refugees started fleeing the region for Europe.

The leader of our battalion was a woman named, Cyrine, a Tunisian battle-hardened warrior with the fiercest gaze I've ever seen. Her voice was loud and tyrannical. When she met the four of us, I already knew. There was a silent nod where we understood on some psychic level, Cyrine was a full-fledged Sword of St. Catherine.

For two years, our battalion wreaked havoc on ISIS insurgents throughout the Fertile Crescent. The fighting was intense. It was actual war. There were days where I didn't eat. Sometimes I had to sleep in rat-infested basements while mortars bombarded sections of a city. Everything was a potential IED. Sand got everywhere. The heat was unbearable. Toilet paper and clean water had more precious than gold. It was a battle of will. When vets say they have PTSD, I believe them. You'd be crazy not to.

The Protégé named Allison Tuney was the first to die. It was a reality check that hit all of us harder than we could possibly imagine. This wasn't just training. This was real. It wasn't guaranteed that I'd ever see home again. Up till her death, we had considerable success. Some battles lasted for days, but one by one, we'd win. And with each victory our egos inflated. We were four young ladies outperforming the tough rugged men in terms of kills, courage, and competence.

But when Allison fell to a sniper, it was a turning point. I'll never forget it. We were on watch, and I was sitting with my back against the rampart of a tower. Allison was scanning the frontlines with night-vision goggles. Just for a moment, she looked down and smiled at me as she was trying to say something. That's when a bullet passed through her temple. Her body slumped over and Shelly screamed so loud that pulling an alarm would have been redundant.

All the sudden, it's like everything was turned up to hyper speed. My heart rate increased. Lights and faces blurred and my vision tilted as I scrambled for my Dragunov. Cyrine ordered us to evacuate. I refused. I was angry. I had to kill someone. I NEEDED to satisfy my rage. Cyrine pulled on my shoulder, and I reacted by hitting her with the butt of my rifle.

That was a mistake.

The next thing I remember, I was waking up in the back of a sandy sun-blasted truck with Shelly and Sanya looking over me. The back of my head was swollen, and I could still feel where I was kicked in the ribs.

Two nights later, Cyrine summoned me. She was sitting by a fire outside our encampment on the banks of Lake Assad. It was on the other side of a ridge, underneath an acacia tree. Out of view from the others.

Cyrine told me to take off my hijab. I refused. She laughed. Cyrine and the ten other women in our unit were from countries ranging from Egypt to Pakistan. They didn't need to conceal their appearance. The Middle East was their home, but when Cyrine spoke English it was always with a British accent.

"You know I should kill you." She said. "On the battlefield, a soldier is not permitted to disobey her CO. It's called insubordination."

I didn't respond. Up to this point, my respect for Cyrine was only so-so. I acknowledged that she was an adept commander but too callous. She didn't bat an eye when she shot a child for delivering what looked like a bomb when it turned out to be a can of beans. That struck a chord with me.

She let down her hijab. Her black hair was pulled back and she had an even olive tone. She smiled before leaning back with her hands in the sand. "Where you come from, are all the girls like you? Imbued with spite and impudence?"

"Where I come from, there is no one like me."

She chuckled. "Celeste was right. Rage...Although, I would also add naïve and full of shit to your dossier as well. Have you learned nothing from all the blood and bodies we've littered across the desert? Anything at all?"

"What else did Celeste tell you?"

"Cheeky..." She smirked. "Well...I heard a certain Andalusian cares deeply about you. Perhaps that's why they assigned you to me. They know I won't go soft on you. Cross me again, and I'll not hesitate to put you down."

I rolled my eyes and turned to walk away. And the moment I turned my back, I heard this fast, aggressive shuffle. Cyrine launched from the banks and tackled me from behind. She ripped off my hijab and shoved me face-first into the sand. I whipped around to claw at her, but she evaded and came down with both hands on my throat, squeezing hard.

"Go on! Scream!" She whispered.

I grabbed a handful of sand and slung it at her. She laughed and turned away in time, but she was no longer on my throat. I kicked her off before we started to circle each other like territorial cats, each wide-eyed with excitement.

"Come on then. Let's see this rage!" She said.

I went at her with everything I had. I belted her ribs, punched her face, and even pulled off a crescent kick that connected with her jaw. She wobbled to her knees, but grinned and dusted herself off.

"Trained well," She said as she checked to see if her jaw was dislocated. "You're impressive, love. But here's what you need to learn."

She charged full-bore before scooping me up and slamming me in a double-leg takedown. I saw it coming but she was too fast. Once I was down, she mounted and grabbed both of my wrists to keep me pinned. And then, she flattened out to bring her entire weight on me, belly to belly, breast to breasts. She pecked me with kisses to my neck and cheek, groping, and grinding her pelvis into mine as she moaned and giggled in my ear.

"It doesn't matter what you do, you'll always be weaker. Without your guns, without guile, you are powerless. Any brainless oaf can do what I'm doing now and there's not a damn thing you can do about it."

She grabbed my face and clenched hard to force my jaw open. "This is what it means to be a woman in their world. The only way to survive is to reverse the roles by force. Like this!" She said before grinding into me.

"And like this!" She said, grinding again.

"And this!"

"And this!"

"GET OFF OF ME!!!" I screamed at the top of my lungs.

Cyrine forced her tongue into my mouth. I bit and drew blood. It didn't stop her. She just laughed before sucking on my neck. I finally managed to get one of my wrists free and punched her as hard as I could in the kidneys. She yelped and I wrestled free.

I scurried over to where I dropped my rifle, whipped it up, and immediately turned to aim my sights at the center of her fuckin' throat. She was breathing hard, laying on her back, ecstatic. I thumbed the safety switch, fully prepared to shoot.

"Anyone who kills a Sword can never become one." She said. "More importantly, to kill a Sword is to sign your own death warrant. You'll be hunted from the capitals to the Himalayas. Now put the gun down. Put it down. Before I really get mad."

I was about to vomit, grinding my teeth to hold back the queasy, nauseating feeling agitating in my stomach. I could still feel the residual warmth of her body against mine. So badly I wanted to kill that bitch. I fired a single shot. It hit the ground and popped sand in her face. Shelly and Sanya must have heard. They came running.

"Touch me EVER AGAIN...and I'll kill you." I shouted with tears rolling down my face.

"Gladys! Your hijab." Sanya reminded.

I hurried to cover myself before others in the unit came.

"Don't worry. We're just sorting some things out." Cyrine told them. Then she dismissed us. And for all I knew, she just laid there under that acacia tree for the rest of the night, smoking a cigarette.

Allison's death compounded by Cyrine's sexually assault really did a number on me. It changed my view of the world. Once, I was willing to put aside my own needs for the betterment of others. I used to feel bad for the screams, the women who were taken advantage of, the public executions, the homosexuals being tossed off rooftops.

I won't go so far as to say I no longer cared. It's more like it hardened me. I stored up those injustices like fuel in the tank and used it like coal in a furnace. It intensified my rage, my relentless drive to keep working, to get better, to get stronger. I wouldn't realize until later, but there was this sick, almost excited anticipation of evil that I hoped to encounter. Without evil, without a need for revenge…why else would I even exist? What else did I have to live for?

Those were dark thoughts that permeated for two years during my time in the Middle East. I felt no love. No happiness. No joy. Just bitter ire and an outlet for my violence. Shelly was eventually killed when a building collapsed during the battle to retake Raqqa. Sanya succumbed to an ambush during a raid on Mosul. I was the last Protégé.

Every day I wished for some IED, some ambitious sniper to take out Cyrine, but no luck. I ended up fighting side by side with her in some of the most savage gun fights that would never make it to the evening news or some history book. Once, we stopped a group of jihadis from a mass beheading along the Murat. And by "we," I mean me and my mounted machine gun from the other side of the river.

We heard about a sect of jihadists who had kidnapped over two hundred girls from a school in Pakistan. They planned to make them brides, to produce a new generation of war-mongering hate spawns.

Cyrine, I, and two other commandos from Singapore infiltrated their camp in the cold desert of Katpana. Armed with just my twin Glocks, I must have dropped at least eighteen before running out of ammo. I helped the girls escape and escorted them back to their villages, but even there, I could tell from the way the elders looked at me that I'd get no gratitude or appreciation.

Those innocent schoolgirls…they were like shells occupied by a timid ghost. I spotted maybe one or two who were independent free thinkers, bold enough to ask a question or two, but the rest…

The strange thing was, I never had any nightmares. I wasn't tormented by the faces I sniped from afar. My hands didn't quiver from pulling the trigger and I wasn't paranoid about raids or IED explosions. This wasn't normal. Something was wrong with me. And every day I saw Cyrine…it'd make my skin crawl and I'd have the insatiable urge to go out and kill some more. It was evil. There's no other way to describe it. I was evil.

On my 21st birthday, after three years of what could only be described as sheer hell on earth, Cyrine entered my tent and said I had a visitor. In walked Breanne, Anna, and Scarlet dressed in Army fatigues, not covered by hijabs. Their hair and ethnicity were open for all the world to see.

I didn't get up from my cot to greet them. I just lay there with contempt for everyone. Anna, the beautiful 5'10 Colombian walked over and sat beside me. She put a hand on my stomach and asked if I was all right. I politely removed her hand and said I was fine.

Anna…so badly, I wanted to ask her, "What were you thinking by sending me here? With *her*?!" Whatever they were training me for, I knew I was ready. Because I wasn't afraid of anything.

"It's time, Gladys," Breanne told me. "Your family hasn't seen you in three years. They're beginning to ask questions and there's only so much your proxy can say that'll convince them you're still in London."

I didn't respond.

"See what I mean?" Cyrine said as she plopped down on my duffle bag.

"Don't tell me you actually want to stay here?" Scarlet said.

"She doesn't. Look at her. She's miserable." Anna noted.

"Doesn't matter. You're to report home at once." Breanne ordered.

I sat up and took in a deep breath, inhaling through the nose. "Breanne…I'm not that same girl who ran up and down that stupid mountain in the posh hills of Canada. You better be careful telling me what to do."

Breanne, her blue eyes and long black hair…you could tell they had no idea they'd be waltzing in here barking orders to a stone-cold killer. Cyrine and Scarlet glanced at each other before bursting out with laughter.

I snapped and reached for my field knife. Anna caught my wrist, but I simply dropped the knife and caught it with the other hand, swiping at her but missing. She shoved me. I toppled over the cot but rolled to my feet, the knife at the ready.

"Gladys! Stop!" Anna barked.

I was ready. I didn't blink. I remember because my eyes were starting to get heated and dry. Anna was shocked. She must have recognized my trauma because she immediately cast her judgmental glare on Cyrine.

"What did you do?" Anna growled.

Cyrine stood up and approached her. "Nothing serious. We had a little fun is all. Didn't we? I think she…"

Before she could finish, Anna knocked her out with the most vicious left hook I'd ever seen. Cyrene's body went limp and collapsed.

"Get your things. We're leaving." Breanne said before she and Scarlet stormed out of the tent.

I sheathed my knife, collected my Glocks, and strapped the Dragunov over my shoulders. Then I ripped off my hijab and let it fall over Cyrine. Somewhat liberated, I emerged from the tent and looked up at the sun before letting my long golden hair sail in the wind.

Interlude

…

The flight back to America was…peculiar. I was on a private jet with all the first-class trappings. I was so used to running in cargo pants with a rough sheet over my face that wearing a designer skirt, a white blouse, and a matching light-jacket, I felt somewhat exposed, naked, and uncomfortable.

I peered out towards the mustard-colored clouds that blanketed this rotten world when, suddenly, a familiar tune played over the speakers. Erik Satie's "Gymnopedie." My favorite, the one I mastered when I was but eleven-years-old. How quaint. Once upon a time, the melody would wash over me like a warm breeze on a nice autumn afternoon. Now…there was nothing.

"I remembered. Your favorite, right." Anna came bringing a glass of orange juice before taking the seat next to me.

I nodded my thanks for the juice.

Scarlet and Breanne occupied the seats facing us. Breanne was the type to smile in the spirit of being polite, but by then, I knew it belied skepticism and doubt. She examined me with invasive eyes. And Scarlet, the woman in the bob cut who used to scare the wits out of me, she seemed more domesticated than before. It was all just so peculiar.

"How do you feel?" Breanne asked me.

My first thought was, "How the hell do you *think* I feel?" My second was, "as if you have the right to know."

I said nothing.

Breanne smirked. "Your initiation is nearly complete, Gladys. There is but one more test before we can draw you as a Sword."

"Another test?" I seethed.

"The ultimate test. To show whether you're dedicated, committed to the cause."

"Breanne…I don't even know what the cause is."

"All these years and you haven't figured it out?" Scarlet scoffed. "Why on earth do you think we had you read Emma Goldman or Virginia Woolf?"

I sat on the edge of my seat, "Listen, I like that we are all women. I like fighting against the patriarchy. There's nothing more important to me than joining your organization. But it's been six years and I'm still a protégé despite everything I've done! All the blood I've shed! Shelly! Ally! Sanya! All dead! I almost died myself out there and for what?! What more do I have to prove? What is our ultimate goal?"

Breanne just sat there scanning me with those diamond eyes, her hands resting on her lap like some boarding-school teacher.

"Just tell her." Anna said.

"No!" Scarlet objected. "She hasn't leaped the final hurdle."

"You'll find out soon enough, Gladys," Breanne said. "You're almost there. When we disembark, you'll reconnect with your family. Repair the bridges deteriorated by your absence. Of course, this goes without saying, you can't let on anything related to your ordeal, your recent trials and tribulations. You have to convince your family that you're still their youngest daughter. Meek, modest, vulnerable."

Anna grabbed my hand. She felt the calluses in my palm, at the base of my middle and index finger.

"You've come so far. You're almost there." She told me.

A heavy sigh expelled, but one tenth of the nervous anxiety was related to my family reunion. Breanne's directions were easier said than done. How does one look into the eyes of their loved ones after having slaughtered close to a hundred people? Just...how?

...

It was a Monday afternoon. Just after Easter. I knew the entire family would be together. They would've returned from their traditional cruise across the Mediterranean.

With each step I took in approaching the mansion's two-leaf doors, it felt like my knees were about to buckle. I left the bags in the car. My hair was braided to the back. I was wearing white with a new fragrance Anna picked out for me. For all intents and purposes, I was a new woman.

I rang the doorbell. The maid answered. She gasped, covering her mouth and backing up as if she'd just seen a ghost. I smiled as I entered threshold and almost immediately, the weight of heart-wrenching nostalgia hit me. The foyer, the grand staircase, the massive family portraits and the antiques adorning the walls, everything was exactly as I remembered.

"Holy shit!"

Standing in the entry of the library was a taller more physically endowed version of myself. Clarice, she had to be about 27-years old by then. As angelic and gorgeous as ever, but there was something different about her. It's been three years since we last saw each other, but my childhood memories were replete the torment she imposed. The last face I wanted to see was hers. And yet there she was, beaming with such gladness.

Even as she ran for me, my hand instinctively moved to the back of my skirt, where my gun usually was. She hugged and I exhaled sharply as if a bomb had gone off in the distance. She held tight. It was genuine. It was peculiar.

"I missed you so much!" She gushed.

I didn't know what to say. Astonishment doesn't even begin to describe it.

"Puppet! Is that you?"

That's when I lost it. The sound of my father's deep, sincere voice reduced me to a puddle. It chiseled through the ironclad walls I worked so hard to build around my heart. Into his arms I ran, and it was like a dam had burst. I cried so hard and let it all out. I wailed, whimpered, and keened, paying no mind to whether it looked weak or pitiful. I just let the floodgates go.

Felix Domina Vandelay II was his name. Right there in the middle of the foyer, in his big wooly robe, he cradled me to the floor. And I cried and cried. My mother, my six older brothers Thomas, Fredrick, Michael, James, Alistair, and Gregory, as well as my sisters Emily and Victoria, all of them joined us in one huge, huddled embrace. Only Clarice stood from afar, watching the beautiful scene.

For the rest of the evening, I refused to leave my father's side. He hit me with one question after another about my time abroad and, to my credit, I answered each with detailed insight, having studied the ins and outs of the London School of Economics primarily for this moment.

It wasn't until after supper when the entire family was sitting around the fireplace in the Great Hall, that Papa asked me, "Darling, have I done something in the past to upset you?"

I stared, almost dumbstruck.

"Have I done something to wrong you or cause you distress? For you to be away for so long, I can only surmise that…"

"Oh no, Papa!" I said, tearing up again. "I'm so sorry I hadn't come sooner. I just, I felt it was one of those things that as a young woman I needed to do. So badly, I wanted to come and visit. But for me, for my individual growth I would say, I couldn't jeopardize that by having my heart softened by your presence, by the sacred love I covet so much. Believe me when I say these past three years, it was the hardest thing I ever had to do."

"Was it worth it?" Clarice asked. "If you don't mind my asking?"

"To go and find yourself..." Gregory scoffed with a playful chuckle.

"Yes, actually!" I told them. "That's precisely it. I know it sounds cliché, but you have to admit, we live a very posh, comfortable life here. How does one know who they truly are if they're not tested, if they're not pushed beyond that which they don't know?"

My father smirked under his mustache. I was compelled to hug again.

"Sounds familiar," He said. "It's akin to the speech I once gave your grandfather. I thought it was foolish in hindsight, considering my brothers never considered whether the grass was greener on the other side. But it's in you. Isn't it, puppet? The inquisitive heart of an explorer."

"I don't know. I guess," I said with my voice muffled into his shirt.

Everyone laughed.

"Yes, well while you've been gallivanting across the Thames, Fredrick and I have been wrestling with corporate lawyers and hedge fund managers trying to maintain some semblance of the empire our father built. I was hoping your experience in London would prove to be a valuable asset in the boardroom." My brother Thomas said.

I turned and looked. He was sincere.

"The boys are up and coming executives." Papa added. "I still remember you running up and down the halls. Now that you're grown and educated from one of the most prestigious institutions in the world, I was hoping you'd join them. Clarice will show you the ropes."

"Clarice works there too?" I asked.

"I have a few accounts, here and there." Clarice said, a little too modest.

"So, what do you say, pumpkin? Are you ready to join the family business?" Mother asked.

"Yes!" I said with glee. "Nothing would make me happier!"

…

The next morning, I woke up before everyone else. It was just before daybreak when a blue fog enveloped the estate. I saw the air move like tiny grains of sand, dictated by the sporadic whispers of the wind. I found a pair of gray jeans and a white cotton shawl and ventured out for a stroll.

The view of the grounds, the open fields, the trimmed hedges, the garden statues, the tree line beyond the creek, and the mist that surrounded all…everything seemed so unreal, as if caught in a dream. The cool moisture caressed my skin and a soft gust propelled me forward.

It was bliss, a heavenly dream I never wanted to end. I remember seeing a mallard lead its chicks towards the pond. It was so endearing and I wanted to cry all over again. I think deep down I knew, with everything I've done, I'd never have true peace or serenity. I didn't deserve it. This estate would never be my home. To even let my heart settle on the idea would've been foolish.

On the wooden walk bridge overarching the stream, I leaned on the rails and watched as the pearl sun peeked over the horizon. The foggy woods were to my left. And to my right, the corner of my eye picked up on a sliver of gold that penetrated the blue like a candle in the night. It was my sister Clarice in a navy jacket with a gray scarf. She seemed so innocent, waving at me with this timid smile.

"May I? May I join you?" She asked.

So peculiar. The old Clarice wouldn't have asked for anything. The old, entitled Clarice would've tread on my tracks as if everything belonged to her and I was the nuisance, as if I was the thief who dared to breathed in the same air without asking for permission.

I can't remember if I beckoned her over or just continued to stare in a trance. But she came and leaned next to me, shoulder to shoulder. She was so tall and beautiful. I confess, the warmth was welcomed. After a moment of uneasy silence between us, she did something she's never done before.

"I'm sorry." She told me. It was sharp and piercing. Our blue eyes met. It was sincere. I felt it.

"All the times I bullied you, it was mean. It was a mistake. I'm your big sister. I should have been the one protecting you from bullies. Instead, I was president of the club. I can't tell you how long I've been racked with guilt and regret. All this time you were away, I honestly thought it was because of me. It reminds me of the story of Joseph from the Bible. I might not have sold you into slavery, but I did cast you out. You didn't deserve to be treated like that, truly. From the bottom of my heart, I really am so sorry."

Tears glossed over. I couldn't believe it. I had nothing, no words. I didn't want to cry. I didn't want to lie and say it was alright. So, I just stood there as the tears rolled down my cheeks. And just when I was about to unload and convey all the pain and torment I've carried for so long, Clarice reached out and embraced me, gently placing a kiss on my forehead.

"I'm sorry!" She whimpered.

I found my hands sliding around her waist to hug her back…but something happened. That queasiness agitating in my stomach. I could feel her heartbeat. It reminded me of another woman who once pressed her breast against mine and the rage resurfaced. My eyes opened wide. I could barely see over her shoulder and she suddenly hugged tighter.

"I should have brought my camera!" said another voice.

It was so sudden. I turned to see Papa walking across the wet grass in his royal robe. "It really does my heart good to see the two of you finally getting along." He said out loud.

As the flood of emotions and inexplicable confusion clouded over, a sharp zip cut through the frosted air. I recognized the sound and, in an instant, the hair on the back of my neck stood on end. Clarice looked to her shoulder. There was a dart sticking out of it. Her eyes rolled back and she fell unconscious in my arms.

"Clarice! CLARICE!" I shouted.

"Good heavens! What happened?" Papa said as he hurried over.

"I don't know, Papa. There's this dart and…"

My instincts kicked in. Again, I reached for my back and the Glock wasn't there. Looking around with alert eyes, a frozen terror began to course through my veins. We were surrounded. Standing on the lawn, around the creek, emerging from the hedges, and even from the woods, there must have been twenty female soldiers, half shrouded in the fog.

"What's going on here? Who are you people?" Papa said.

I recognized one of them. "Scarlet! What are you all doing here?!"

She jutted her chin for me to look the other way. Breanne…She was coming from the other side of the bridge. Her snow-white visage and those diamond eyes seemed to glow. Whilst everyone else wore dark combat uniforms, Breanne was wearing a rich hooded coat with a fur trim. She tossed field knife my way and I caught it.

"This is it, Gladys." She told me. "The final test. In order for a Sword of St. Catherine to be drawn, she must kill the man she loves the most in this world."

My eyes widened with terror as the knife slipped from my fingertips. I mumbled, "You mean…"

"What is this nonsense?" my father said. "Gladys, who are these people?"

"We've all done it." Scarlet said as she approached from my rear. "It's the only way to shed our former selves. Being a Sword is about the sisterhood. We can't have the love of one jeopardize us all."

"THEN I QUIT!" I shouted. "I don't want to be a Sword of St. Catherine anymore! I renounce my initiation! I quit being a protégé! Where's Anna!?"

"It's too late, Gladys!" Breanne said with a fixed gaze. "You really think I brought all these women here to accept your resignation? You've come too far. You know too much. Felix Vandelay II is the only thing connecting you to your former self. He's the only thing keeping you from reaching your full potential. Don't you see? This is your baptism! Take up the blade and be born again. A free woman! A real woman."

"As long as he lives there will always be doubt. You'll always second-guess yourself." That came from Celeste. Even she was there.

I looked for Anna and screamed her name. "ANNA!!!"

"The Andalusian can't help you, you stupid bitch!" Scarlet barked.

"Anna was a basket case herself," Celeste said. "But even she got the job done. If you really care about Anna, if you really want to join her, this is the only way."

"No! It can't be! He's not the one that I love the most! There's another man! A secret love I've had since I was little girl."

"We're wasting time." Said Scarlett.

"WAIT!"

I flinched as father's hands settled on my shoulders. I turned around and it hurt so much to looked into his eyes. "Puppet, I get the impression these women want you to kill me. Why is that? Did I hurt you?"

"No, papa! Never! And I would never do that!"

"HA!" Scarlet scoffed. "You should see the bodies she's scattered all up and down the Euphrates. We have pictures."

"Shut up!"

"She decapitated a man who begging for his life. I saw it with my own eyes." Scarlet chuckled.

"SHUT UP!"

"What?" Papa gasped.

"No papa! He was raping an innocent girl, I had to stop him!"

"What are they talking about? What have you done?"

"I'm afraid your little angel ain't so angelic, Mr. Vandelay." Celeste chimed in. "She's one of the most savage gunslingers I've ever seen. Put a fully automatic in her hands and she'll clear out the whole stadium. Rage issues, so I hear."

Papa shook his head. "That's nonsense. I refuse to believe…"

"KILL HIM!" Scarlet snapped. "And you better hurry the hell up!"

I whipped up the dagger and hurled it at Scarlet. She dodged and chuckled as she came charging forward. She threw two punches. I parried both and reached for the pistol on her hip. She also had an assault rifle around her shoulders, but I palmed the muzzle and shoulder-checked her over the railing. She went tumbling into the creek.

Immediately, I dropped to a crouch and aimed at the ladies on the lawn. They dispersed like rabbits to a swooping hawk, showing off the same training I had. I managed to shoot two in their legs. But then…

A sharp of line of blood sprayed across my face. My father hunched over with a deep gash across his midsection. I stared and screamed, clutching at him to stay alive. His lips were moving but there were no words. He wasn't looking at me. He was staring in horror at someone else.

Clarice…I couldn't believe it. She was up. She was up and standing over us with blood dripping from a long narrow knife, a misericord. That cold, unmoving expression. As if her eyes were devoid of a human soul, hollow, and dead inside.

My eyes were red with tears and grief. Papa groaned as he tried to sit up. Cradling Papa in my arms, I babbled with spit drooling from my lips. "Clarice! What are you doing?"

"What's happening?" He whispered.

"I'm sorry, papa! It's my fault. It's all my fault!"

"Damn right it is. This was supposed to be your kill!" Clarice said before launching on us, driving that narrow blade through his chest, the tip, piercing through his body and into my clavicle. I was at the bottom of a dog pile and Clarice had both hands on the misericord, digging it deeper into Papa's chest as she leaned over to snarl at me with utter contempt.

"STOP IT!" I cried.

"Fuck you, you weak cowardly bitch! I wasn't supposed to do this! This is your fault!"

"CLARICE! GET OFF!"

Clarice yanked the blade from father's chest with an eruption of blood. She brought it back down in an attempt to stab me in the face, but I moved just in time.

I shimmied free and rolled to get away. Clarice slashed me across the back and the burning pain caused me to stagger to my knees. I wasn't sure how deep the laceration was, but I could feel the blood already soaking through the shawl.

All the training in the world was useless at that point. I couldn't focus. Papa's body was a distraction that slowed my senses and delayed my reaction. Even with the cut to my back, I was still so disoriented that I could barely brace myself when Clarice casually walked over and stomped me in the face. All I could do was cry like a baby.

Clarice shook her head. "Wasn't supposed to go down like this. You were almost there!"

"You're a Sword of St. Catherine? You knew they'd ask me to kill our father and you let them?!"

She leaned over me with a knee to my chest, the misericord still in hand. "I've been sending him death threats for weeks. You had one job and we would have framed it on a disgruntled employee, but no. I told them. I freaking told you, Breanne! Gladys is a waste of time. Every one of us is born of oppression. Every woman here has sufficient reason to hate men. But Gladys…Gladys just hates everything, don't you? You're no different from a terrorist on a killing spree or a mass shooter hitting up a mall."

With each word that came from that bitch's lips, my rage grew and grew. "No…You're wrong. I don't hate everything. Just you. It's always been just you."

Clarice smirked as she pressed harder into my chest. She looked to Breanne and said, "You know, this actually works out better. We could say that the death threats came from her."

"I was thinking the same," Celeste added. "Gone for three years doing God knows what in the Middle East. Only to kill her father under the guise of some hidden grudge. No! Islamic indoctrination! Yes. That checks out."

Breanne nodded. Clarice yanked me up and slugged me so hard that I went tumbling back towards my father's now lifeless body. A bullet zipped by my ear. Celeste fired again and it scraped my shoulder. Frightened, I took off running the other way. Breanne simply stepped aside and let me pass. They all did. I didn't question it. I just kept running.

The woods seemed endless. The blue haze persisted. The dream had turned into a nightmare and I was now trapped in a rush of heat, sweat, pain, and fatigue. Occasionally, a shot would pop off from a distance and strike a tree nearby. Huffing and puffing, I ran as hard as I could.

After what seemed like hours, I emerged from the woods and tumbled down a steep slope rolling towards the interstate. I hit a guard rail and just laid there with my arms covering my head. I cried and wept, so heartbroken and utterly destroyed. I had no plan. No direction. Both of my worlds had caved in. If I bled out and died…it would have been mercy.

Suddenly, I heard sound of screeching tires. Someone had just done a U-turn and was accelerating my way. I pushed off the grass and stood up. A silver sedan with the headlights on. The driver came to a skidding stop just inches away. With blood and grass sticking to my face, I watched almost in a catatonic state as Anna raced from the car to come and grab me.

I said nothing as she tucked me into passenger's side and strapped me in. My eyes were on her, but I said nothing, as if my brain was in the process of rebooting. Anna got back behind the wheel and drove off. I must have just stared at her with unblinking eyes for well over five miles. Then, my head rolled to press against the window, the cold, refreshing window.

Papa…the pain of losing him was unbearable. He didn't deserve that. Clarice…my most hated enemy. She must have known I'd never kill him. She must have known I'd fail. Bitch. That sadistic, cold-hearted bitch. All she's ever done was ruin me.

Just thinking about her…it got my heartrate going again. The rage brings about a certain clarity, a certain focus. As I rode in the car with Anna, the helplessness and the lack of direction, those feelings faded and were hijacked by a new goal. With each breath I took, my resolve hardened.

"Gladys are you okay?" Anna asked.

I keeled over and vomited through my mouth and my nose.

"Gladys!"

After expelling the contents of my stomach and spitting out what was left of the taste, I let out the most epic of all meltdowns, screaming up at the windshield, pounding the dashboard and kicking. "AAARGGHHH!!!"

"Gladys! Stop! GLADYS!

"RAWWR!" I reached over and slapped at her. She slammed on the brakes and tried to pull to the side, but I was all over her. The car slid into a grassy ditch and rolled over. Anna was caught by her seatbelt, but I ended up flying to the backseat with the car upside down.

After some time with nothing but the sizzle of a blown engine, Anna whispered, "You didn't kill him, did you?"

"No..."

"You need to disappear."

"I can't. I have a sister to kill."

"Gladys...She's a Sword. You can't kill her."

I squirmed on my knees until I was in front of her. "You knew?" I asked with blood and puke clumped in my hair. Anna had her eyes closed. She was bleeding from her hairline.

"Anna, did you know?"

She didn't respond. I reached over and checked her pulse. It was faint. I felt her pockets, found her phone, and called for emergency services in a disguised voice.

I kicked out the window and crawled to get out. With each step it felt like fire bursting in my knees. My shoulder was dislocated, and I was hunching forward as if I no longer had strength in my back.

I hobbled through the forest with no sense of direction. Every turn looked the same. Leaves. Branches. Vines. Gray sky and the nasty feeling when one's body heat blended with the moist frosty air. That was my condition. And once again, I let myself drop to the ground and cried, utterly hopeless and helpless.

I cried...for the last time.

I know it's cliché. Revenge is always cliché to people who don't know what it means to be driven by it. They killed my father. You don't get to flourish after that. From that point on, nothing else mattered. The sole purpose of my existence, my impetus, is to destroy these whores. I am the villain in this story. It's like what Anna Marie said long ago. We really are monsters.

I survived that day and went into hiding. They framed me for the murder of my father and I was hunted by nearly every state, local, and federal law enforcement agency in the country. Clarice even went so far as to put up a $5 million reward for information leading to my arrest.

Months after the murder, a scandal broke out. It was alleged that my older brothers had hired hookers and forced them to use cocaine and perform sexual acts during a number of lavish boardroom meetings. CEOs and shareholders were implicated. My brothers had to step down in disgrace, clearing the path for Clarice to take over the leadership role of my father's company.

She'd go on to establish a number of influential foundations to raise money for the victims of sexual abuse, single mothers, and spread awareness about the lewd and insidious behavior that goes on behind closed doors of corporations. Clarice Vandelay was the beautiful face, the strong and independent voice, the powerful poster child with the potential to one day enter the political arena.

My two eldest brothers committed suicide after the scandal and three more had become degenerate alcoholics to cope with the depression, divorce, and having their kids taken from them.

As far as I knew, my other sisters Emily and Victoria were innocent. They even spoke up on behalf of the youngest brother, Gregory. They vouched for his character and claimed he would never hurt a fly. But Clarice sided with the accusers and condemned Emily and Victoria as women who were too blinded by familial ties to see the truth. Even their careers took a hit as Clarice made calls to block investments to anyone who would hire them.

Clarice became the unofficial Queen of Wall Street. I don't know who her paramour was. I don't know if it was difficult for her to complete the initiation, but none of that mattered. She killed Papa. For that, she must die. All the money in the world can't stop me. That's how I know. I'll never be Paramour. Never.

...The Perennial War of Paramours...

06. Jake Buchanan – The Hopeless Commander

"There was this girl. Her name was Jamie. We went to the same school. Seen her around campus, but it wasn't till my sophomore year that I found out we stayed in the same housing complex. Lived just across the hallway.

"First time we spoke, it was like magic. Pretty eyes. Sandy blonde hair. She had a sweet smile. Contagious. One day, we were walking out at the same time and I introduced myself. I remember my voice was shakin' like crazy. But she seemed smitten, ya know. Her cheeks lit up bright red. We talked about this, that, and the other, and it was cool. I thought we hit it off.

"Then I went and did a Google search on her. I know that sounds creepy or whatever but, I dunno. I just wanted to know more about her without asking all these invasive questions. I didn't have the 'right' to know. But still, I wanted to know. I clicked on the images tab and scrolled down to find her. And that's when I was floored, man.

"There's a selfie of her in her bathroom, like a webcam. Turns out this girl was using Backpages to hook up with sugar daddies all over Denver. I couldn't believe it. She seemed so pure and innocent. Like, if you talked to her, you'd never guessed she was into sex work. That's not the impression she gives off.

"I kept it to myself for weeks, but it was just by coincidence we ended up in the same class that semester. She was crazy about the environment. All up in arms about that pipeline going through some reservation. Again, my point being, sugar baby is the last thing you'd expect. And the truth is, I was madly in love with this girl. Like, heads over heels. She was so beautiful.

"One night I came home from the closing shift. And I saw her crying on the steps. Someone had beat the shit out her and, man, it pissed me off. Her face was swollen, black and blue. The neck hole of her shirt was all stretched out. I could see scratch marks on her shoulders. Just thinking about it now...it's like setting me on fire, you know.

"I asked her what was wrong, but she wouldn't tell me. She just said she wanted to be left alone. So, I did, at first. I left her alone. But, I...I couldn't just go in and rest easy knowing the girl of my dreams needed help.

"Bout half hour later, I went back out with a bottle of water and she was still there. She let me treat her injuries. I had like, gauze and Neosporin or some shit.

"The way she looked at me, it's like a puppy I just took in from the freezing rain. I tried to get her to open up and tell me what happened, but she wouldn't. She just said she was going through some things and everything would be alright.

"And that's when I messed up. It's like a thousand voices in my head screaming 'NO! Don't do it!' But that one voice in my heart was like, 'Do it, she needs help!' So, I did. I went ahead and told her that I knew she was on Backpages. She didn't deny it. If anything, she seemed relieved.

"I told her that she was ten times more precious than she probably knew. I told her how impressive she was in class. I said she was beautiful, smart, and so full of potential. There are better ways to earn money. Whatever she was getting paid, I told her it was pennies on the dollar for what she was worth!

"She cried. And I cried with her. I would've given her a hug right then and there. I should've wrapped her up in my arms and told her everything was gonna be alright. But I didn't. I thought that would be...I thought that'd be taking advantage of her. I didn't want to do that. Didn't seem right.

"So, I helped her up. Escorted her to her apartment. And I never went in with her. What I told her was, 'Jamie...I stay right there. If you ever need any help, if you ever need someone to talk to, just let me know. You have my number. I barely sleep. So just call anytime.

"And she smiled. I thought we were cool. I went to my own apartment thinking, you know, I did something good. I was proud of myself. Not only for consoling her, but my discipline of not thrusting myself on her in such a vulnerable state.

"Well...as you can imagine. No good deed goes unpunished. About a week later, I was called into the Dean's office. Jamie had accused me of rape and sexual battery. She had the bruises to prove it and there were neighbors to testify to seeing me with her the night in question. So, I was evicted. Expelled. Spent two years in prison and now I have to register as a sex offender wherever I go. No one will hire me. Fucking terrified to even look at another girl. Essentially, my life is ruined.

"I never got a chance to face my accuser. She didn't have to show up for trial. I never saw Jamie again after that night. I couldn't ask the questions that would eventually torment me for years. Why? Why'd she do it? Was she ashamed? Did she think I'd go out and tell everyone she was an escort? It really got to the point where I thought about killing myself. Out here. Out on these mountains. All it would take is one jerk of the wheel to end it all. Death would have been sweet. That's honestly how I felt.

"But that's when Jake found me. I think he was sent from God because that morning, I made up my mind to end it all. I was leaving the pharmacy with a bunch of oxys when I saw Jake on his Harley. He was parked next to me, looking all badass and what not. I thought he was talking on his phone when he said, 'God has a plan for you.'

"I stood there in place, frozen, stiff as a board. Jake told me, 'consider the words of Joseph. In Genesis chapter Fifty, do you remember?'

"Joseph, poor Joseph, his brothers had sold him into slavery. His master's wife falsely accused him of taking advantage of her. Then he spent years in jail because of it. But throughout it all, he never lost faith in God. God granted him the power to interpret dreams, helping him gain favor with Pharaoh, prompting his ascension to become the second most powerful man in Egypt. Thanks to Joseph, Egypt had prepared for a famine, which saved the lives of thousands. Hundreds of thousands!'

"But one mustn't forget the hardships he endured. One mustn't forget the trials and tribulations he faced. And what did he say? In Chapter Fifty when his brothers feared his wrath, when his brothers feared that one day Joseph would exact the vengeance they felt he was so justified to take? Joseph said: 'As for you, you meant evil against me. But God meant it for good. To bring it about that many people be kept alive as they are today.'

"Jake told me, 'Everyone has their trials and tribulations, my friend. Remember Jesus Christ, who was persecuted and died for our sins. Know that the world accepts what is theirs, but as for you, because you are no part of the world, but one claimed by Christ, they will persecute you. Have strength. Be strong and ever faithful in the word of God.' That's what Jake told me in the parking lot of a pharmacy."

...

Trent recounted his experience with tearful repose. We gave him a standing ovation, an ovation worthy of his ordeal, his pain and recovery. After concluding the meeting, I saw everyone out, locked up the church, got on my Harley and drove north on 25 along the Rockies.

Trent was but one of hundreds in our support group. It was just for men. It had to be. In my day, men were taught to be strong, tough, and reliable, but we still had emotions. When our fathers and father's fathers told us we couldn't cry, that we couldn't appear weak, we knew. We understood what it meant. They were trying to make leaders out of us. Preparing us to protect and provide for our families. If the leader is weak, incapable, and too yielding, it trickles down.

My generation understood this. Trent's generation…I know people like to harp on Millennials and give 'em a hard time about why the country's gone all to hell, but where do they think they get it from? Do they think Millennials just hop out of the womb, born with a sense of entitlement? Or has someone instilled them with the mentality, that the world owes them everything and if they don't get it, it's not their fault, it's the worlds? The institutions. The "man".

The problem with Trent's generation is a virus, getting worse by the day. Trent's but one of millions across the country suffering debilitation from the false accusations and offenses taken. And that's what the public doesn't get.

If Trent really was the villain society made him out to be, the criticism would've rolled off his back like rain to nylon. He wouldn't have become so broken. But because he is a good guy, one of old school chivalry, the stuff of gentlemen, not extinct but no longer appreciated, it took the grace of God to give him the strength to pick himself back up.

Young men like Trent get no sympathy. They're called INCELs, Betas, Simps, and White Knights. There's no recourse for false accusations. If he went online and posted his sob story there wouldn't be a line of people waiting to lend a helping hand.

Maybe he did rape her. Maybe he didn't. Once upon a time, we believed in the concept of innocent till proven guilty. Nowadays, to even question the victim could land you in hot water in your pursuit of the truth. They'll accuse you of advocating rape. They'll shame you for shaming the victim. It's all a bunch of nonsense and it only encourages me to strengthen my faith in God. This world really is wicked. Everyone knows the truth, but they refuse to live with it. So, they hold fast to the lies.

That's why groups and grassroots movements began popping out of the woodwork through various mediums. Men's Rights Activists, the Manosphere, Men Going Their Own Way…these are just a few. But the media's careful about acknowledging their existence, lest more people find out and actually be enticed to an alternative that makes more sense.

Furthermore, they shamelessly confected boldface lies to discredit the leading figures of these movements, associating them with the likes of the KKK and various hate groups so no one will take them seriously, or that to agree with them would mark you as a supporter of hate and bigotry. It's nothin' new. Sowell and Buckley can attest to that.

All of it was pushed and promulgated by an underground society of hardcore feminist hell-bent on supplanting men from power and influence. Sadly, they're winning.

It was the Society who was behind that cat-calling video that made good men reluctant to so much as blink at a woman. Thus, it's mostly bad boys who could care less about being falsely accused who end up procreating. The Society knew damn well these men would make dead-beat dads, leaving the children to be raised by single-moms who know nothing about instilling their sons with masculinity, weakening an entire generation of men who could dare oppose the Society. Weakening an entire generation of women who never knew the love of real father, so they go on perpetuating single-parent households by choosing the wrong men.

It was the Society who was behind the slut walks, the celebration of abortions, and brainwashing our students that a rape culture exists on campuses. They had the top singers, actors, and directors flooding the entertainment industry with female empowerment, deceptively teaching women that men, particularly white men, was the source of all their problems.

It ended up isolating individuals and inadvertently creates segregation by preference. Men are more likely to stick to men, and women to women, all in an effort to keep from offending each other, to keep from making each other feel "uncomfortable".

And to that end, I feel sorry for the innocent women as well. It's not like all that female empowerment encourages women to be the ones to make the first move in courtship. Nope…that task is still behooving of men.

And what about the women who actually like the traditional roles of being a housewife? The ones who want nothing more than to be a loving wife and a nurturing mother. I'm referring to the women who don't give two shits about rising in power or breaking that glass ceiling but would rather have a strong husband to take charge and actually lead. Even they feel the pressure, frustration, and confusion.

Everything, all of this…it's all to destabilize the infrastructure so the Society can swoop in and replace CEOs and world leaders with their own proxies. Meanwhile assholes like the president, and big-name producers in Hollywood only get bolder, thinking no one would suspect them of corruption because they donate to the political party that's supposedly on the right side of history.

Either way, this is the virus plaguing Trent's generation. A conflict of contradicting realities, of post-truths, force-fed by the slanted media and a biased education system. And my generation wonders why young people rather stare down at their phones than look someone in the eye and extend a simple greeting. We wonder why they'd rather order from a kiosk than an actual human being. We wonder why Millennials still live at home with their parents as opposed to moving out. We wonder why they lack the drive, the sense of setting goals and working hard to accomplish them.

It's okay… The Bible foretold these sordid events in 2 Timothy Chapter 3. All we can do is that which is in our power to do. That's why I'm a Paramour. Because I don't shy away from the truth. More importantly I sense there's a great hunger for the truth. Problem is, sometimes the snake bites the hand that feeds it. Being a Paramour requires a great tolerance from that kind of pain.

As I rode my motorcycle with wind biting my face at 65mph, these were the thoughts that permeated.

…

A transport was waiting for me, the blades already spinning with rotor wash kicking snow across the ridge. The custom white-painted Chinook was a veteran used in Vietnam and Iraq. A unit of six Army Rangers were waiting inside. Hired escorts. Alongside them were three of my fellow Paramours, all adept and more than capable of holding their own behind enemy lines.

The Paramour, Ravi Naranjo, was a former narcotics agent from Colombia.

Paramour, Jessi Dobson, had studied to become a schoolteacher. She had no idea she was sleeping with a member of the Society and when Jessi started asking questions, the girlfriend shot her and left her for dead.

And then there was Lincoln Holcomb, a longtime friend whom I had come to trust with my life. Lincoln was one of the few Paramours who wasn't declared dead or hunted by the Society. Thus, he held a public job without fear of being shanked or having his car explode upon ignition. We needed people like him to acquire and move civilian assets who had no knowledge of either the Paramours or the Society. That's how we were able to have an escort of Rangers. Lincoln's clout as a high-profile attorney in the JAG Corp afforded him a few perks here and there.

As soon as I strapped in, we lifted off from Fort Benton, Montana. Our destination was somewhere in the rugged wilderness of Alberta, Canada. In the dead of winter. Not ideal. But we had reliable intel that was too good to pass up.

"Why on earth you ridin' your Harley in this weather?" Ravi chuckled.

I smirked. "You're from the tropics, kid. I was born in the alpines. I could go skinny dipping in this. When I was a kid, we used to use the bathroom in the middle of the night and the toilet water would be frozen. Called it breaking ice."

"Oh god..." Jessi groaned while everyone else laughed.

I turned to Lincoln. He sat there looking all official with his aviators and that leather jacket zipped all the way up. As Jessi and Ravi continued their banter, I reviewed the dossier. The first thing I noticed was the picture of a girl who looked no older than thirteen. Blonde hair. Blue eyes. Ivy League threads.

"Don't tell me this is who we're after."

"Read the profile," Lincoln told me.

"Yeah or you could just tell me. We got time to kill."

"You just don't like to read, vato!" Ravi chuckled.

"Nah. He's just mad the Council wouldn't let him bring his precious Ellie along." Jessi added.

"Hey! Mark my words, Elliot's gonna prove himself vital in the coming days."

"I dunno, vato. Looks like any other Asian kid to me." Ravi snickered.

"Linc…" I said. "Is this really the target? Seems a bit much to have four of us out here."

"That's what I said," Jessi added. "What is she, in middle school?"

"Yes, Ms. Dobson. I'd bring four of us and a squad of Rangers to take out a middle schooler." Lincoln quipped.

He continued, "As far as we're concerned, this middle schooler is the holy grail. She was trained by the Society and ruthless to boot. To date, three ghost squads were sent by the Vandelay Corporation and of the twenty-six deployed, only one man returned. He's awaiting trial because he was still officially a Marine. But his deposition revealed some interesting details.

"According to the him, his team was ambushed by a single gunman. A girl. This girl. After some legwork, we concluded she was either with the Society and defected or she's still with the Society and this whole thing is just an internal dispute. Either way, we need to get in there and bring her over to our side before it's too late."

I nodded, "And your money is on the defector angle, I presume?"

As soon as I asked, Lincoln flashed a grin.

"Makes sense." Jessi said. "The girl is none other than Gladys Vandelay. Y'all remember that crap that dominated the headlines last year. Her brothers were caught up in a sex scandal, one committed suicide. And badda-bing-badda-boom, the new CEO is the posterchild of 'strong and independence,' Clarice Vandelay. Now for Clarice to contract hit squads to take out her own sister, as fucked up as it is, it reeks of dissension."

"And if that's the case," Lincoln said, "Then we're looking at our first Society defector in over a hundred years. The last one was Emily Davison's cousin from the Suffragette movement. After Davison was killed in that horse race, her cousin turned on the Society. Most of what we know about the Society's existence, their structure, their initiation, we got it from her. But even she didn't know everything because she wasn't a full-fledged member."

My interest was piqued. I read the profile. This girl…she looked thirteen, but she was twenty-two. She was accused of murdering her own father. Her brothers were pariahs and the two sisters who stepped up to defend the brothers had their reputations shot to pieces. Something about Gladys's picture, taken from the Marine's helmet cam…something in her eyes told me she was going to be a lot of work. The idea of planting the seed of forgiveness in her would be about as tedious as pushing a seed through concrete. But still…it's as Lincoln said.

Our first defector in over a hundred years.

"Listen up!" I shouted to get the Rangers' attention.

"As you all know, our target is a young woman named Gladys Vandelay. She may be dainty in appearance but let me tell you this target is cold as ice. To date, her body count is twenty-five plus. Good men and women have died trying to bring her back to answer for her crimes in the states. We're not going to add to that by underestimating our target! As soon as we touch down, consider yourselves in enemy territory. We stay frosty. We have each other's backs. We take this bitch down!"

"YES SIR!"

I sat and stared out at the snow-dusted pine trees sprinkled along the mountains. It never ceased to amaze me how powerful these women were. They really do run the world. Either because men are terrified of them or because we've come to love women more than we love God. Either way, I won't let myself fall into that trap. Never again.

…

"ETA to LZ, fifteen minutes!" said the pilot over the intercom.

We zipped up our white coats, locked and loaded our weapons and strapped on our goggles. All I could see was gray gradients for miles on out. We had about two hours till sundown. It wasn't good. That unnerving feeling crept into my gut. We were still airborne, but already it felt like I was being stalked by a lion.

BOOM

Something exploded overhead with the rotor blades. We banked hard and some spilled from their seats. Alarms went haywire and suddenly we were at a ninety-degree angle where I could see ground, looking to my right, while the overcast was to my left.

"We're hit! We're hit!" shouted the co-pilot.

"No shit, cabron!" Ravi shouted. "MIRA! MIRA!"

Lincoln clutched a handrail. "Brace for impact! It's go time!"

It wasn't my first air crash, but it was by far the most violent. We flew into a brush of towering sequoias that turned our descent into a classic game of pinball. Whiplash and concussions galore. After hitting a number of solid objects and rolling for what felt like an eternity, we stopped at the edge of a stream that wasn't yet frozen. I remember because I was upside down and ice-cold water was trickling in.

I could still move my legs. Other than a few bumps and bruises, myself, the Paramours, and all eight Rangers staggered out. The pilot and co-pilot weren't so lucky. Tree branches impaled them through the windshield. I thought that's what had killed them until Lincoln pointed out the headshots.

"Sniper!" I shouted.

Everyone got low and hustled for cover. My warning couldn't have come any sooner because two bullets just zipped by and pelted the snow inches from my boots.

"Fan out in teams. We'll rendezvous at this position at 2000 hours." Lincoln ordered.

"SIR!" everyone responded.

It reminded me of Baghdad, how calm and collected we were. I went with Lincoln. Ravi paired with Jess. The eight rangers broke up into two teams of four. In a smooth steady ascent, we scaled the slopes.

BOOM

A dull explosion went off six klicks east. Lincoln and I turned to see a massive sequoia falling in the distance. We exchanged glances, mutually conveying, "What the fuck was that? Are we even going the right way?"

Suddenly we heard the rapid taps of a machine gun going off in the same direction. It didn't make sense. I was certain the sniper was to the north. So, what the hell was going on in the east? We communicated through our earpieces.

"Sir!" Ravi called in. "The sniper's a .40 cal on a mount. It's remote controlled."

"Be advised! Terrain's laced with booby traps and detonators!" Jessi warned.

BOOM!

Another explosion occurred two klicks to the west.

"AGH! Man down! Man down. We need a medevac!" shouted a Ranger.

"Jansen, Banks, tend to the wounded." Lincoln ordered. "Everyone else, press on. Stay frosty! Let's move!"

I sprinted along a narrow ridge, controlling my breath, trying to keep from slipping off the packed snow. We covered probably 800 meters before a spray of automatic fire hit me across the back and I went tumbling down the hill. I looked up and saw smoke and white dust pluming from the muzzle of a machine gun stationed just twenty feet above the ridge.

"Jake! You hurt?" Lincoln said as he rushed over.

Body armor stopped the penetration, but it still hurt like a mother. Simply raising my arms felt like hot coals raking my back. A gunfight was intensifying in the distance. Grenades were thundering left and right.

"That don't sound good." I said as I leaned against a tree.

"Ravi, Jess, do you have a copy?" Lincoln called. "Have you made contact with the target?"

"Negative. Eighty yards and closing...we think." Jess responded.

Lincoln turned to me. "What kind of Ivy League school did this kid come from?"

"God knows. Help me up." I said, latching onto his shoulder.

Then, it dawned on me. We could hear an intense shootout underway, but Ravi, Jessi, and the Rangers hadn't reached the target yet.

"Be advised, be advised!" I warned. "Another team might be in play. I repeat. We are not alone. The target is engaging them as we speak."

I started sweating. For all I knew, it could've been members of the Society coming to take out the deserter. And if that was the case, our chances of survival were decreasing by the second. Determination kicked in. We couldn't lose Gladys. We had to keep moving.

The gunfire was relentless, like a downpour of pelting rain. Trees were falling. Clouds of snow burst from the branches.

"Contact!" Ravi shouted.

I heard him, both on the radio and within earshot. Like a tornado, the entire battle was raging from east to west with Lincoln and I directly in its path. Then...as sudden as lightning on a clear day, this white blur of motion came darting from the bushes. And there she was. I saw the blue of her eyes before the glint of her pistols. She had one in each hand.

I shoved Lincoln out of the way as she discharged shots that would have tagged him in the chest. Another soldier emerged and wrapped her up from behind, lifting her clear off the ground. Gladys swung her body and raised her legs to push off away from a tree. She caved back onto the man's chest before rolling to her feet and putting two shots in his face.

Another soldier emerged and unleashed a spray from a G36. Gladys kept low and dove, sliding in the snow as she pelted the soldier with at least six shots all ripping through his chest. Then she got up, raced to grab the G36 that was still strapped around his shoulders and disappeared into a brush before the soldier even dropped to his knees. It was that quick.

Lincoln and I hid behind an outcrop, completely dumbfounded.

"That's a fucking pit viper." Lincoln whispered.

"No, no. She's scared. Backed into a corner. I sense it."

"We fall back" Lincoln ordered. "We fall back and come up with another plan. All units! Fall back! I repeat, fall back! Jake? JAKE!"

It was too late. I heard him calling my name, but I was already after her. She kept bouncing in and out of my sights as if she had sprinted through these slopes a hundred times just for fun.

She started taking fire from her left and it didn't take me long to realize she wasn't exactly trying to escape. With the G36 assault rifle, she took cover behind a massive tree with roots the size of a car, ducking in and out to return fire on a unit of six that was steadily closing in.

I crouched behind a ridge and threw a non-lethal flashbang designed to disorientate the enemy. It worked. They started shooting all over the place. One even shot his own man by mistake.

Gladys emerged from the sequoia and started picking them off like fish in the barrel. They didn't stand a chance. After she dropped the fifth man, I suddenly felt responsible for this massacre, so I advanced and tackled the remaining soldier out of her way. The soldier was younger and stronger. He showed his gratitude by rolling on top and pummeled me with punches.

I grabbed one of his arms, banged his head up against a rock, and pulled him in for a chokehold. In no time at all, I put him to sleep. The victory was short-lived. No sooner had I lowered the soldier to the ground that I heard the metallic click of a pistol cocking back. She was behind me. I was on my knees.

With caution, I raised my hands.

"Jake! Jake, come in."

She swiped at my neck and severed the cord to my earpiece.

"I've seen this before." She told me. "Save the damsel. Gain her trust. Dispose of her when she's outlived her purpose. So, I'm going ask you once and one time only. Did they send you?"

"Gladys…"

"ANSWER THE QUESTION!"

"I know you're innocent!" I shouted. "I know you didn't kill your father. Your brothers didn't hire hookers and Clarice isn't the feminist she pretends to be. I know all of this, because I am just like you. I'm a Paramour! A rebel against the Society!"

I nearly choked as she yanked me close and pressed her blade so deep that I knew I was bleeding.

"That's good. Let me guess. Celeste told you say that? Or was it Breanne?"

"You're not the only one with a bone to pick with the Society." I strained to say. "They took my wife. They ruined my life!"

She shoved me to the ground, and I turned to look at this kid. She was hooded but man... the stone-cold look in her eyes could make a therapist salivate at the hours she'd need to bill. It wasn't the look of a survivor, but of a child soldier. As if all she's ever known was pain and suffering.

Aimed at my face, she whispered, "Go on..."

"About eight years ago, I finished my last tour of Iraq. It was supposed to be a new chapter for me. Just me, my wife, and our three daughters nestled in a ski town not far from Denver. But my wife...the whole time I was away fighting for my country, she was cheating on me. Flying out to New York on business. Hooking up with another man behind my back.

"And of course, she's one of you. To be a member of the Society, she had to kill the man she loved the most in this world. The only reason I'm still breathing is because it wasn't me. The man she loved was the bastard she had an affair with."

"Then, you should be happy," said Gladys.

"You're wrong. A massive scandal broke out. It was all over the news. Someone hacked into the website she used to facilitate her affair. It exposed the thousands of married men and women using it to cheat on their spouses. She was using a fake name to protect her business, but she came out and told me the truth. It was the worst day of my life."

"Did you kill her?" Gladys asked.

"I couldn't! I can't! She's the mother of my children."

Gladys winced and clutched the gun with both hands. "Likely story!"

"I'm not lying! Google my name! You'll see me come up as a sex offender."

"What?"

"My wife...she's the one who cheated on me. And she's the one who filed for divorce. And I don't know how she did it, but she convinced my daughters to lie in court. They accused me of molesting them. No evidence. Just their word against mine. I was convicted. Spent six years in a federal penitentiary. I lost my pension. My benefits. All custody rights to my girls.

"Meanwhile, my wife's thriving as the president of one of the top five publishers in the country. Pumping stories full of degradation to teenagers, brainwashing them, encouraging them to explore their sexuality, corroding all sense of accountability and depicting religion and morality as the chains holding them back."

"Yeah? And what about you!?" Gladys barked. "Where's your accountability? Huh? What did you do to her? Why would she do that to you?"

"I was selfish! I admit it! I chose duty to my country and conscience over her, over my daughters. Those are my sins. But I've repented. I seek atonement for my crimes. I no longer live to serve myself but to serve others. Now, tell me. What are you gonna do? How are you going to redeem yourself? You may not have killed your father but don't kid yourself by standing on the soapbox of innocence."

Gladys stood there. I couldn't tell what she was thinking, only that she was thinking. It seemed like my words threw a monkey wrench in the gears. I didn't rehearse it. I never planned on laying out my sins to sway her over to our side. But there we were.

"Get up," she said, before whipping her gun to aim at Ravi. He and Jessi were there, watching this whole time. Ever so casually, Jessi approached and checked the dead soldiers.

"Don't worry, Gladys. They won't hurt you. That's not what we do." I said, cringing from my aching knees.

"Who are you people?" Gladys asked.

"We're the Paramours, chica." said Ravi.

Lincoln appeared. "Alright captain, we'll rendezvous at the Chinook in half an hour. Prepare your Rangers for extraction. The target got away. No. Everyone's whole."

Lincoln then turned to Gladys and said, "Obviously we can't have the others thinking we have you in custody. Otherwise, we'd have to turn you in to the authorities as soon as we crossed the border."

Gladys aimed at Lincoln as he continued to read, "Gladys Vandelay. Youngest daughter of Felix Domina Vandelay II. Virtuoso with the piano. Spent the last three years at the prestigious London School of Economics, just to come back and whack the old man. Doesn't sound right, does it?"

"Because it isn't. Clarice killed my father."

"We know. That's why we're here, chica." Ravi said.

"Stop calling me that! What do you want from me?"

"Hey!" Jessi called out. "These guys are contractors. Blue Steel out of Oregon. We gotta get out of here. These guys are like ants, man. Trust me. I ran into Blue Steel during that thing after Katrina. They're gonna call in the fuckin' cavalry."

"This one stays with me." All eyes turned to Gladys; she was talking about me. She finally had her rifle lowered and before we could agree, she was ushering me through the woods by the shoulders.

I nodded and conveyed I'd be alright before the Paramours let me go.

After a fifteen-minute hike, Gladys brought me to this makeshift bivouac of a tent set up near the edge of a cliff with a river rushing beneath. She lowered her hood. Long blonde hair pulled back in a messy ponytail.

This girl…Everything about her was deceptive. Young, but carried herself with more confidence than most sergeants. Short and petite, but strong enough to yank me up with one hand. Looked like an indoor girl but outfitted the entire battlefield to work in her favor. Also, she was wounded in the gunfight. I hadn't noticed because she gave no indication. But when she started taking off her garments, the contrast of red was all too apparent.

I remember standing there, unnerved. Not just at her potential, but at the likelihood that nearly everyone in the Society was trained like her. Including my ex-wife.

"Sit down. You're freaking me out." She told me.

I did as commanded with my back against the wall and the trickle of the river to my left. She kindled a fire and wrestled up a pot of oatmeal.

"I'm astonished, Gladys, truly. How long have you been up here?"

"Tell me more about these Paramours." She said.

"Actually, I was gonna ask you about your organization. It's draconian initiation process. Determining one's loyalty by being disloyal to the ones you're supposed to be loyal to the most? Sounds counterintuitive."

"It has little to do with loyalty." She said. "The Swords of St. Catherine value commitment above all else. When a woman commits her heart to a cause, whether it be family, the home, her job, religion, or a movement, it's absolute. Unbreakable. We are fierce. We'll defend it to the death. Therein lies the true loyalty. But commitment comes first. The only way to break the covenant is through betrayal."

She pointed at me, "At the altar, when you got married, I imagine you stood before the eyes of God and man and said 'I do' to your wife. Did you not? And, what did you do? You went and broke your vows by putting your job before her. You lost her commitment, and along with that, the right to her heart, her honesty, her truth, her loyalty."

"Gladys, you don't really believe all that, do you?"

"Men…" Gladys scoffed. "So simpleminded."

"Men are fools. I'll give you that." I chuckled. "Why do you think God gave us women? It wasn't to drive us insane. You think men built cites, fast cars, and towers that reached for the sky for our own egos? Or rather, why do you think we have egos in the first place? We are engrained with the spirit of competition. Yes, some men compete for greed and power, a need to control and dominate others. However, all men, all men compete for love."

"You're babbling."

I laughed. "All I'm saying, is that without women, the motivation of men would diminish by roughly eighty percent."

"Oh yeah? What about homosexuals?"

"It's not all about sex, darlin. It's the companionship, a nurturing element that all men need."

"And…"

"What's that?" I asked.

"Here's the part where you tell me what we women need. Right?"

"I don't know. I'm not a woman."

She handed me a bowl of oatmeal and said "Well, you're convincing. I'll give you that."

"Convincing?" I asked.

"I know you're with the Swords. So, what do you want? Why'd they send you? It clearly wasn't to kill me."

"Darlin, I already told you…"

"Enough with this darlin, shit! Enough with the Paramours! Just tell me, what you want?!"

"I want you to join us."

"Who?!" She barked.

"Let's put it this way. If your father had survived, he'd be one of us."

"Careful…You're playing a dangerous game. Mention my father lightly again and I will literally rip out your eyes."

"I don't blame your skepticism, Gladys. But everything I told you is the truth. You really think the Society would send a convicted child molester to come and give you a motivational speech?"

"There are no depths the Swords of St. Catherine wouldn't stoop."

"Gladys, this bitterness in you. If you let it, it will swallow you up and eat you raw. How many more men are you going to litter across these mountains? The way I see it, right now you're at the bottom of a well. I'm extending my hand, by the grace God, to lift you out. I won't force you out against your will. It's up to you come out if you are ready."

She slouched back against a rock, squinting those vindictive eyes, ever on guard, so full of doubt. "What's your name?"

"Colonel Jacob Buchanan of the United States Army, 737th Infantry Regiment."

"When were you in Iraq?"

"03 to 07."

"So, before ISIS?"

"Before ISIS."

She smirked, "Tell me more about the Paramours."

"Tell me more about the Swords of St. Catherine."

07. Elliot Chan - Domestication

"You can't be serious."

"I am."

"You brought a living breathing weapon into our sanctuary. Buchanan, have you lost your mind?"

"Well, technically, she isn't a Sword. She flunked the initiation."

"And she's already been scanned. Her biometrics came up negative for any sort of tracer. If there was a bug on her, she'd already be dead."

"Precisely. Which is exactly why I brought her here."

"To do what, exactly?"

"Make her one of us."

"She will never be one of us, Buchanan. She's a killer."

"As was I. Or do you think I was merely a medic during my three tours."

"You know what we mean, Buchanan. Stop prevaricating."

"Gentlemen! All I know is that this is our first dissident in nearly a hundred years. We should take this opportunity and use her to our advantage."

"Brother, you know I'm usually on your side of these debates, but the old adage of playing with fire does come to mind."

The Senior Council of Hollow Rock had been in session since noon. There were eight of them, high-ranking members debating the direction of the Paramours. Us newbies had some input, but never while council was in session. So instead, we lined the walls of the auditorium, just beyond the pillars that circled the seniors. We observed. We listened. We learned.

"Gentlemen!" Jake stressed. "Your concern is duly noted but unnecessary. Gladys doesn't know where we are. I made sure of it."

"My chief concern is that she's playing you, Jake," said Capt. Benaiah. "With due respect, we know you have an affinity for girls who look your daughters. For all we know, she could have been cast out or set up to fail her initiation only to have the Paramours track her down, bring her here, and have her tear us apart from the inside out."

Lincoln scoffed. "That's reaching, Benaiah…"

"Notwithstanding," Benaiah asserted. "You know this is all too plausible. You underestimate the Society and it'll come back to bite you."

"There's also the fact that you brought her here without our consent. You go too far, colonel," Lord Dathan scolded.

"It was a judgment call." Jake nodded. "The girl was wounded and another wave of Blue Steel Mercs were closing in. We couldn't leave her out there."

"I support his decision." Lincoln added.

"Well, she seems to have recovered rather quickly. If I'm not mistaken, it was just a flesh wound," noted Alekzander in his Middle Eastern accent.

"Gentlemen…" Jake said in a lighthearted chuckle. "What are we, if not a countermeasure for an ongoing war that's lasted for nearly two centuries? How can we call ourselves soldiers, how can we call ourselves men if we're too afraid to step out on the battlefield? Everything we do involves risks. Everything!"

"And if you're so eager to die, then take your leave!" Benaiah boomed. "It's not your place to make decisions that jeopardize us all."

"I think that's his point, gentlemen." Lincoln said. "We all know Col. Buchanan to be a man of convictions. The fact that he put his life on the line for the service of his country is proof positive that he's willing to sacrifice everything for the bigger picture, the greater good. If things go sideways, he and I will take responsibility and do what's necessary."

"Sirs, none of us want it to go so far," Lord Dathan said. "The Paramours will never leave its own out to dry. We only ask for transparency and an acknowledgment of the clear and present danger."

"Rest assured. It's acknowledged." Jake said, almost in a grumble.

Despite Lord Dathan's reluctant support, everyone sat sullen and dismayed.

"A domesticated tiger is still a tiger, colonel. That's all we're saying." Alekzander noted.

"She'll purr one minute. And the next she's mauling you in your sleep." Benaiah added.

"And if that's what happens, that's the way it should be." Jake concluded before abruptly rising from his seat and storming off. Lincoln followed.

They were walking my way when I could see it in Jake's eyes that he didn't mean his closing remarks. Those were the words of a man who was willing to fight and die for some secret plan he's yet to divulge. It seemed unusual from what I knew about the old-timer. To be honest, he almost sounded like myself. Childish. It was strange.

For the rest of the afternoon, I confess, I was gripped by the uncertainty. I wandered the English country estate of Hollow Rock with a freezing light rain falling in sporadic mists. Still, I endured it just to venture out to my favorite spot by the cascading stream.

All that talk about Gladys Vandelay… Jake had so much hope, so much faith in her. Jake's not an idiot. Just a hopeless romantic. Who was she? What did she know? What if she knew nothing and all this drama was a waste of time and stress? They did mention she flunked her initiation. From my understanding, only full-fledged Swords knew the deepest innermost secrets of the Society's infrastructure. So, what could we possibly gain from this one girl? I had to look into it myself.

After combing the enormous estate for most of the afternoon, I found her in the first place I should have checked. I heard she was crazy about guns but damn. By the time I got there, about ten minutes past seven, she had already gone through fifty magazines. Three sniper rifles had jammed, and the gears of an antique machine gun had dislodged from its cogs.

She pretty much had the whole underground shooting range to herself because her relentless pace annoyed everyone else. A guy who was leaving told me that she didn't talk to anyone and good luck. She just stayed in her lane and popped off rounds. I approached and pulled up a chair, letting her know that I wasn't going anywhere.

She glanced out the corner of her eye before replacing a target sheet and wheeling it out to 30 yards. I heard she was 22, but she looked like she was in middle school. Baby blue eyes. Long blonde hair with curls at the ends. From her skirt and stockings, I could tell she was athletically gifted by the bulge of her calves, the way she barely shook from the recoil. Her accuracy was also something else. She hit the X on eight out of the ten shots fired from a fully automatic.

"I'm glad to see your injury hasn't affected your aim." I said as she reloaded.

She didn't respond.

"You were wounded, right? I'm giving Col. Buchanan the benefit of doubt that he isn't completely off his rocker in bringing you here."

"Scared?" She asked.

"Naturally." I grinned.

"You should be. I'm only barely containing the urge to turn my Glock your way. Now leave me alone."

"Are you here to destroy us? Or do you really want to take down the Society?"

She slapped in a new magazine with an attitude that sent chills down my spine.

"If none of you believe me, then why the fuck..." She chuckled. "You should get rid of me. Honestly, it's so simple it's stupid."

"You're right!" I said, standing up. "It is stupid. However, Jake isn't dumb and neither is the council. But unlike them, I know all about false hope. I know what it does to a man. They'll sacrifice their entire lives for that which isn't true, plunging headfirst in their graves blissfully at peace with the 'hope' and 'faith' that everything will work out. I learned that lesson long ago. Hope, faith, belief, these are like batteries for martyrs. I'm not a martyr."

"You think I give two shits what you are?" She growled.

"I heard they killed your old man right in front of you."

She aimed at me and clicked the hammer.

"They killed my father in front of me too. Both of my fathers, actually. The biological one and the one who adopted me. Honestly, you bitches make me sick. Initiated or not, you're one of them. I can see it in your eyes. You all have it."

"Have what?"

"Selfish. Every single one of you thinks you're the center of the universe."

"Puh-leeze! Grow up, alright! Everyone's selfish! You have to look out for yourself because no one else will. I swear, you guys say the dumbest shit. If all Paramours are like you then none of you stand a chance. The Swords will carve through you like cake."

I shook my head and walked away, kinda pissed.

"You're selfish too, you little punk!" She kept barking. "You're just too stupid to see it! That 'correct the course' philosophy is nonsense! It's pointless. It won't change anything. If you don't kill them! If you don't kill every single last one of them, they'll only multiply and they won't stop until they get their revenge! And it will go on! On and on! It's insanity you stupid blockhead!"

I could still hear her shouting as I boarded the elevator. It's not that I didn't believe or understand where she was coming from. I suppose that's the difference between the Paramours and the Swords of St. Catherine. The women perpetuate the hate. The men are prepared to end it by laying down their lives. It begged the question, am I really a Paramour? Because I'm not about to die for these bitches. No way.

The next day was colder. I wished it would go ahead and snow already. With my cover blown and the Society hunting me from sea to shining sea, I was confined to Hollow Rock and limited in aiding Paramours on their missions. Of course, in my downtime I still wrote scripts and movie ideas. I was a film student after all. That passion never faded.

"Jesus!" I shrieked.

I was crouching by a pond with music blasting in my earbuds when I spotted Gladys's reflection. She was bundled in this white pearl coat with the wooly hood on. That, added with the gray overcast, she really did look like a ghost. Creepy AF.

I took out one of my earbuds for a moment to see if she had anything to say. My curiosity had dried up from our last conversation, so if she didn't have anything else, I'd prefer to enjoy the rest of my day.

"I'm not selfish." She said, almost in a pout. "You just…You have no idea what I've been through. That's the look in my eyes, that's what all Swords have. It isn't selfishness, it's pain. We've all been oppressed. We've all been antagonized and preyed upon."

"By whom, Gladys?" I asked with heartfelt sincerity. "And before you answer, consider this. I think you're about to plead the case that all Swords aren't the same. And if that's the case, why can't you apply that same logic to everyone else. Whoever oppressed you, whoever attacked you and inflicted you with this eternal pain, consider that they, even they, are individuals. They don't represent all of humanity."

"You're not making any sense!" Gladys argued. "Then why do you want to end the Society! If you really see everyone as individuals, then why hate them as a group?"

I smirked, rising to a stand. "Is it really so hard to grasp? On the battlefield, when you see soldiers comin' at you, I think it's reasonable to assume everyone in that uniform is out to get you. All men aren't the enemy. Just like all women aren't the enemy. Just the militant ones out to destroy us and reduce men to impotent puppies on a leash. And I assume it's the corrupt, abusive men who's your enemy, right? The ones who still think all women are all inferior slaves. But that doesn't mean all of us and I refuse to believe it applies most."

"Yeah, thanks to us women." She said. "If it wasn't for us putting our foot down, forcing civilization to progress, we'd still be in the Dark Ages."

"Maybe, but I'd think Jake would give Christ a lot of credit if he was here. Listen, we may go up against a Society dominated by women, but every Paramour here will tell you that their love for women is still paramount. The Swords of St. Catherine are evil. That doesn't mean all women are. We know that."

"Tell me, this. Why do you think the Swords are evil? Not the Paramours. I want to hear what you think."

"Because they murder, Gladys."

"Spare me. As if men don't murder."

"And those men deserve to be punished. In fact, a lot of them are being punished. Not sure if you noticed, but the prisons are filled to capacity."

"So naïve." She grumbled.

"Maybe. But I'm not wrong. And pointing the fingers at everyone else doesn't change the fact that your little group of girl scouts are the worse of the bunch. They kill and ruin everyone who gets in their way. They'd rather replace love with hate. If that's not the pinnacle of evil, I don't know what is."

"You're wrong. They're not replacing love with hate. They're replacing the love of men with love of-"

"Themselves?" I asked. "I don't think it's for the love of God or any other deity I ever heard of. And if it's for the love of women, why would they force you or any other woman to commit these rotten, unspeakable acts. Like sleep with a man to get close to him. Or kill your own father. If you ask me, that's no different from the so-called Patriarchy, or kings who send entire vanguards out to slaughter just to lure the enemy into a trap."

Her blue eyes glossed over as the breeze pulled at her bangs. "What do you guys want from me? I keep asking over and over again. What do you want?"

I chuckled. "Well, I can tell you what I want. I want to see the Society and all the Swords fall flat on their faces. Whatever they got planned, whatever my mother's up to, till the day I die, I want to fuck it all up."

"Your mother's a Sword of St. Catherine?"

"Yep."

"And you don't want to kill her? You just want to fuck up her plans?"

"Yep."

"You don't want to kill her because she's your mother?"

"I guess. Don't get me wrong, I've thought about it. But she's a tough cookie, let me tell ya. Bite her the wrong way and it'll break your teeth."

"What if I killed your mother for you?"

"Geez, kid…What is it with you and death?"

"BECAUSE, YOU DOLT! That's the only way it ends! That's what I don't get. It's so stupid! Fuck up with her plans? What are you, twelve? Don't you feel guilty for the countless lives she'll ruin, that she'll destroy everything because you and your butt-buddies are too busy twiddling with your fucking thumbs, snickering behind closed doors at all the plots you foiled like it's a goddamn Saturday morning cartoon? GROW UP!"

Gladys…sure was something else. I could still hear her fuming as she trudged off towards the mansion. Still…she had some good points.

…

The next day, again, it got colder but still no snow. And my dumbass carried a cold bottle of soda that made my fingers numb as I ventured out to the cascading stream. Again, Gladys eventually showed up in her pearl white coat, still wearing that same scowl. I took out my earbuds and waited for her begin.

"Truth be told, I'm not onboard with this stupid 'undermining them and steadying the course' nonsense."

"You don't say..." I scoffed.

"You have to admit, it sounds idiotic. For the love of God, please admit that."

I nodded. "It's not like I don't get where you're coming from, Gladys. But we're all given a choice. Being a Paramour isn't a badge or some title they bestow on us. It's who we are when we're faced with that choice to live or let die. We truly do live up to that name because it all boils down to love. My mother killed my father. But I still love her. I wish I didn't. I bet half the Paramours in Hollow Rock wished they didn't love their women. But they do."

She shrugged. "There's only one person on earth I loved, and they killed him. So, what do you think happens now?"

I smirked. "Well, consider this. Just because you lost a loved one, doesn't mean you'll never love again."

"Sounds like hope to me. Thought you said that crap was for martyrs."

"Would you believe me if I said you changed my mind?"

"Over the course of a day?"

"Yes, Gladys. We can do that. It's called intelligence. We adjust our views based on what's observed, based on new knowledge we attain. Go figure."

"More like, wishy-washy," she grumbled.

"Whatever."

"You know, you never told me your name."

"You never ask…forget it. My name's Elliot. Friends call me El, or Ellie or whatever."

"Ellie's pretty."

"Do I look pretty too?" I asked, fluttering my lashes.

"You're weird."

"Look who's talking, kid."

"El!" someone shouted.

I looked up towards the house and saw Jessi running my way. "I thought you'd want to know. He woke up!"

"Really, Jess? I'm supposed to know who…"

"Marcus! He's awake!" She said before running off to tell someone else.

It caught me off guard. I completely surprised.

"Marcus?" Gladys asked.

"Yeah. If it wasn't for him, I wouldn't be here. Come on! He's been in an induced-coma for God knows how long. What the Swords put him through, let's just say you'll never catch me complaining about a stubbed my toe. Come on!"

"Okay, but who is he?" she said as we hurried over the frosted grass.

"A journalist from New York. He was investigating the possibility of an underground feminist cult. Basically, he was on to you guys. Had the Paramours known about him before he started publishing his essays, they would've saved him. But Marcus was too fast. Too smart for his own good. I read some. The historical references, the current events, it's provocative. Bound to ruffle feathers.

"Anyways, when I sought him out, they told me he died. I thought he was dead. The Paramours had him shot, beat him to an inch of his life, and hit him with a car. The Paramours found him in the gutter. Literally. I went to Kentucky to find out what happened and that's when Jake found me."

"My Jake? Buchanan?" she asked.

"Your Jake? Oh look. Now it's snowing."

…

A small crowd had gathered by infirmary. As much as I didn't want to join them, I confess, I did see Marcus as my own personal hero. If it hadn't been for him, if it hadn't been for his courage to investigate and post his honest thoughts online, I might not have found my mother. I owed him a debt. More than words could explain.

All this was going through my head as I shouldered through the huddle to reach his recovery room. The door was closed but everyone could see through the observation window. He was alive. Looked thin and frail. His contusions had subsided, and he was now sitting up with lively facial expressions.

Jake, Lincoln, Ravi, and Lord Dathan were all in the room with him. I could tell conversations were light by the spurts of laughter, but no one could hear what they were talking about. I didn't need to hear. Simply knowing he had survived and was finally out of a coma was good enough. I was confident I'd have plenty of time to get to know him later.

"So that's him? Your lord and savior?"

I looked over my shoulder, then down at the shorter Gladys. I also noticed almost everyone else had backed up to keep a safe distance her.

"That's him. Marcus Angel. The man I owe my life."

It was strange. I expected more questions or a snarky comeback, but there was silence. So, I turned and saw that she had this far off look on her face. Others started to murmur with increasing agitation. And Gladys caught me watching her.

"What's up? Do you know him?"

"I do now." She told me. "Let's go."

Before I could say anything, this little girl was grabbing me by the arm and pulling me with a display of strength that was a bit disturbing. I almost tripped over my own shoes as she more or less dragged me down the hall.

When we got outside, Gladys let go and stared off with her hands on her hips.

"What's wrong, kid?"

"Speak softly and carry a big stick." she whispered.

It was faint but I could have sworn I heard her say that.

"Elliot…If you say what you mean and mean what you say, then come with me. Let's get out of here, someplace safe and remote where I can train you, out from under their supervision."

"What? Why?"

"Because, oddly enough, I don't feel like they trust me here. Strange, I know. And I believe what you said about wanting to stop the Swords without killing them. But to do that, you need to defend yourself against a Sword. What better way to learn that than to have a Sword coming at you no holds barred."

I smirked at first. Didn't take her seriously. That was, until her smile faded and was replaced by this cold blue-eyed stare that reached in and grabbed my soul by the throat.

"Are you in or out? Right now!"

Couldn't understand where all this was coming from. I'd only known her for a couple of days, but already she thought she could trust me? Did I trust her? Was this even safe?

I would confess, however, that there was something very exciting about Gladys, her fearless conviction. She and I were the youngest at Hollow Rock. Running off and getting into trouble should have been somewhat expected. In the end, I think I just trusted my instincts. If I was wrong and Gladys ended up murdering me in my sleep, I'd have no one to blame but myself. But I could live with that.

I nodded, "Alright. I know a place not far from Surrey. But I think you should know--"

"Perfect. Pack your things. I'll meet you at the front gate."

"Gladys, wait!"

"And El! Don't tell anyone."

This kid…I wasn't so stupid so as to abscond without leaving some hint as to where I went. So, I sent Jake an e-mail, which I knew he barely checked, but eventually would. It was to let him know I was with Gladys and still in the country. And to Surrey, we went.

Interlude

…

On the outskirts of the rural Borough of Runnymede, there was a gang boss who delusioned himself as the king of the streets…even though he was a smalltime hood. His name was Bruce Lorry, a hefty man who spoke in a fast cockney accent that was hardly coherent. Bruce was gay, lived like a gypsy, and was very sensible yet emotionally fragile despite his intimidating physique.

A couple of years ago, a bunch of lads in Bruce's crew were arrested for breaking into commercial truck full of smartphones. I just so happened to be near the station when I heard Bruce pleading to police on behalf of the young boys. I saw how much he cared for the boys who were already living hard knock lives, so I impersonated a lawyer and convinced the police to let the boys go. Bruce owed me a favor.

He allowed Gladys and I to stay in the 2nd floor flat above his boxing gym. He didn't ask a lot of questions and for some reason he took an instant liking to Gladys. Every afternoon, he'd check on us and gift Gladys with sugar cookies from the bakery. I'd sit there and listen to their endless drabble about the latest fashion trends or how they thought pop music was all starting to sound the same.

We trained in the gym and if anyone gave us crap for being outsiders, Bruce would show his face. For two months, Gladys put me through the ringer with her version of some kind of hell-on-earth boot camp. I bulked up from 160 to 180 and it really started to show. I was getting ripped.

Gladys was a proficient pugilist, like…ridiculously good. Almost every day, after sprinting through the hillside with a modified jacket that was filled with rocks, we'd practice boxing drill after drill. And then after I was good and exhausted with nothing left in the tank, we'd spar. Everyone would stop what they were doing just to watch this Little Bo Peep beat the shit out of me. I could barely land a punch and when I did, she'd get even angrier. And once, I'm not ashamed to say, I literally ran to my corner and just rang the damn bell myself.

Then, at the end of the day with my body hot and swollen, she'd make me carry a duffle bag with enough ammunition to land us in prison for the rest of our lives. We'd travel to the water meadows not far from where the Magna Carta was signed. It was here that we practiced our shooting.

I already knew how to handle sidearms, but Gladys…it's like she got off on it. The smell of gun smoke was catnip to her. And I noticed she had a habit of exhaling ever so softly every time we snapped in our magazines.

I never knew when she was impressed, but I always knew when she was disappointed. If I missed enough times, she'd snatched the gun away and just stare at me like I stepped on a kitten.

This girl. It didn't matter if she was working with a 9mm, a scoped rifle, or an AK-47, she hardly ever missed.

It was in those moments where I watched her in action that...well, let's just say I acknowledged she wasn't a middle school student. She may have been petite and youthful in appearance, but the way she handled herself with this serious intensity and blue eyes that hardly blinked...Gladys was indeed a grown woman. In so many ways, my superior. Feelings began to manifest. It was here that my heart began to flutter.

Just picture it, the auburn sun setting over the slopes of golden wheat that waved with the wind. Then Gladys, with her yellow, blonde hair loosely pulled back in a ponytail. Wearing this oversize dirty green army jacket, reminiscent of Vietnam. Crouching on one knee, with the stock of an assault rifle planted firmly against her shoulder. Those blue eyes and her soft, unblemished rosy visage. The lack of emotion when she pulled the trigger in short bursts. That painting will forever be in my mind.

At night, Gladys would ask me all kinds of questions about previous missions and my mother. I revealed my mom's name and that she was a powerful network executive. I told her about the years of angst, the visions and reoccurring nightmares of my father's murder. I told her about the night I finally confronted Jaida, and Gladys laughed.

She said I was lucky to get out by the skin of my teeth. She bragged that the Swords hardly ever failed once they sank their teeth into a prey. But I suppose, the most reassuring thing Gladys told me was that Jaida must have loved me. She said Jaida must have known I'd be in the writer's room that night. It was interesting. I never once even considered that.

When I tried to flip the conversations over to her, Gladys was reluctant to tell me anything about her past. Even when she gave me the headlines, she only said enough so that the secrets remained secrets. For instance, she told me that her sister killed her father...which was heavy. But I wouldn't find out until later that this was Gladys's initiation and that she failed by refusing to kill the father herself.

Also, I'd learn on my own that she fought in the Middle East. That was crazy. I've performed escort missions around Turkey, but I never did any hard fighting. After so many conversations, her deflections and obvious prevarications were starting to wear thin.

By the end of the second month, I finally had the courage to ask Gladys if she even trusted me. It was a beautiful spring day. We were on our way back from shooting practice when we stopped along the Thames. The sun was setting with an orange, pink-clouded sky. It took her a while to respond as we both stared out at the horizon with the sunset glow cast upon us.

"Ellie, there are some things I just don't want to talk about."

"Yeah, I've heard that before."

"Because it's true. I'm glad you feel comfortable in telling me things. I'm honored and do consider you a good friend. But I'm sorry. I just can't reciprocate. The scars around my heart...maybe one day, when they've healed to the point where I can acknowledge them without boiling with rage, maybe then I'll tell you."

"Say no more. I understand."

"Do you? Because you sound annoyed."

"Because I am annoyed." I chuckled. "But I mean, all that shit that happened to you was last year, wasn't it? I've had more than enough time to heal. And not everyone heals the same way. So, take your time. I understand. I can't stand it when people tell me I should be 'over' something. I'm like, really? Thank you, I hadn't thought of that. Also, fuck you. My name is Elliot, not whoever the hell you think you are. I'll heal at my own pace if you don't mind. So, you can take your expectations and shove it. How's that?!"

She smiled. It looked like relief. I wondered if she was afraid I'd resent her. But, how could I? I know what pain feels like. And I wasn't trying to get in her pants. I respected her. She knew who she was. No delusion. No doubt. It was refreshing.

When we got back to the boxing gym, we were in for a surprise. All the boxers were huddled around the TV. The volume was turned up and we could sense the air of excitement. Gladys and I hopped into the ring for vantage view over everyone's heads. Bruce spotted us out and shook his head.

"Bit a shite yous boys be in now, roite."

I think that's what he said. I just nodded like I understood and paid attention to the TV. It was breaking news. Scrolling in the lower third read the words: "FIRST LADY FOUND DEAD IN THE WHITE HOUSE, PRESIDENT TAKEN FOR QUESTIONING."

The media was in a frenzy. Massive crowds were on the verge of rioting in front of the White House. In uproar, they called for the president's impeachment.

The most damning news was the leaked autopsy report. Every outlet clamored over it. An anonymous source claimed ligature marks were found around the First Lady's neck. Murder was on the tips of everyone's tongues. Speculation of economic collapse and anarchy crowded out the fake concern and commiseration. Cameras zoomed in on those with the most emotion, the angriest, the loudest.

"Gladys, I think it's about time we returned to Hollow Rock."

She didn't answer. She just glowered at the screen. All of it reeked of foul play.

08. Elliot Chan – Assembly

Paramours from around the world descended on the country estate of Hollow Rock. It was a beehive of activity. By the time we got back, the roads leading up to the front gates were lined with clean cars and big SUVs. Attendants stood by to provide directions.

As soon as we entered, oddly enough, my first thought was that my room had been commandeered to accommodate the influx of visitors. Selfish, I know.

For the first time since my orientation, the halls were packed. Paramours I'd never seen were there in groups, entourages with their assistants and teams that may or may not have been official members. Everyone dressed important. Everyone hurried to and from. It was crazy. I sensed panic in the air.

I looked over my shoulder and down. Gladys and I were like stones in a relentless stream of urgent faces. She looked to me for answers, as if I'd experienced this level of pandemonium before.

"El!"

It was Jake. I heard his shout before I saw him. I wasn't exactly the tallest guy in the hall. The crew cut colonel came shouldering towards us as he waved off questions. I wasn't sure how many Paramours Jake had sponsored over the years, but I imagined there were quite a few. He encouraged everyone to just hurry into the auditorium.

As soon as Jake was within arm's reach, he yanked me up and ushered me into a private library. He tried to close the door, but Gladys was there to catch it.

"Um, darlin, could you give us a second? I need to speak to El alone."

"If it's about me, I'd rather I stay."

"GET OUT!" Jake snapped.

"Don't yell at me!"

Jake shoved her out the door and slammed the door close. It scared the bejesus out of me...the sight of Jake getting aggressive with someone so small. He turned and set his frazzled sights on me.

"Look, I'm sorry I didn't get your permission, but I was sure I'd be safe."

"Where'd you go?" He asked.

"Surrey. You know Bruce Lorry's place, right?"

"Yes. What have you been up to?"

"Training." I said, squinting, somewhat offended.

"Training. What kind of training?"

"Jake, I've fought the Swords before. My mother is almost twice my age and she whooped my ass like she was still in her prime. So, I asked Gladys to train me to prevent that from happening again. She was gracious enough to...Dude, what exactly is your problem with this? Are you really mad I didn't tell you? Check your e-mail!"

Jake nodded with his hands on his hips. Lookin' like a high school principal.

"Honestly, why are you pressing me on this. We're just friends, Jake."

"You gotta be real careful, El. Ya understand? I know you're ten times brighter than I was at your age. But if you've learned nothing from our brothers, beauty can blind us. It can compromise our personal constitutions and coax us down a path by which there's no turning back."

"Hang on," I cringed. "I thought you said you trusted her."

"Elliot, I trust that Gladys will do exactly what Gladys wants."

"So, you don't trust me then?"

"Would you?" He asked. "How can any man know what they'll do when they step into uncharted territory?"

"Dude, what the fuck!?" I whispered. "Wasn't I trained specifically just for that? To fend against deception and seduction?"

"We both know there's no substitution for the real thing. The love of a mother is not the same as the love of a potential mate."

"Buchanan! They're starting."

The call came through his earpiece and loud enough for me to hear.

"Just be careful, would ya? And I don't care that you left without telling me. You're a good kid. I don't want to lose you, alright."

138

"Damn…" I thought. I had no idea Jake cared so much. When he left out through the hallway, I noticed it wasn't as noisy as before. I suspected everyone had found their way to their seats. Meanwhile I was leaning against a bookcase, spinning a globe with the nudge of my thumb, pondering his words, questioning myself. Gladys entered and stood in the doorway, her blonde hair shimmering in the light.

"Are we going?" She asked.

"You're not going to ask what he said?"

"I have a good idea. Let's go."

I smirked. Of course, she did.

…

The auditorium was large enough to house 3,000 and every seat was occupied. Gladys and I were down near the bottom, fourth row from the stage. Lincoln was giving the presentation with the Senior Council sitting in a row behind the podium.

A big screen flashed the headlines we saw in Surrey. The First Lady was indeed dead. It was declared a homicide and the President of the United States was being questioned in connection with the murder.

Lincoln spoke, "Our sources confirm that the First Lady was strangled to death by an instrument, most likely a belt or a tie. The evidence against the president looks damning and you can bet your ass his political opponents will drop breadcrumb after breadcrumb, slowly frothing the mainstream into a frenzy, turning it into the biggest conspiracy since JFK.

"What the public doesn't know, though I suspect they soon will, is that the First Lady was having an affair with the Vice President. It's likely the opposition will keep this under wraps until election season, therein guaranteeing victory for the first female president in U.S. history. As we all know, the former Secretary of State never fully left the spotlight following her previous defeat.

"She's been publishing tell-alls, mudslinging her own party, and jumping on every scandal to pontificate to an audience, all susceptible to emotions and blind to the facts. And after this, the people will call for the President's head and she'll be right up there waiting, holding the ax.

"Now we've known for a while now that the Society has backed the Secretary, silencing her critics, facilitating her ascension despite the numerous blunders that's plagued her administrations. Ladies and gentlemen. Mark my words. If we do not correct this course, she will be the next president of the United States. It will be the end of Western Civilization as we know it."

"So, what if it is? Are we in the business of protecting America or the innocent?" said an Israeli nationalist from the audience.

"How many innocents do you think will die if the cornerstone of civilization crumbles?" replied an American.

"Bullocks, mate," shouted an Australian. "Always leaving their allies out to dry. Never keeping their word. The United States ain't the center of the universe!"

"Actually, it is gentlemen." said the elderly Lord Dathan of English Parliament. "As one who's old enough to have seen the entire world engulfed in flames, I can assure you the United States' role in global prosperity is pivotal.

"Look back to the second World War. After the first, the United States adopted an isolationist sentiment. Many Americans believed the government should take a step back, stop policing the world, meddling in foreign affairs and all that.

"However, my friends, that is exactly how a madman like Hitler was able to rise to power in the first place. It started with the invasion of Austria and Czechoslovakia with very little recourse. The world was so timid about intervening after the first war, they did nothing to stop Hitler or undermine his advancement."

"Then look what happened!" Lincoln said, jumping in. "Hitler invaded Poland. Millions of innocent people lost their lives."

"Spoken like a true Imperialist." Benaiah said. "As if America's the answer to all our problems. Lest we forget their inability to act against Saudi Arabia after 9/11 all just to keep relations with their oil supplier intact. Don't get me started on Vietnam."

"Classic strawman, Benaiah." Lincoln retorted. "The point I'm trying to make...the hell with it. In this world, in this modern age, every country, citizen, and community on earth is connected now more so than ever! There has to be a nation to step up and take that leadership role. If not the United States, then who? The U.K.? China? Russia? Whoever is number one, it is incumbent upon that nation to intervene and do what it can to prevent another world war."

The assembly grumbled.

"Is this what it's comes down to?!" Jessi, the former schoolteacher shot out of her seat to shout. "Does the council really believe that having a female president in the White House will result in another world war? Is that what we've come to?"

"This isn't just any female, Ms. Dobson." Lord Dathan answered. "She's a proxy. Women can be stern, powerful leaders. I speak for all England when I say that. But anyone in office who's bought and paid for, where their every decision that effects an entire nation is dictated by a shadow organization…this is evil. This is corruption!"

"My point exactly!" said Benaiah. "By your own admission, you reveal the futility of interference. What you've just described is no better than what's already happening in American politics. As if the career politicians don't already serve a master the supersedes the will of the people."

"His point, Benaiah, is that it can always get worse. And with the Swords of St. Catherine…well, I challenge you. Other than the Third Reich, can you name a greater threat to prosperity?" Lincoln questioned.

Again, the assembly grumbled.

"A room full of SMALL-MINDED MEN!" Gladys's roar rose above all others. It brought the hairs of on my arm to stiffen up. Little Bo Peep projected so well, loud enough for all to hear. And she was still sitting down.

"The Swords of St. Catherine don't care whether or not the world's falling apart. What the society, what the Swords care about more than anything, is control. The desire to dictate culture, policies, education. Conflict is just an ingredient for the caldron, a concoction by which such results are produced."

"Gladys…" I groaned.

"For those who don't know, Ms. Gladys Vandelay here used to be one of the Swords of St. Catherine." Lincoln introduced.

Almost at once, a wave of shock and horror befell the bemoaning Paramours like a ripple in the lake. I kept hearing, "she can't be trusted" or "You can't be serious. She's a poison aimed to infect us from within. Why is she here? She shouldn't be here!"

Gladys continued, "If everyone's dead, there'd be no one to rule. The Society isn't out to start a global war. They're aim is to replace man atop the hegemony. They've already done it in the U.K. They're doing it in Australia. United States is next. Russia and China won't be far behind. And it's like magic. If the world knows the trick, the illusion has no effect. If the world knows that there's a secret society hell-bent on world domination, they won't let it happen.

"That's why the Swords tried to kill your Marcus Angel. That's why they put every opposing voice in the same category of lunatics like the supremacists or the alt-right. That's why they want a female president, a puppet controlled by Society leadership. Once they latch their talons into politics and control legislation…there's no stopping them. They've won."

"Don't you mean you win as well? Once a Sword always a Sword as far as I'm concerned," Benaiah told him.

"Believe what you want. As for me, I can't stomach another word of such stupidity. And sadly, this auditorium is filled to the brim with it."

The place exploded in uproar. Gladys stormed through the aisle and down to the exit as Paramours wagged their fingers and slung accusations. It was hard to watch. More than that, her logic struck a chord with me.

After another thirty-minute debate, Lord Dathan took to the podium and encouraged everyone to delve into their resources to get to the bottom of the White House scandal. Everyone was instructed to contact their people, their agents, their sleeper cells, any staffers, anyone in national security or the private IT sector to dig up whatever they could to exonerate the president and counter the accusations levied against him. Even if it meant hacking into classified files or stealing encrypted data.

Everything was a go. They were calling in all cars for this one. I've never seen anything like it, a mission where the entire assembly would combine their efforts on a single objective.

As everyone prepared to depart, I found Jake and Lincoln being followed by a huddle of Paramours. I couldn't hear the gist of their conversation, but I did pick up that they were going to D.C. They almost seemed excited, like it was a competition and they'd be damned if they were going to lose to the Swords.

Then, Jake spotted me out of the corner of his eye. He stopped in the middle of the hallway with his attendees folding around us.

"What should I do? How can I help?" I asked.

Lincoln and Jake exchanged glances as if they had been talking behind my back.

"We need you to stay here, Elliot." said Lincoln. "I know you want to help but with a scandal of this magnitude, you can bet your ass your mother's network will have hundreds of cameras scanning every nook and cranny. The last thing we need is for you to get spotted and have to divert the brothers for a rescue mission."

"Hang on!"

"Don't argue. Now's not the time. Just stay here and dig up anything you can that will aid our brothers in the field. That's an order." Lincoln commanded.

I wanted to remind these jerks that this wasn't the military, but I understood where they were coming from. I simply nodded and off they went. Jake and Lincoln had just turned a corner when I saw Gladys standing by my side. She was dressed rugged for travel.

"Are you coming?" she said.

I threw up my hands. "Where to?"

"To take down the Society, of course. Come along." She said with this ambitious grin that should have been my first red flag to run the other way.

We were in a hurried stroll when I asked what she meant and I admit, I was running out of breath just to keep up.

Gladys explained, "You heard what I said in there. I wasn't just blowing smoke. It's good that everyone's taking me seriously. They have every right, but they're going about it the wrong way. Even if they find a way to clear the president's name, it won't stop the Society from completing their mission. It'll only prolong the inevitable. The only way to stop the Society is the same way all societies have fallen throughout history. From within."

"And I don't suppose you'd like to explain your grand plan to do that? It can't be you. They'll kill you at the doorstep?"

"You know, you sure can be dense. All this time, you guys had the key. You just didn't know it."

Suddenly, I realized we were in the medical wing. When we got to the recovery rooms, Marcus was wide-awake and sitting up, watching the news. He turned to us with a puzzled look.

Gladys smiled, so sweet and innocent. My hands begged for an explanation but all she did was usher me in with that freakish strength before closing the door behind us. Without saying a word, she went to each window and closed the blinds.

"What's going on?" Marcus asked. "No one's told me anything. Is this the Society? Did they do this?"

I scratched my head, "Yeah. Almost everyone is deploying to get this situation under control."

"So, messed up." Marcus groaned. "I heard the First Lady was strangled. It's supposed to be all about female empowerment, yet they'd do this to one of their own."

Gladys gave his bedrail a sharp tug and said, "Being born a woman doesn't make her one of their own. In the eyes of a Sword, they're just punishing the First Lady for marrying an idiot like the president to begin with."

"Who are you?" Marcus finally asked her.

Gladys shook his hand. "Gladys Vandelay, at your service. The ward here is my lackey, Elliot Chan. And you sir, are the highly coveted Marcus Angel. I've heard so much about you. And I hope I'm not being too forward in saying this, but you have no idea how many lives you've touched. If it weren't for you, this world would truly be a lost cause."

"Alright, Gladys," I grumbled. "Don't you think you're laying it on a bit thick?"

She leaned over the bed and stared at Marcus like an object in a snow globe. "Tell me, Marcus, by any chance do you know of a woman named Anna Marie?"

Immediately, Marcus's eyes widened. His chest deflated. He started to look around as if he was in danger. In a panic, he squirmed, kicking in the bed to sit up before Gladys took hold of his wrists.

"Calm down! She's not here. No one's here to hurt you. I just had to make sure you were the one."

"The one?" I stressed. "Gladys, what are you talking about?! Enough with this cryptic shit!"

"When I was with the Swords of St. Catherine, I befriended one of their most formidable operatives. And when I say formidable, let's just say I'm willing to stake my life on the fact that she could easily kill ten men on her own. Her name is Anna Marie."

"My Anna Marie?"

"That's right!" Gladys whispered. "Now ask me, how do you think *I* know your name."

"She told you?" Marcus asked.

"Yes! As I said, Anna and I became good friends. And as Ellie can attest, that's no easy feat, being my friend. She confided in me. Because I caught her in a moment of crippling depression. She was sad. Sullen. Heartbroken. Over you. She told me that she killed the only one who ever knew the real her. She told me his name was Marcus Angel."

Marcus's eyes began to gloss over with tears. It was my first time hearing of this Anna Marie person. Another one of Gladys's guarded secrets. But the wheels started turning and everything started making sense. It wasn't until Gladys saw Marcus a couple months back that she decided to train me. Was this her plan from the get-go? And what was even stranger was that Marcus didn't ask any questions. Was he so naïve, or was everything Gladys saying so true and spot on that he was utterly speechless?

I stepped closer and asked with all seriousness, "Gladys. What are you doing?"

She was still leaning over his bed when she turned with that look in her eye. It was a paralyzing stare that conveyed, "you know damn well what I'm doing."

I turned for the door and as soon as I touched the knob, I heard the metallic click of a Glock.

"Just listen." She said.

"Or you'll shoot me?" I said, my temper flared.

"Just listen! Marcus is the main reason you were able to learn about the society, right? You owe him. Not the Paramours."

"Marcus is a paramour!" I shouted.

"He is not! Nor am I. Marcus was brought here unconscious. He had no say in the matter."

"You deceitful bitch!" I said, almost laughing through my frustrations. "Jake was right. He was right about you all along."

"Just listen! Listen to what I have to say and if you still want to run like a little emasculated whelp, then go. But forewarning, I won't be stopped. You'll only be leading lambs to the slaughter by trying to interfere with my plans."

"Do you even know what you sound like? You sound like one of them!" I shouted.

"I told you the society could only be destroyed from within! With Anna on our side, no one can stop us. Believe me!"

"You really want to kill them. All of them. Don't you?"

"Well, as many as I can. I suspect I won't survive long, but Anna will. You don't know her. She's the only one who can do it. Think back to the night she shot you, Marcus. That was only after you were already shot up and struck by the car, right? It was her initiation. She shot you because she thought you were already dead and there was no other option. Don't you see? Out of all the men in her life, the hundreds who've come and gone, she loved you the most. She loves you still. I've seen it. Anna may have everyone else fooled, but at heart, she is not a Sword of St. Catherine. I suspect there are others like us, but with Anna, there's no mistake. I willing to stake my life on it."

"Can I go now?" I said, unimpressed.

"If you must." she told me.

Just as I opened the door, I heard, "Wait."

It was Marcus.

"Elliot, I understand how you feel. Your sense of loyalty and duty. I don't want to impede on that. But if what she says is true and you do feel indebted to me, I have a favor to ask. Please."

I shook my head, "What is it?"

"I'd like to see her again. All this time I've spent cooped up in here, she's all I ever think about. Her eyes, her lips, her voice. I just want to see her one more time. I promise I won't convince her to kill anyone. Whatever this one has planned, I doubt it'll happen all in one day, so you'll have plenty of time to warn the others. But please, only after I see her. Consider it my mission as a Paramour. Just give me one last time."

...the Perennial War of Paramours...

146

09. Gladys Vandelay – A Daughter's Rage

My father's company. It was just after closing time on the Upper Eastside when the city appeared to be made of pure electricity, all contained in tall spires of glossy stone and steel. We were up on the 16th floor of a parking garage just across the intersection from my father's building. Staring at it brought back memories. Sadly, those weren't fond memories.

Every time I closed my eyes and tried to picture my father, I saw his death. Not his embrace, his smile or his gentle voice. No...what I'd see is him falling over with a bloody gash in his stomach, a lethal laceration delivered by my own sister, a sister who was now CEO of the investment firm he built from the ground up. So badly, I wished an airplane would fly into the building. I'd relish the thought of it collapsing with her and all her minions inside.

A thudding bump brought me back to reality. Marcus woke up. He was sleeping in the back of our unmarked van rented by Elliot. Elliot himself was parallel parked in a black sedan a block away. I asked him to keep his distance just to be safe, among other reasons.

I entered the van's driver's seat and looked to the back. "Hey. You hungry?"

"No. Just anxious more than anything else." Marcus said.

He was brushing his hair, primping himself using his phone as a mirror. He looked dapper in his black blazer and white collared shirt. I'll admit, there was something cute about him. The way there's something cute about the bug face of a pug.

He caught me staring and asked, "Gladys, why are you wearing a bulletproof vest?"

"Well...I didn't exactly tell her you'd be here. Only that I needed to talk. I trust she'll come alone, but you never know. It's been a while since I've seen her. For all I know, that tough exterior had only hardened with time. Like cement."

"Tough exterior...Heh." He smirked. "You know when I first met her, she had a hard time making friends. Everyone thought she had this huge wall around her. Unapproachable. As if she was some goddess they weren't fit to address."

"But you didn't see her that way?"

"Well, sure I did," said Marcus. "But still…she's the most beautiful woman I've ever seen. I'd be remiss if I didn't at least try. Whether I was rejected or not, there'd be no shame in it. I'd merely point her out and say, see!? And others would understand. Might even applaud me for so boldly reaching out of my league."

He continued with, "I dunno. I just saw something in Anna that… I knew she wasn't all armor and spikes. I think she had to protect herself, her sister, her mother, to guard her heart. But deep down, she was looking for someone to simply put up with all that and take a chance on her. To show a little backbone. Stamina, not so much physical, but more so the mental endurance to tolerate the idea that she could never be completely contained. She's not looking to submit to anyone, but at the same time, she wants to be conquered. This is all conjecture, of course."

Listening to his words…I brought my legs into the seat and sighed before telling him, "Marcus…I really do think you just her equal. I mean, it's all great, your little psychoanalysis of the dichotomy and what not. But plainly put, human beings are all different. Everyone can't be equal in everything. I'm good with a gun, sure, but she can beat my ass and a room full of Marines by herself. I don't care for prognostications. But she does. Theories and conjectures, the mental stimulation.

"Think about it, Anna could have any man she wants. From the star of the football team to the hottest rapper. She's had them all sexually, but none of them really had her. If you know what I mean. There's a certain appeal that comes from within. That's what she was looking for. Not the money, status, or materialistic things. She was looking for someone who respects themselves enough to tell her no even if it means losing her. Someone with principles, morals and convictions. I think that's you."

His face was transparent, like dozens of tiny muscles reacting to each point I made. Marcus didn't need to tell me whether he agreed or not, the tightening of his lips, the pull of his eyebrows spoke volumes. Marcus was indeed cute. And…perhaps too honest for his own good.

"What about your man, Elliot? Do you see him as your equal?"

I slumped against the seat. "Elliot's weird. In a good way, I guess. Overly cautious and thinks the worst is always gonna happen all the freaking time. He even made me bring that duffle bag full of ammunition just in case. Don't know if I like that, someone constantly fretting and fearing for my safety. Feels like he's the woman in our relationship. You know? It's just weird."

Marcus nodded, "But you do like him."

"I guess."

Just then, the squeal of grinding tires screeched from the winding turn of an approaching vehicle. I shushed him and told him to lay flat. Then I exited the van and cocked the Beretta I had tucked along my waistband, straightening my coat, making sure I appeared as cordial as possible.

Anna drove up the ramp in a black luxury sedan, crossing over parking lines as if she had every intention of smashing me into the side of the van. She came to a smooth stop just ten feet away, blinding me with those high beams. I couldn't tell it was her until she turned them off.

After shutting off the engine, she just took a moment, sitting there staring at me like a disappointed parent who had come to pick up her child from detention. Last time I saw her was over a year ago. My heart rattled like a drum. For all I knew, her loyalty and commitment to the Society might have grown even stronger during my absence. My life was indeed in her hands.

She exited with an exasperated sigh, about a foot taller than me and impressive with that perfect posture and long raven hair. She had broad shoulders for a woman, but it fit her figure. Dressed like a corporate girl but probably hiding a pistol and blade underneath her coat, she had the air of someone who's had to manage an entire team all day, putting out fires, making things happen. Anna Marie, the fierce Colombian more infamously known by her code name, "the Andalusian".

She took three loud heel steps forward. "I know why you're here, Gladys. Can't let you do it. Clarice is too important."

I sighed with relief. As intimidating as she was, there was still that twinkle in her eyes.

"What are you doing here, Gladys? Why'd you call me? If anyone else finds out about this, I'll have no choice but to put you down. And this time, I swear to you-"

The van doors opened. The sound of grinding metal startled both of us and Anna instinctively whipped out her 9mm, aiming it at the now gaping abyss that gradually widened as the doors opened.

"Crap!" I whispered. I wasn't ready for him. I swear my heart was about to jump out of my chest. I had no idea how this was gonna to go down, but out trudged Marcus Angel. He still had to use crutches to hold himself up, but he managed to not make it look like a struggle.

When I returned my sights to Anna…it was unforgettable. The gun was down by her side, barely hanging from her fingertips. Her caramel complexion had turned pale. She looked like she was about to collapse as if she was witnessing a ghost. Her jaw slacked and the sheer…I wanna say horror, but more than that, it was sorrow, a widow longing for her husband who was lost at sea. The sparkle in her eyes intensified just before the tears rolled down her cheeks. I heard whispers, perhaps in Spanish, barely audible. Anna Marie stood frozen in time as she watched Marcus come closer, one metallic crutch at a time.

"Hey, missy. Long time no see."

The gun fell to the pavement. It was so loud. All was so quiet.

"It's okay." He told her. "I know you did what you had to do. I know it sounds crazy, but in my heart of hearts, I think I forgave you as soon as you pulled the trigger. Haha."

"Dios mio!" she gushed with hands rushing to cover her mouth.

She turned and walked away towards a railing overlooking the city. She cried. Anna Marie broke down in a hard way, so much grief and possibly remorse. And Marcus…for some reason he kept laughing. Not a taunting, "ah-ha" laugh, but it was more like he just thought the whole thing was endearing. There were tears mixed in his chuckles.

"Anna, honestly! You did what you had to do. Stop crying." He told her.

"STOP! Don't come any closer. Just stay back!"

"You know I can't do that."

"WHY ARE YOU HERE?!" She screamed. "You shouldn't be alive?!"

"But I am. I am alive. And you're right. I shouldn't be here. Not after that shit you and your people put me through. But I survived. And even if I die tonight, even if your group hunts me down like a pack of wolves, just seeing you again…Sweetheart, it's worth it. I told you a long time ago, I don't mind dying if it's in your arms. Sounds stupid and I'm pretty sure I didn't know what I was saying at the time. But I wasn't lying. I love you. I'll always love you."

Anna had her arms crossed, trying her level best not to look at him.

He continued, "I keep replaying that night. Over and over again. You were trying to save me, weren't you?"

"Marcus stop. Please…" She whimpered.

Oh Anna. Seeing her puddle up in a ball of emotions gripped at my heart. Marcus approached and put a hand on her back. She shuddered at the touch just before he flattened his palm and massaged firmly. He was slightly taller than her. Seeing them together, I just thought they were a perfect match. Anna Marie wasn't in need of protection or some big brute shielding her from enemies. She was in need of comfort, assurance, and stability. From the mere touch, I saw with my own eyes how much Anna had truly missed him. His voice. It was pleasant, sincere, and soothing. To both of us, I think.

"It's true, isn't it?" He said. "You were trying to save me. And like a cat afraid of water, I fought back. That's why I almost died that night. That's not your fault."

"Marcus!" She whimpered, finally turning to meet his gaze. "I've done all kinds of horrible, horrible shit! Like, bad. Just really, really bad things. I've killed dozens, if not, hundreds!"

"Anna…Ever since we were in our early twenties, I knew you'd do whatever it took to accomplish your goals. I don't judge you by the path you've taken. I can't. I should, but I don't. You are who you are. I don't know what you've done, but it's not the end of the world. As long as you're alive, it's not too late to redeem yourself. To repent."

"I CAN'T!" She cried.

"Yes, you can! With God, all things are possible. You're stronger than you give yourself credit for. For fuck's sake! Everyone can see that! Why can't you?" He said as he wiped at her tears with the soft nudge of his thumb.

It was heart-wrenching. Part of me was glad to unite her with her paramour. Another part was extremely jealous in the saddest kind of way. That kind of love…I've never experienced it. They started kissing but I didn't sense lust. It was genuine, natural affection. A nurturing kiss. Tender, the peak of compassion.

"You guys, I really think we should get going." I told them.

"Go where, Gladys?" Anna said with reddening eyes.

"Anywhere!" Marcus said.

"It's not that simple," Anna said. "Gladys is a marked woman, but she was only a protégé. I'm a full-fledged Sword, they won't stop until they've wiped us from the face of the earth, and I won't let that happen. I can't let them get to you! Not again! NOT EVER!"

"Anna."

"No, Marcus! You guys need to get out of here. I can't be seen with you!"

"Anna…"

"Marcus, you said you loved me. Now I confess, I love you too. Always have, which is exactly why I'm pushing you away. We can't be together. Understand? I wish we could, but we can't! Alright? It's too dangerous."

"I don't give a shit!" Marcus barked. "Don't you see? I really just don't give a shit. If I can't be with you, I'm dead already."

Anna's face cringed up something fierce. They embraced once more, but the hairs on the back of my neck stood on end. I heard the faint sounds of screeching tires coming from the spiral ramp in the corner of the garage. Cars were approaching at an aggressive pace. We were found. We had to get out of there.

With haste, I stepped over and grabbed them by their shoulders. "Guys. Seriously. We really need to get out of here. They probably put a tracker in your car, Anna. They're here. I hear them."

Anna helped Marcus to the van while I whipped up the crutches and threw them in. And then…

This is…. this part is a bit difficult to write. I um...

It was faint, but I heard the buzzing zip of a sniper's bullet glance past my ear. It was unmistakable. The scream that followed haunts me to this day.

"AHHHHHHHHHHHH!!!!"

I turned around. Anna was struggling to hold Marcus up. She lost her grip on his jacket and he fell onto the pavement with a bloody gash where his heart used to be. His eyes were still open with shock and horror...but he was gone.

"NOOOO! NO GOD! NO!" Anna screamed.

Frustration, guilt, and panic had me wringing my fingers through my hair. I turned around and scanned for the sniper and it was just by some pure fucking happenstance that I looked up to where my father's executive office used to be.

It was Clarice, my sister. I caught her as she was moving the rifle away from the window. The scathing heat came over. I don't think Clarice knew that I spotted her, but she knew I was there. And instead of killing me first, this bitch thought it'd be best to get rid of Marcus. So yeah, something came over me, boiling rage and blind fury.

As Anna's wailing screams reverberated through the garage, Elliot was calling through my earpiece. Even he could hear the screams from a block away and badgered for an update. I didn't reply. Saying nothing, I walked to the nearest pickup truck and retrieved my stashed bag of ammunition.

Whipping off my overcoat, I put on a shoulder harness that could holster two pistols and six clips. I equipped myself with the following: 2 Walther P99 semi-automatic pistols, a lightweight 2016 Uzi variant, three grenades, a Beretta ARX 160 A3 assault rifle with laser scope sighting, and one more AK-47 that I brought for Anna.

"Anna. We need to go. They're coming."

"Let them." Anna snarled. Her back was to me as she remained keeled over Marcus, but I felt the grumble in her voice, like the growl of a mastiff.

They came. Three armored vehicles charged up the ramp with a screeching halt. It was a team of private contractors, ex-military, the likes of which I had to contend with in Canada. And leading them was a familiar face. I expected at least one Sword would show up. But here, there were two.

One was Mandee. I remembered she was always following Scarlet around as if the two were partners in crime. She was a fearsome little cunt who shattered a girl's jaw with a single palm strike during our training. Next to her was Jazmin, a Mexican senorita who was a little too top heavy for our line of work in my opinion. The eight mercenaries and two Swords filed out with fully automatics trained on us.

"Should have stayed in Canada, Gladys! Too bad." Mandee taunted.

"And who's this?" Jazmin said, as she approached and stood over Anna's shoulder.

Anna said nothing. On her knees, she continued to embrace Marcus with her long black hair covering her face.

Jazmin aimed at me. "Who is this man?" she said.

"Anna…" I whispered.

"You know what…" Anna sniffled as she slowly rose up. "I don't think I can be part of this group anymore."

"What?" Jazmin asked.

Before Jazmin could follow up, Anna slapped away Jazmin's muzzle with one hand and slit her throat with the other. It all happened in a flash and before anyone could process what happened, I dropped to my knees and opened fire with my Beretta ARX. A steady, horizontal spray cut through the knees of three before the rest ducked for cover.

Mandee charged at Anna, kicking her in the back. Anna hit the side of the van, bounced off and engaged Mandee in this fierce gun/knife battle. The likes of which I'd only seen in cage matches back in Syria. It didn't last long. As fierce as Mandee was, Anna was a fucking beast.

Mandee managed to disarm the gun, but Anna slashed at her thigh, elbowed her nose and slung Mandee over the concrete barrier of the parking garage. I witnessed the tail end of their brawl while skirting along the perimeter, keeping the soldiers contained with 7.62 Soviet rounds.

Anna had lost it. I don't think she feared anything. As the men shot at me from behind their black SUV's, Anna charged from their blind side and just started kickin' ass. Her kicks dislodged knees and broke ribs. Her field knife sliced through arteries and exposed veins.

And just when I was about to join her, two crisp knocks came from my right. Chunks of concrete pop up from the floor. The sniper had returned.

I spun to train my muzzle on the executive floor of my father's building. Sure enough, there was my bitch-ass sister trying to take me out. I fired what was left of my clip, blowing out three windows before I saw the silhouette of her body drop from sight. I knew she wasn't dead.

Leaving Anna to vent her frustration on the remaining mercs, I took off running for the stairwell and crossed the street. In the intersection, people were already on their phones calling the police. The sight of me running with an assault rifle only added to their hysteria.

"Gladys! Wait!"

Elliot's shouted over the noise, but I didn't turn to look. I had tunnel vision on the entrance doors of my father's building. The elderly receptionist recognized me. She was on the phone when she saw me sprinting through the lobby and her jaw almost fell to the floor. Two loud bangs came from my rear. I spun around and shot the security guard. The receptionist screamed. Sorry she had to see that.

Alarms blared. The staff was alerted and a lockdown was in effect. All elevators were shut down and access to the stairwell was restricted without a keycard. Thankfully, I was already in the stairwell sprinting up the steps. So was Elliot. I could hear him calling my name from two floors down.

Just as I passed the 7th floor, I heard the doors open behind me. Three soldiers had entered the stairwell and opened fire. I got hit in the back, but it got the Kevlar. It wasn't until I was halfway up to the 8th that I returned fire. Two headshots and I got a third soldier with four slugs to the chest.

Grunting, I pulled myself up. The tips of my hair were dripping with sweat, and my quads were burning from the ascent. But still, the fuel tank of determination kept me going.

The building was seventy-stories, but the executive floor was the 32nd. With just six steps away from this 32nd floor that I used to run around and play as a child, I paused and took a deep breath while reloading with a fresh clip. I listened to discern how far down Elliot was. Couldn't hear him. He could have been dealing with his own ambush of soldiers. Either way, it was better this way. This was my problem. This was my mission.

I aimed at the locks and fired before kicking the door open. Dashing out onto the slick tile flooring, I rolled as a hail of bullets came from what seemed like every direction. As expected. Private military, all armed to the teeth with black-market weapons. Clarice wasn't stupid. I'll give her that.

But what the soldiers didn't know was that this was my personal Vietnam, and they were unwelcomed invaders. I knew every office, corner, hallway, and column of the 32nd floor. I knew where the counters were, where the partitions were. I knew where the walls were thick and where the locations of the railings where I could jump over. This was my playground. They fanned out and followed.

Like a competitive gamer in a first-person shooter, I directed my muzzle with nerves of steel. I heard which shots came from where and it was a cinch picking these bastards off. All them were big and sturdy. They didn't have my agility. They were too slow, and they called themselves trying to hide behind partitions with the top of their heads, their foots, or their asses exposed. I took any inch they gave me and tore them a new one.

Blood splattered and pooled everywhere. Men were screaming and some bumped into each other trying to get away from me. I must have killed at least twelve before depleting the last of my ARX. It was a shame because I was fond of that gun.

The Uzi had a pistol grip but no stock, so I used one hand to mow down two men pursuing me, wasting a ton of ammunition. Another one came into view. I chased him, sprinting as I turned the corner, sliding on my knees as I shredded into his back while gliding into an adjacent office.

"Grenade out!"

Idiots. Nice of them to warn me. I threw my entire weight to break through a conference room window and took cover behind a table just in time to shield against the explosion. The overheads went out. Emergency backups came on.

As the deafening blast fizzled out, I poked out into the hallway and rolled two of my own grenades toward a group of men with green laser scopes that stood out like a beacon in the fog. I pushed off the ground and took off running the other way. They started shooting but the explosions put an end to all that.

A severed hand flew by my shoulder. I aimed at it, ready to fire. Then another hand gripped my shoulder. I swung my Uzi but it was palmed by Elliot just in time to keep from clocking him.

Elliot… I'm sure I looked possessed in his eyes. He pulled me away from a column and sat me down against a copy machine.

I was about to scream at him for interfering, but he covered my mouth and tugged on my shoulder straps to let me know I was bleeding. I was shot but I didn't feel the pain. He looked around as if he was searching for an exit, but I knew I wasn't going anywhere. I punched at his throat and kicked him away.

As soon as I stood up and peered down the hall, I locked eyes with her. We had the same blue eyes and blonde hair. However, in the peach-colored emergency lights, Clarice looked like a demon the way she wore that malicious grin with a Javelin anti-tank missile mounted on her shoulders.

She fired and I swear my entire life flashed before eyes. Like a deer caught in the headlights, I stood frozen in place almost as if I had accepted my death.

Elliot tackled me through the glass walls of a conference room as an explosion, the likes of which I never felt, ripped through the building. It wasn't a direct impact, but I felt the heat. It burned, searing my pants into my calves. We were thrown across tables and chairs before rolling against a perimeter wall.

A section of the floor had collapsed. It was a twenty-foot drop into the next floor down. The building was on fire. Sparks flew from exposed wires. Debris, glass, and chunks of marble were scattered everywhere. And Elliot, Elliot had shielded me. His arms were wrapped around my head. The sprinkler system showered over us, but I knew it wouldn't stop the blaze.

"We can make it. It'll hurt but we can make it." Elliot said, almost out of breath. He was referring to the twenty-foot drop down to the 31st floor.

"El…"

"Come on!" He said as he tried to lift me up. I wouldn't let him.

"Go." I told him.

"Gladys! This whole place is gonna come down!"

"THEN GO!"

"Not without you!"

I drew one of my P99s and aimed it at his forehead. "I'm not leaving!" I was deadly serious.

A loud pop came from an electrical unit, but Elliot didn't flinch. He just stared at me with this growing fervor. Even with the gun aimed at him, he leaned over me and grabbed me by the straps of my vest.

"Alright, you listen to me! I'm not leaving without you! I know you want to kill her! I understand! I really do. But you're better than them! You're better than you think you are! That's why I believe in the Paramours! Understand?! GET UP!" He shouted as he yanked me to a stand.

"I won't let you go down that path. Now we're gonna get the fuck out of here! And you and me, we'll have each other. I love you and I know you love me even though you're too stupid to admit it. That's what separates us from them. They live for a cause. We live for the sake of each other. For people! For life!"

At that moment, I grabbed this stupid, idealistic man and kissed him with all the passion and affection he showed me. I really did love Elliot Chan.

I just hated Clarice even more.

It was slow motion the way I shoved him back. He fell into the open 31st floor with his arms spread out like a sparrow trying to catch the wind. I wish I was as great as he seemed to think I was. But I just couldn't do it. I couldn't forgive her.

With a pistol in both hands and tears stinging my eyes, I emerged into the hallway and sprinted as fast as I could for my father's office. I was screaming some horrific war cry, fully aware that at any time I could drop dead from that TAC-50 I knew she still had in her possession.

Suddenly, something hard and metal battered the front of my shins. I tripped and hit the floor, knocking the wind out of me as I went sliding. Clarice had just thrown the Javelin launcher at me and I screamed from the pain.

"Shut up." She said. "All that screaming and for what?"

I pushed up to my knees and aimed one of my pistols. She kicked it out of my hand. I spun with the momentum of her kick and aimed the second. Before I knew it, she caught my arm and slammed me to the floor in a brutal hip toss with half her weight landing down on me. She tried to break my wrist, but I let go of the pistol and wiggled free. Just as I got back up, she hit me with a spinning back heel kick that sent me sprawling over a desk.

Clarice leaped over the toppled desk and whipped out a blade, the same French dagger she used to kill my father, a misericord. All I had on me was a field knife. The exhaustion was setting in. My body was overheated and the flames had spread to the ceilings above. So, what happened next made no sense to anyone with a tactical mind. Goes to show, I didn't plan on surviving. But if I was going down, I for damn sure was gonna take her with me.

I flung my field knife. She deflected it with her blade. And in that split second, I did this crazy mad dash to jump on her back like a velociraptor. And like a velociraptor, I sank my teeth into her neck, biting as hard as I could. She screamed and flailed her dagger. Finally, she had the wherewithal to smash back me into the wall, ramming me twice before I let go.

She turned and tried to drive to dagger into my stomach. I sidestepped and the blade got stuck in the wall. From there, we went at it.

It wasn't a catfight. It was an all-out, bare-knuckle brawl. She clobbered me with blows that might as well have come from a bat. I used my tai chi to redirect her strikes. And whenever I could, I'd grab the back of her head and send her face-first into a desk or some hard surface.

Our fight spilled from conference rooms, to the bathroom, and back out into the hallways. The hatred was mutual. I saw it in her eyes and I know she saw it in mine. The scorching heat didn't faze us for an instant. Every time we separated, we'd pounce at each other regardless of the crackling wires or collapsing walls. Hair was pulled. Ears were torn. Two of my molars were dislodged and I managed to dislocate her left elbow.

It wasn't until I took her to the ground and held her in a triangle choke that the tide of the battle turned. She used her superior strength, shouting with all her might as she picked up my entire body. She meant to slam me back down, but before she could, I slipped out of the hold, hooked my arm around her head, and smashed her face-first into the tile floor in a devastating DDT.

Clarice's forehead was busted open and the blood spilled from her bangs like syrup. She started to stagger off, but I grabbed her ankle. She retaliated with a stomp to my face that ended up breaking my nose. I remember whimpering something fierce as my eyes welled with tears.

I watched as she staggered towards the elevator doors and willed them open with her bare hands. The lift wasn't there, but she jumped onto the cable wires and slid down. I cracked my nose back into place and followed.

...

On the streets below, civilians had gathered behind the yellow tape in the intersection, watching as the fire had spread across six floors. Emergency services were already on the scene. Most of the first responding police officers were in the parking garage investigating the initial calls of shots fired.

"HELP! HELP ME PLEASE!!!"

Clarice hobbled toward a pair of ambulances and a team of paramedics that were already tending to the injured soldiers that Anna beat. I suppose the sight of this blonde corporate girl covered in blood made everyone change their priority. She was halfway across the intersection when paramedics started running to her to help.

TA-TAT! TA-TAT! TAT-TAT-TAT!

That was the sound my gun made as I riddled Clarice with seven rounds. I remember the slapping sound her face made when her body smacked the asphalt. Everyone screamed and the crowd ran like ants in a mound that was just stepped on.

Then...something happened to me.

I was standing on the sidewalk in front of the glass entrance to my father's old building. How do I put it? I thought there would be a catharsis, a release of anguish and rage. I thought there would be triumph or relief. Instead, there was this sick, nauseating feeling that immediately churned in the pit of my stomach. The pistol slipped from my fingertips and I didn't even hear it hit the ground.

I turned around and looked up at my father's building. The amber flames waved like banner flags to the night sky. Windows were cracked and shattered. The structural integrity of the stone façade appeared as if it was just one explosion away from a total collapse.

Someone tackled me from behind and I didn't resist. A knee was planted into my back and my cheek was pressed against the grainy concrete. There were two, maybe three of them. I didn't resist but they were super aggressive. I could tell from the way they wrangled my limp wrists into the cuffs.

I stared at my sister's body lying in the middle of the road. It was over. And for some reason, I started crying. It may have been the unbearable trauma throbbing through my nose but I think it was something else. I don't know. I don't know why I was crying but I was. So sad, so empty, so wretched, so…pointless.

Faded in and out of consciousness. They kept me on the scene for a while. I saw a lot of angry men pointing at me, shouting at me, but I heard no words. Paramedics were reluctant to treat me. I was put on a stretcher. Blinding lights from a helicopter shined down on us. And that was the last thing I remember of the crime scene.

…

I woke up two or three hours later in a hospital room. We were still on the Upper East Side because I could make out Park Avenue from my window so high up. The beep of a heart monitor was a good sign. At least my nose had stopped bleeding. It was taped and I couldn't breathe from it, but still, it wasn't bleeding.

I started to diagnose how badly I was injured when I noticed I was cuffed to the bed railing. Two deputies were stationed outside my room. There was a commotion in the hallway. It sounded like reporters and some police rep giving a statement. Escaping in my condition was futile. So, I just laid there, replaying the events over and over in my head. Melancholy lingered, but not as badly as before.

Just as I contemplated sleeping off the rest of the night, a pair of detectives barged in. The bald one closed the blinds while the shorter stout one with a three-day stubble just looked my body up and down and grunted with disgust.

"I've heard of sibling rivalries. But shiiiet." said the stout one.

"Gladys Vandelay," barked the bald one. "The same Gladys wanted in connection with the murder of Felix Vandelay of Vandelay Holdings United. You wanna talk about one fucked up family…"

I squinted my eyes. I knew these cocksuckers had no clue but still…talking down to me like that was enough to spark the ignition switch in me.

"Where'd you get the guns? Better yet, where'd you learn to shoot like that? We got sixteen phones recording you tearing into your sister right there in the middle of 67th."

"SPEAK!" the stout one shouted.

"Don't speak. Last I checked, she still has the right to remain silent." In walked a woman in office attire with her hair tied up in a bun. She was accompanied by two other women, smaller, younger, less impressive in stature.

"Detectives. I'm sure we don't need to go through the usual routine." She said.

"No! Not this time, counselor! This time we have the suspect dead to rights! Captured on film with dozens of eyewitnesses."

"No doubt factors leading to her arrest, sure. But she still has a right to legal counsel and a fair trial." Said the woman.

"Let us do our jobs! We're investigating, goddamn it!"

"Then do your job, detectives. Collect evidence. Build your case. If my client wants to speak to you, she is well within her rights to do so. Ms. Vandelay. Do you wish to speak to the police? No? There you have it. You may leave now. Good evening, gentlemen." The woman said.

"Yeah don't get too comfortable counselor. The DA's on his way. This is a shitstorm! Looks like Beirut out there!"

The detectives stormed out of the room. Upon closing the door, the lawyer and her two paralegals turned and looked at me with the same creepy expression.

"My oh my. We have been a busy girl. Haven't we."

"A thorn in our side."

"A fly in our lashes."

"Whatever are we to do with you?"

Each took turns saying their lines like they were rehearsed. The attorney with the bun leaned over and whispered, "You should have stayed hidden like a bunny in the snow where no one could find you. As soon as these cameras are gone, you're a dead wabbit. But first. Where is the Andalusian?"

So stupid...If I was already dead then why in the hell would I give her up? I deduced that these women weren't full-fledged Swords, but probably pawns or protégés. Either way, they were wasting my time. I just wanted to sleep.

The lawyer put her hands on my neck and squeezed.

"Listen to me!" I whispered. "You really don't want to be giving me a reason to…"

The door opened and someone else entered. It was Mandee. The last time I saw her, she was scrapping with Anna in the parking garage. Immediately, panic set in. Mandee was no joke. I struggled with my handcuffs as the attorney giggled.

"No, no. Please finish. What were you going to say?" the attorney taunted.

Mandee walked around to the other side of the bed. Her face was bruised and swollen with a patch over her left cheek. She was pissed, the kind of angry that didn't care about logic or reason.

"What are you doing?" the attorney asked her. "We're supposed to wait for Breanne to--"

"We can't wait. We're doing this now." Mandee said.

With a crazy look in her eye, Mandee took a syringe from a small case in her pocket and filled it with a clear, translucent substance. I saw her face light up with satisfaction as the fluids dripped from the needle. And just when her eyes focused on me...

BOOM!

A high-pressure crash came in through the window. I barely saw what happened as my bed went tipping away from Mandee and pinned over the lawyer's legs. She screamed in agony. It was Elliot. He repelled down the building and came bursting through the window. It was awesome!

Mandee was hunched over the railing with the syringe still in her hand. She saw my wrist still cuffed to the railing and grabbed it. Before she could inject me, Elliot kicked her away and shot her in the thigh. The two paralegals had regained their bearings and drew their weapons, but Elliot shot them both before they could take aim. Another shot freed me from the railing.

The stout detective hurried into the room but fled back out after a quick glance of Elliot's Model 22A.

"Hang on!" Elliot shouted.

I wrapped my arms around his neck, my legs around his waist. Then, he jumped out of the window and latched onto his rappel line with one arm.

He grunted something fierce. I felt it. The same arm he used to latch on to the rappel line had just popped out place. We were forty floors up. A plummet from this height would have killed both of us but somehow, he was still holding on as we slid down at a safe speed.

Elliot…I could see the torture from his grimace and sweat. So determined. His own weight on a dislocated arm would have been hard enough, but he was carrying both of us. I held tight and embraced him. I should have whispered thank you or kissed him or something. But I never got the chance.

Shots rang out and echoed off neighboring buildings. I looked up and saw Mandee glowering as she aimed at us. I saw the muzzle flashes and then she disappeared.

We reached the sidewalk. Elliot was still carrying me in his arms. But then, ever so slowly, he slumped over and laid on top of me. I felt the deflation in his chest. It was strained as if he was hiccupping, struggling to retain breath. My hands slid across his back, upward towards his shoulders and there it was. Two entry wounds, one on each of his shoulders.

"No! No no no no, not you!" I whispered.

"My keys. Two blocks north." He struggled to say.

"NO! Please. Please, come on. COME ON!" I shouted with hands on his face.

"Go. Get out of here."

That was his last breath. Ellie…my Elliot.

"NOOOOO! OHH!!! ELLIOT NO!"

I squeezed him tight. Didn't want to leave him. Not like that. Not in the middle of the fucking sidewalk as people with their stupid, fuck ugly faces huddled around.

"Get back!" I shouted with his gun. "Get back or I'll kill you! I'll fucking kill you all!"

I shot the closest person in his chest. I honestly didn't give a shit. He staggered back as the rest fled like dogs. Sirens were closing in. We were on the hospital's west façade. The entrance and emergency exits were on the other side. I had to leave him. As much as it pained me, I had to let go.

I took his keys and hobbled as hard I as I could, stopping for nothing, not street signs, not for anyone staring at the gun or my naked ass flapping from in the hospital robe. Nothing. North, he said. So north I went.

After crossing the two blocks, I started pressing the key fob and saw the flashing headlights coming from his silver sedan parked on the corner. Then, another shot rang out. It hit me in my back and I was flung forward to the sidewalk. The bullet passed cleanly through my lower back and it felt like molten lava pouring through my pelvis, from my hip to my thighs.

Mandee... Even with a slug in her leg, somehow this relentless bitch had been behind me the whole time. Now, here she was stalking me, her wounded prey. I sat up and clawed myself closer to the car, but she was closing in.

All seemed hopeless until I saw a blur of motion come out of nowhere. Anna Marie tackled Mandee like a grizzly bear and savaged her neck over and over again with a field knife.

Then she got up and approached me with the same murderous stare she had for Mandee. I pointed and begged. "The car! Hurry!"

Anna…I had no idea what was racing through her mind. She looked like she had every intention on killing me and I wouldn't have blamed her. But after looking around, she hurried over and helped me into the vehicle.

Once she was in the driver seat and rolling down the street…I allowed myself to pass out. So much had happened. The emotion, the pain, the bloodshed, it was all too much.

10. Anna the Andalusian – The Cult

My life begins every time he dies, and I'm getting sick of it. I thought he was dead. I thought I killed him. This time I know he's not coming back. I suppose the only solace stems from the fact that he finally learned the truth. Truth is, I loved him. I'll always love him. That's all there is to it.

I don't want everyone to know all about my family upbringing or whatever. It's nobody's business. So, I'm going to skip all that.

I met Marcus in my early twenties. We worked together in the same building, at the same company, an up-and-coming media outlet focused on entertainment. He was a journalist writing op-ed pieces on the ever-changing culture, while I made my bones on the forecast projections of album and box office sales. I heard he gave me credit for how much I changed him, inspiring him to grow. I suppose I should do the same.

...

I dunno… Marcus was really shitty at small talk. I think our first conversations were about God. That's how deep and straight to the point he was. It was kind of annoying at first. I thought it was creepy and invasive. I was like, "who the hell are you that I should tell you all these deep and personal things?"

But after a while, I dunno. It kinda grew on me. I found myself thinking about crap I never would've.

He talked about stuff like North Korea or the slave trade in Africa that still persists to this day. And when he spoke, it was so full of passion. Like, he honestly cared, as if he had a family member out there or some stake in the matter. It was a spectacle, actually. Always so animated and full of histrionics. Caught myself smiling a couple of times. He'd notice, turn and blush. If black people could blush.

Then he'd ask for my opinion. I wouldn't have one. I just liked listening. But he encouraged me to think. He was in my head. That's how the bastardo got me.

Of course, when you're young you never realize these things. Like, who actually takes the time to analyze why they're hanging around another person? Other than Marcus, who takes the time? I know I didn't.

As engaging as he was, I didn't think Marcus was all that attractive at first. He had a big camel nose, tall and goofy-looking. And yeah, he lost weight overtime, replacing fat with muscle, which was kind of nice. But still, his eyes. He had puppy eyes that expressed too much emotion. I didn't like that.

Back then, I went for the strong silent types who looked like mysterious vaults begging to be pried open. With Marcus, he was already open. Too easy and painted with desperation. And when he told me he loved me after just five months of meeting me, I thought it was so stupid.

He called it being straight-forward and honest. But where's the fun in that? So many times, I tried to tell him, "Instead of showing all your cards at once, let the other person peel back the layers on their own."

He wouldn't let me. He'd counter with crap like, "If you think I've shown all my cards by this one conversation alone, you're sadly mistaken. My well runs deep and I've merely doused you with a bucket from the ocean."

So arrogant and full of himself. Well…sure of himself. Either way, I suppose the reason why I'm writing all this is to convey how much I changed. Back then, as much as his overconfidence repulsed me, it never ceased to amaze me.

With him, every day was different. Always a new topic, always a new thought or some interesting story to discuss. Not just the main topics that dominated talk shows, but he'd read between the lines and bust out his own theories of ulterior motives for everything. It wasn't boring with Marcus. But at the same time, it wasn't fun.

You see how confusing that sounds? Only Marcus could elicit that kind of reaction in me. With anyone else, I could sum them up in 140 characters. With Marcus, I'd need a couple of afternoons to explain. And even when I did, I'd probably confuse myself.

So, when it comes to how much Marcus had changed me, I credit him with turning me into an independent thinker. Someone who not only sees what happened, but why it happened. And even when I heard explanations, I wouldn't take it at face value, but consider the possibility that the speaker may be mistaken. Not lying, but oblivious to how wrong they are in their evaluation.

But like I said…when I was younger, I took all that for granted. I wanted to do more with my life whereas Marcus seemed more settled. I come from Colombia. I knew there was more to the world than that, more the world had to offer, so I decided to venture out.

It was tough and scary and I left a whole bunch of friends behind in New York. Marcus was especially pissed. I could tell because he didn't even come to the farewell party. He sent this block of text, and I wasn't about to read all that.

I remember my last day, walking by his cubicle as he worked. It made me smile, because as much as he's changed over the years, when Marcus worked, he had a habit of listening to loud metal music through his headphones, bobbing his head with his hood on like a total creep.

I thought about scaring him like I used to but knowing him…It was a happy day for me. Marcus had a way of pissing on my parades. So, I didn't do anything. I must have stood there for about three minutes just watching him type. And then I left.

Marcus…I honestly believed that one day he'd change the world with his thoughts. I prayed for him and wished him luck.

My next stop was Los Angeles. It didn't take long to find a job as an event coordinator with the LA Bulls football team. I was at the epicenter, a wheelin' and dealin' world of two-timing agents, backstabbin' promoters, and all the hunks you could eat. I loved it.

Everything was high stakes and fast paced. Here, women had to walk the walk and talk the talk. You had to keep up and dish as much as you got. I worked directly under the Marketing Director so I was in charge of coordinating with vendors and making sure everything was set up for all the parties, social events, and conferences leading up to the big game. There was a lot riding on my back and it's exactly what I wanted. The responsibility. The power. The constant fear of failure. Knowing that one single mistake could cost millions. I loved it!

And the thing is, I knew from an early age that I was more attractive than the average woman. As a child, I was taught to have good posture, arch your back, stand up straight, take care of your skin and all that. I don't think there was a single day that a man didn't hit on me, or a girl didn't sneer at me with envious eyes. It didn't bother me. I knew my looks were a blessing and I had every intention of using it to my advantage.

I could get any man to do what I wanted them to do, no matter the inconvenience. All it took was a smile and a stroke of their ego. When it came to women, I knew how to befriend them and get them on my side. The trick was to show them that you're down to earth, to convince them that you don't want to be known for your looks or assets.

Show 'em that you're a driven worker, tolerant and expecting of the prejudice while keeping your complaints to yourself, shutting them up by outperforming them all. That's why women have it worse. We have to work harder. It's also what's makes us better.

Being in a hub of professional athletes, I've dated football players, basketball players, athletic trainers, even managers and coaching assistants. They're all the same. I won't go so far as to say all they care about is sex, but it's the main thing they cared about. And to be honest, it's all I cared about too.

I admit it. I was addicted to sex. The flutter of the flesh. The heat, the stimulation. I used to tell people, "Good sex is like morphine to the misery of a bad relationship." It was the only way to explain why I was with an obvious dunce or some jackass whom I clearly had no intention of spending the rest of my life with. They were just hobbies I played with to pass the time.

I could care less about their dreams or aspirations or how they felt about me, so long as they quenched my desire. The problem was when they caught feelings, or as Marcus would say, "they loved me so much that they started to hate me."

I'm talking about hard dudes built like iron, made of muscle and so tall that they had to duck to avoid the door frame. These monsters on the field were soft as teddy bears when they got to opening up. It made me sick to my stomach. I didn't go after them to hear about their adversity or the obstacles they had to overcome. News flash! Everyone has obstacles. I didn't care! I just wanted to have fun for fuck's sake, a man with stamina who could handle me in bed. That's it!

But no! The stereotypes are full of shit. They say women are all emotional but from what I've seen it's the other way around. These gorillas lose their shit and flip over tables if you don't compliment them enough or notice when they're trying to impress you. And for some fucking reason, everyone wants to have children. Like, right away!

I don't mind children, but first, let me live a little. I always made this clear from the get-go. And because they can't wrap their tiny little brains around it, they'd lash out. I've had men put hands on me and I fought back. I actually trained in MMA and us Latinos know how to work our legs. I've keyed cars, broken windows, and smashed bottles to defend myself. At the same time, I've come to work with swollen eyes and busted lips but I never felt embarrassed. I took pride in knowing I defended myself well.

Over the course of five years, I've had fifteen men propose marriage to me in elaborate fashion. I wouldn't feel a shred of remorse when I'd tell them "no" even as a crowd looked on. It's because they insulted me. They were either stupid or foolish for ever thinking they could contain me. And that's what it really boiled down to. All men wanted to possess me. They wanted to own me, mind, body, and soul. To cook, clean, and conceive. And of course, we all know men like to talk, bragging about exploits in the boardrooms and locker rooms.

After a while, I was tempted to quit the business. If I weren't such an effective producer, I probably would've been fired.

Then, everything changed when a star quarterback was traded in from Philadelphia. He was probably the most gorgeous man I'd ever seen in my life. He was tall with sharp eagle eyes, curly brown hair, this German African breed who looked like he belonged on the cover of a men's health magazine. His name was Jason Turner.

The first time I met him was at the welcome party at a packed nightclub out in Malibu. We locked eyes on the dance floor and gravitated like magnets. It was the best sex I ever had in my life. I knew he was married with children, but none of that mattered. In fact, I think I liked it better so he wouldn't expect to have children with me.

This probably went on for seven months. Jason had a stellar season and led the team to the playoffs for the first time in six seasons. But the night before the conference championship, Jason went out with the boys. Cameras caught him making out with a stripper in Miami. It didn't bother me that much, but it pissed the hell out of his wife and they ended up losing the game.

Jason returned to Los Angeles a disgraced train wreck. His wife filed for divorce and much to my horror, Jason wanted to move in with me to start a new life. I wanted none of that. So, I started ignoring his texts and screening his calls. I avoided him whenever I could, but the night after a Mardi Gras party, Jason came staggering into my West Hollywood apartment with two of his teammates. All of them fuming with alcohol, stumbling one foot after the other.

I didn't want them to stay the night. It had been months since I talked to Jason, so I started to call him a cab. He wrestled the phone from my hands and demanded that I talk to him.

"You're drunk, Jason! You need to go home!" I shouted.

"I am home, bitch. I paid for this couch. I paid for that TV. That bedspread's mine!"

"You want it? Take it and get out!"

I ripped the sheets from my bed and threw it at him. "Take it and get the fuck out! All of you! Go!"

Yes, I was pushing him. I shoved the comforter in his arms and started pushing him towards the door when suddenly he punched me in my face. It was full force. I saw the look in his eyes. His intent was clear. So of course, I fought back. I clawed at his face and threw hooks but he was too strong. He grabbed my arms and wrestled me to the carpet right there in my living room.

His boys sat there laughing. It was the first time since I was a child that a man overpowered me. That feeling of helplessness no matter how hard I struggled, no matter how hard I fought back…it's the most wretched feeling in the world. This blinding rage overcame me and I started screaming. The teammates laughed louder, pointing like sick twisted gargoyles.

Jason flipped me over, pulled down my pants. He started to rape me. I clawed at the carpet, screaming, trying to crawl away, but he had my right arm pinned down, with his other arm coiled around my head, his hand clamped over my mouth, muffling my screams as he thrust himself into me again and again. He was grunting like a wild beast. My heart must have been beating at 200 rpms because I was convulsing, trembling with sheer rage.

Then, out the corner of my eye, I saw the beer bottle he dropped. I grabbed it and was able to turn around to smash it into his face. Before he even hit the floor, I was on him, jamming the broken bottle into his neck. Blood gushed and sprayed everywhere, the curtains, the wall, the couch. I stabbed him again and again…as if I was cuffed and had to dig the key out from his throat.

Next thing I know, his friends got up, cursing as they ran for the front door. Only, they didn't open it. Someone else did. A number of suppressed shots zipped through the air before their bodies hit the floor. I whipped around. I remember my blood-soaked hair slapping my shoulders like a wet mop.

In walked a group of women all dressed in black overcoats and business attire. The one with the pistol came and stood over me. She had long black hair with crystal clear deep blue eyes.

"I'm Breanne." She said as if that was supposed to mean something. "Perhaps you should get off of him now."

I looked down. It was strange…killing a man. You really don't realize what you're doing until it's done. Crimes of passion are real. Jason had circular lacerations all over his neck and face. His right eye was stuck in the bottleneck of the beer bottle still in my hands. I tossed it.

When I looked up, Breanne had tucked her pistol and was now extending her hand my way. I accepted and she helped me up. Another woman came and wrapped me in a black coat. Another four ladies were packing the teammates in body bags. I watched as three more ladies entered with soap buckets and brushes. Another woman had a police badge on her hip. She was speaking some command into a radio handset.

Breanne said nothing as she observed me watching everyone else. Of course, the first question to mind was "who are they," but I never asked. I think Breanne was waiting for it and when the question didn't come, she simply took me by the hand and escorted me away from my apartment.

Everything seemed so coordinated and rehearsed. None of my neighbors stuck their heads out to inquire about the ruckus. There was a woman waiting by the entrance of the stairwell. Another waited by the exit door. The reception desk was vacant. A black limousine with tinted windows waited out front. It was late night, but I still expected to see a pedestrian or two. There was none in proximity. A lady opened the door for us and as soon as Breanne and I were inside, the limo pulled off.

"We've been watching you, Anna. I knew it was only a matter of time before something like this happened. I was hoping to pull you in beforehand, but alas, I'm not an oracle," she said.

"Where are we going?"

"Somewhere safe. To get you cleaned up."

At the other end of a limo was another woman, in her early twenties with a computer in her lap. This one had a sassy look about her, black hair, red eye shadow wearing a black choker.

"My associate, Scarlet." said Breanne. "She's new. Like you, Anna."

"Who are you people?" I finally asked.

"We're a sisterhood of women determined to take charge. Our society has lasted for centuries. No one knows we exist. No one will ever know we exist. Just like no one will ever know it was you who killed the Bulls' star quarterback, Jason Turner."

"You're going to blackmail me?"

"Absolutely not. Merely illustrating that when it comes to realities, we're quite adept at manipulating them to be whatever we want."

"A sisterhood?"

"That's right!" She whispered. "From here on out, your life will only get better. I will teach you to drive thousands of chariots with one hand. You will learn the extent your full potential and impose your will as you were born to do. Anna Marie, you are a goddess among men. You don't have to hide it anymore."

Breanne Cunningham, a member of the Society's prestigious Armored Front. She might seem calm and collected, sophisticated and civil. But when it came to bloodshed and violence, Breanne was a professor of it. Her words struck a chord. I pretended like I was enamored, but the truth was, I knew she was catering to my ego. If I were in her shoes, I would've done the same.

And here's the strange thing…even though I had just killed a man, I wasn't traumatized by the experience. I didn't even try to justify it in my mind. It didn't bother me being cold and sticky with dried blood. I didn't ask any more questions about this so-called "society" or how or why she had been watching me. My mind was just blank.

I suppose, deep down, it was in that moment that I realized nothing would ever be the same. The alternative was prison. Instead, I was riding in a limo. So of course, I accepted it. Of course, I didn't ask questions or asked to be let out. Whatever Breanne wanted from me, anything would've been better than life behind bars. Thus, it was easy to embrace what was happening.

I went through the same training process that Gladys talked about, except while her vest weighed 40, I had an 80lb vest as I ran through the slopes. I wasn't very talkative. Just driven. Exercise and running came natural to me because I was already well versed to combat training. When it came time to learn a new system of fighting, I chose Krav Maga. I already knew MMA and concluded if your opponent's asymmetrically stronger, all the grappling techniques in the world can't help you.

The Society flew me out to Israel to learn Krav Maga from an ex-Mossad agent who was once an instructor for the all-female Israeli Defense Forces. Her name was Hannah Sjoberg, tough as nails.

Krav Maga was a combination of practical techniques designed for extremely close quarters. Whether you're surrounded by a mob or cornered in an alley, with a knife in your hands and Krav Maga in your repertoire, you're a fucking lion on the Serengeti. It emphasized bursts of ruthless aggression and maximum effort, both of which, came natural for me.

Blades were my best friends. Daggers, field knives, the benthic knife, concealed blades, I was taught how to use them all. I learned the pressure points. I became familiar with the main veins and arteries of the body. You could stab, puncture, lacerate, and saw into flesh to drain the enemy's life force. The human body can lose over four pints of blood in less than a minute from a well-placed puncture wound. This was Krav Maga.

One of my favorite moves was a counter where I'd block high with my left hand and dash low to my opponent's right side while slicing across their obliques. I got good at it. The first time I used it was on an extremist in a bazaar, not far from Jerusalem during one of the many uprisings.

Everything Hannah taught me worked. I trained with her for six months and every time there was a conflict, we'd put on the burqa and involve ourselves for the sake of experience. It was an adrenaline rush. Hannah became like a second mother. She didn't speak much. She didn't ask questions. She didn't judge. She just took care to discipline me, refining me into the fearsome warrior I am today.

When it came to motivation or what drove me…truth is, I didn't and still don't know. I was upset about having to leave my career behind, but it wasn't the end of the world. The so-called friends I used to have didn't mean much to me. Jason's death was manufactured to look like a hate crime not far from Skid Row.

Breanne served as my sponsor, a mentor of sorts. When I wasn't training in the field, she'd try to indoctrinate me with all kinds of ideology about female empowerment and how men have continued to fuck up over the centuries. But again, even on all that, I wasn't really sold.

I think it was the structure, the tradition, a sense of order and organization that made me feel like I belonged. Given my own frustrations with men, it was nice to see women taking charge. Ever since I was little, I always thought of myself as more capable than most of the men in my life, so it made sense.

The Villa in British Columbia was a training facility, but it also served as a headquarters the way the Swords came and went. Even when I was still a protégé, everyone treated me like I was already a full-fledged member. I didn't sense they were disingenuous. These women didn't wear masks or force politeness to make you feel good. Everyone was sincere and full of purpose, so focused on their mission and the greater goal.

Mandee was actually in my training class. We came up together. I think she was a little jealous about how popular I was and right away, she befriended the bitchiest girl in the house, Scarlet. I always thought there was something else going on between them, but that was none of my business.

Breanne kept me close. We were the same height and whenever I was with her, it always felt like…like if it was just the two of us against a hundred bad guys, I wouldn't be afraid. At the head of the table, Breanne placed me at her right. Again, this was back when I was still a protégé. So yeah, Mandee and Scarlet started to hate my guts. But it didn't bother me so long as it was limited to the scowling.

But one night, Scarlet showed just how crazy she was. I had just stepped out of the shower and threw on a towel when this short bitch pinned me against the wall and put a blade to my throat. She started whispering some threat, but I reacted on impulse, ramming her face into the wall and trapping her in an armbar. She kicked away from the wall and landed on my chest, but I used my towel to wrap it around her neck.

Others heard the commotion and rushed in. It took six ladies to pull me off, partially because I was still slippery and the steam was fogging the bathroom. I really was about ready to kill that bitch. It was a good thing they managed to separate us.

I remember Celeste was there. She was the first black woman I saw in the society. She had been with the Swords of St. Catherine for about two years by then and apparently already knew about Scarlet's reputation.

"So, what's this all about?" Celeste said with a smirk. "Somebody give this girl a towel."

"You're fucking dead, you fucking cunt whore!" Scarlet shouted.

"Now, now, Scarlet." Celeste teased. "It's not whether you win or lose. It's what you do with your dancing shoes."

"How bout I dance all over your fucking face!? How bout that?" Scarlet screamed.

"What are you whining about?" Celeste taunted.

"She attacked me! I'm a Sword. She's still a fucking protégé. She's out! You hear me? She's out!"

"You're not the one who decides that. I am."

Everyone turned to see Breanne walking in with two soldiers armed with M16s.

"It doesn't take a rocket scientist to see who provoked whom. Scarlet, this is the last I ever want to hear about you doing something like this again. Do I make myself clear?"

"Why do you coddle her?" Scarlet barked. "It's been two years now! She still hasn't done the initiation."

"Alright listen up!" I said, fucking fed up and stark naked. "I don't give a damn if you're a protégé or the motherfuckin' president. Anyone try some shit like this again and you're getting' stabbed."

Celeste started laughing. Scarlet pushed her and Celeste shoved back.

"ENOUGH!" Breanne shouted. "This is what I'm talking about. This is why women can't get ahead! This is our problem, our biggest problem. Right here. Don't you see? No one can bring us down but us. Look around. Not a single man in sight but we're all ready to draw blood."

Breanne circled Scarlet with a stare that could melt ice. "Why are you so jealous? What is it that you want, Scarlet? Speak!"

"Respect!"

"Respect, she says." Breanne nodded. "And why is that so important to you?"

"It's important to all of us. Even you, Breanne."

"See, here's the part where I should reach out and snatch the ever-lovin' life out of you, but I'm not going to do that. I'm not going to kill you, Scarlet. I'm not even going to threaten you with expulsion. Because this is what we want. We want our women to think and act for themselves, determine of their own freewill what is truth and justice. For that, I applaud you. But one lesson you will learn. Is that every choice has a consequence. Before you make that choice, you must be prepared to accept the consequences. That's called accountability. Do that and you'll have my respect. Come along, Anna."

I made sure my towel was wrapped tight as I bypassed Scarlet on my way to Breanne. Scarlet was about to follow us but was stopped by the women with the M16s. Four more women were out in the hallway, all wearing boxing gloves. Breanne gave them a nod and they entered the bathroom as we continued on.

"Oh what?! Y'all want some of this? Come on then! Let's go!" Scarlet screamed.

I could hear the fast steps of squeaking boots and slapping impacts followed by grunts and shouts of exertion. Anyone who grew up in the inner city could tell Scarlet was getting jumped and fighting back with everything she got.

The next morning, Breanne was sitting on my bed as an assistant reviewed her upcoming schedule. I was in the closet, getting dressed in a black skirt with a white Chinese style collared blouse.

Still heated about last night, I asked, "Is that what happens around here? Anyone gets out of pocket and they get jumped?"

Breanne chuckled. "Scarlet's a hard case. She comes from a broken home and on top of that, she was kidnapped and sold into the Los Vegas sex trade. When I found her, she was fourteen and being charged with the murder of her pimp and three of his associates. In all my years, I've never seen such defiance, so ruthless. Logic and reason won't work on her once she snaps. The only way to keep her in line is with corporal punishment. It's unfortunate but not the first time we've had to resort to extreme measures. The last girl she bullied ended up killing herself. Scarlet carved an X over her face. The girl was supposed to be a model. We had plans to use her as an ambassador and Scarlet ruined it."

"Then why is she still around? Why keep her? Sounds like a loose cannon. I wouldn't trust her."

"She likes to fight..." Breanne told me. "So, do you. But not all of our ladies are hardened warriors. We teach them self-defense, sure, but a lot of what we do requires a more delicate approach, a certain finesse, grace and charm."

"Celeste comes to mind. She has a knack for deceit and trickery. With invaluable managerial skills, Celeste isn't exactly one we'd send out with a sweeper team. Truth be told, I'm building Scarlet up as a name to be feared. Where the very threat of her name gets others to bend the knee without having to resort to physical violence. Speak softly and carry a big stick. Scarlet and eventually you will be our big sticks. So...I'd say we're on the right track."

"Is what she said true? That all we care about is respect?" I asked, staring at her through the vanity mirror as I put on earrings.

"It's not *all* we care about. But respect is a big deal in terms of female empowerment. Take Suzanna here. Suzanna, what were you doing before you joined the society?"

The assistant, Suzanna, answered, "Hygienist. The dentist I worked for was a jackass, skimming money from a children's charity down in Sarasota, Florida. When I confronted him about it, he planted fentanyl in my purse and reported it to the police. I spent eight months in county. Lost my job. My husband left me and took the kids. This is the nature of men. Corruptible. Selfish. Entitled."

"And what did you do to the grubby little dentist and your disloyal husband?" Breanne asked her.

"Took the kids to my parents. I chained my husband to a billboard overlooking the park and made him watch as gators ripped the dentist limb from limb. Call it fear. Call it respect. Doesn't matter. Fact is he now knows what I'm capable of."

"There you have it." said Breanne.

They were still in my room. I was planning to head into town to meet up with one of my first contacts, the son of a bank manager who bought me a cup of coffee. He worked as a loan officer and was already putting funds in a fake account for me.

"You know she's right though." Breanne said. "You haven't completed your initiation yet."

"Yes, you keep telling me. I've mastered Krav Maga. I've done my trials in the Middle East with that bush-eater, Cyrine. What could possibly be worse than all that?"

"Come along." She said.

Five minutes later, Breanne, Suzanna, and I were walking around the pond out back. It was more like a reflection pool not far from where other protégés sparred. But around this time of year, it was so cold out that everyone was indoors. Sunlight glistened over the white slopes making everything brighter than a dream.

"You've been through a lot, Anna. You don't ask questions. You just do what we ask. Makes it difficult to get a good read on you."

"Is that a problem?" I asked.

"When it comes to trust, it is. I wouldn't trust Scarlet with vital information when her blood gets all hot and bothered. But I do trust her to destroy anyone I mark as an enemy. I trust that she'll execute and come back to me alive. I trust Suzanna here with my Social Security number and most of my international contacts. But you…I don't know what you want. I don't know what you believe. You won't talk about your past or what you did before you came to Los Angeles. How can anyone trust you?"

"You can trust me to get the job done. You don't need to know why."

Breanne squinted her shimmering eyes. "You wanna know what I did before Barbara took me under her wing?"

"Barbara Godwin?"

"Yes, one of the Twelve Chairs. My old sponsor."

"Look, Breanne. You don't have to tell me what you've been through. Honestly, I don't care. I don't need to hear all this back-story. I'm not saying that to be mean. I just, I don't like sharing information about my past. Not to you. Not to anyone."

"Not even to Marcus?"

I swear the moment she mentioned his name, it's like every bone in my body just cracked. I held my breath and the mountains themselves seemed to shake. Staring into the deepest blue of her eyes, I saw it, a cold, predatory vault of pure malevolence. I never seen her kill anyone up to that point, but I knew she was capable of it.

"Breanne, how do you know that name?"

She tugged on her coat collar. "My goodness. Has it gotten colder all the sudden?"

"Breanne! How do you know that name?!"

"Should I call security?" Suzanna asked.

"Don't be absurd." Breanne smirked. "It's just to three of us out here. We're all friends."

I yanked her by her lapels. I can't remember what I was thinking. My adrenaline just spiked through the roof and this anger took over. But Breanne showed her true colors. She had to be in her early forties, but she grabbed me with the strength of a linebacker and hip-tossed me to the ground.

178

I didn't try to get up. I just laid there on my back in two inches of snow looking up to the gray sky, wondering what the hell just happened. It was so fast. Breanne kneeled next to me. I remember her black heels and the heart-in-chains tattooed on her ankle. Her eyes sparkled like diamonds.

"You whisper his name in your sleep. Cyrine told me. I think that's beautiful, Anna. Who is he?"

My eyes started to well. Stupid emotions. "I don't want to talk about it."

She sat down in the snow and crossed her legs.

"Once upon a time, I was madly in love with a poet. It wasn't his job. He didn't make money off his scribblings but that's who he was, a poet working as a construction worker. He was gorgeous with the cheesiest smile you ever seen.

"I killed him. I brought him to our favorite spot in the Blue Ridge Mountains, slit his throat, and pushed him off a cliff."

I stared with hooded eyes. "Breanne. Why would you do that?"

"Because of this," she said as she wiped a single tear that slipped from my lashes.

"The Swords of St. Catherine can't have any attachment to the past. Our commitment to the Society is absolute. Every Sword has gone through the initiation process. It's our crucible. It's extreme and not many can handle it. But it's the only way we can trust one another. Because all of us have lost the men we loved the most in this world. We kill them ourselves."

"You can't be serious."

"Suzanna, finish your story." Breanne ordered. "You got your revenge on the dentist. But how is the husband? How are the children?"

"Ah, yes. Not long after, my husband was killed at a country music concert, one of dozens killed during a mass shooting. The children are with my sister."

Suzanna spoke as if she was talking about mailing off a check. My heart palpitated. A fever set in as I got up and paced around. It was crazy. They had to be joking. But after watching them sit there, straight-faced as if they were waiting for me to snap back to reality…I should have run away right then and there.

"We can't make you do this, Anna. You have to decide for yourself."

"And if I don't? Will you'll kill me? Will you kill him?"

"No, Anna. Why would we do that? We don't even know him."

That conversation could have gone on and on. I've dealt with women like Breanne before. They're master manipulators. They're so well attuned to lying that in their heart of hearts, distorted truths, facts, and opinions are all the same.

But most of all, I wasn't oblivious to the inevitable consequence. There was no doubt in my mind that Breanne would have had me killed. And then she would've tracked down Marcus and killed him just to work off the frustrations of having wasted the time training me.

"Ultimately, it's up to you, Anna Marie. We want you to join us but only if you want to."

My back was turned to her. I had to be careful. If I slipped up and gave any indication of deceit, it would've been my last day on earth. I was trapped. It was hopeless.

"Anna?"

I turned around with a heavy heart, "Just tell me what I have to do, and I'll do it."

A wind blew between us as we stared each other down.

"You can start by giving me his full name. And you should know your anger isn't doing much in the way of convincing me."

"That's because I'm pissed!" I shouted. "I'm just now finding this shit out?! Fuck dude. His name is Marcus Angel. Zip code 10001, Manhattan, New York. But I'm warning you. I'm the one who kills him. If I even get a whiff of Scarlet's scent around him, rest assured I will break down the walls of your whole fucking world."

"Well…if that's not love I don't know what is!" Breanne teased.

I stormed off. Meant every word. I didn't give them an exact date as to when I would kill Marcus. I just told them it would be before the end of the year. There was a lot going on, a huge election. I went back to New York and I saw him for the first time in so long…

…

It really did hurt my heart so much. Stupid emotions. He had grown so much, a far cry from the 24-year-old lump of cookie dough I once knew. I watched him for a time, building the courage to approach. I observed as he walked through Central Park, ever deep in thought. I saw him interview professionals. He sparked up conversations with pedestrians, strangers, and city workers. The same goofy smile, the same big nose and expressive eyes. I saw in Marcus, purity. He was innocent. Whereas I was dirty, my hands soiled with blood.

As I watched, I confess, I imagined a life with him, what life would've been like if I stayed and somehow, we found our way back to each other. I stalked him. Even slipped into his apartment one night and stared as he slept on the couch. So stupidly adorable.

Then one day, I just went for it. I decided it'd be the day that I'd reenter his world. And the funny thing is…it's like we didn't skip a beat. I could see in his eyes that my return was like a dream come true. And we talked. Not about how good I looked. Not about what I've been through. He asked about my happiness, how I felt, what I thought, what I wanted to do with my life from this day forward. It's like, right away he got me thinking again. I missed that.

I…I really don't want to go into full detail about the weeks leading up to his first death. Yes, we had sex. He was stubborn about waiting till marriage, but inevitably I took his virginity. We made the most of what little time we had. And the truth is, I tried to save his life. But Marcus was too smart for his own good. He found out about the Society. Someone had tipped him off. He attended a rally in Louisville and overhead Breanne speaking with Celeste and Scarlet. When I went to his hotel that night, he was scared out of his mind. I don't blame him. But I swear. I really tried to save him.

After Breanne hit him with our Escalade, I shot him because I thought he was already gone.

And that was it. That was my initiation. Killing Marcus was the hardest thing I ever had to do. Thinking about it fucked me up because I couldn't decide who I was mad at more, so I simply decided to stop thinking about him. Never again. That chapter was supposed to be closed.

Two months later, I was on a private charter bound for Italy.

It was a grand ceremony with so many rituals and moving parts. Bells and whistles and all that. We weren't allowed to know the name of the private island. It was home to the Palace of the Living Martyr. Only the Twelve Chairs, an elite squad of bodyguards, and a staff of oath-bound servants were allowed to revisit the island after their confirmation. Protégés were kept in the dark about its existence. But once we we're initiated and backed by our sponsors, all Swords were drawn from the same pool.

I know all this sounds confusing, so let me go ahead and explain how the organization's structured, as was explained to me after the ceremony.

The "Living Martyr" is the head of the Swords of St. Catherine. She's believed to be a direct descendant of Syvil, the blood sister of St. Catherine of Alexandria. It was Syvil who founded the Society after Catherine was beheaded as a martyr. This was in the early 4th Century when Christianity was still young and feared by pagans and non-believers alike, basically men struggling to retain their sovereignty, instead of sharing an ounce of it on the belief that a single Jew came and died for the sins of all mankind.

Anyways, the Living Martyr is the head of our organization, the supreme authority, a pope-like figure, worshiped and clothed in immense power. No one knows her real name save for the Twelve Chairs. The "Twelve Chairs" were the seconds-in-command when it came to making decisions and giving orders. These were the generals, women of vast resources and their own private armies. The Twelve Chairs dedicated their lives to the cause, having risen through the ranks due to their competence, grace, eloquence and the blood they've shed.

So far, I only know two by name. One was the woman who sponsored Breanne Cunningham, Barbara Godwin of the prestigious Godwin Dynasty who built an empire on shipping and aviation. Another was a woman named Jaida Fong, a highly influential network executive who was apparently quite popular within the Society for being the youngest of the Twelve Chairs and by far the one quickest to rise. It was she who started the movement of female empowerment in the entertainment industry. I also heard she wasn't opposed to getting her hands dirty. In fact, she preferred it.

Beneath the Twelve Chairs was the "Armored Front". These were the twenty or so elite lieutenants who were responsible for operations in different regions around the globe, sometimes collaborating with each other if necessary.

Breanne Cunningham was one of the three lieutenants assigned to the North American branch of operations. Everything the Swords, Protégés, and Pawns did was her responsibility. Whether we lived or died was in her hands. As far as I was concerned, Breanne was the queen.

With a single word from the Armored Front, entire legions would spring into action. After I learned how vast the Society's network of informants, sources, and sleeper cells reached, I was kinda glad I killed Marcus. As much as I loved him, I also have a little sister. And if anything happened to my sister…it's one of the reasons why I don't like to talk about my family. For her safety. For my sanity.

Beneath the Armored Front, were the "Swords." I became a Sword. The Swords were soldiers, operatives, and agents who carried out missions and answered to the Armored Front. On most missions, we were entrusted with the details, the why, the objective. We were allowed to ask questions, but the final word from the Armored Front was absolute. Disobedience would result in death. I know, because I've had to kill a few insubordinates. I understood and accepted the justification. A Sword of St. Catherine is entrusted with so much. Failure would jeopardize not only the mission, but other operations contingent to their success.

Under the Swords, were the protégés who spent a number of years honing their skills, sharpening their edges. And then there were the pawns, contacts, who could never be a Sword, especially if they were men.

Even before I was a full-fledge Sword I had already had a basket of pawns around the globe. With allure and feminine wiles, I could get any man to rob a bank. I had sources in law enforcement. I had hackers. I had congressmen and half of their staff. I even had other women, like black market fencers and doctors feeding me information, giving me places to hide, supplying me with equipment and supplies if I needed it.

…

It was just after sundown on August the 18th when my inauguration ceremony began. An assembly had gathered in a cave grotto where warm turquoise waters from the Adriatic reached up to my waist. Everyone was holding a torch. And there, I saw the Living Martyr for the first time along with seven other inductees. All seven of us were naked.

The Living Martyr was covered from head to toe in a black and gold cloak. She walked with a hunch in her back as if she was old, but for some reason I suspected it was just an act. I saw a glimpse of her bangs. They were rich, brown, and healthy.

We were instructed to chant the following:

"The wheel will never be broken. We till the earth. We grow the seeds. We've come to collect on all man's deeds. To the martyr. Till the end."

Then, the Living Martyr was helped into the water, and one by one, she baptized us, dipping us in the seawater, bringing us up anew. She was drawing us up as new freshly forged Swords.

Then, each of our sponsors presented us with a silver ring, the Sinaya Ring. It was a replica of the same ring St. Catherine wore when she executed. We remained in the water as the Living Martyr was lifted out and brought to a throne. It was then that I learned the structure, the sacred order of the society. The history I learned was astonishing. I never trusted textbooks the same way again.

An older woman, one of the Twelve Chairs with an Armenian look, whose name I never remembered, stood from a precipice as a Sword held a torch over her. An Armenian read from a thick book that looked like it came from some Egyptian tomb.

As we listened, I was overcome with immense pride to learn how far the society had come over the centuries. Our impact and influence on the world were astounding. Joan of Arc was probably the most famous. There was also Anne Boleyn. Catherine the Great of Russia. Empress Josephine, who motivated Napoleon to conquer half of Europe. Along with other influencers like Mary Surrat, Mata Hari, and Emily Davison.

I was inspired to cement my own legacy, to do something, to start a movement or make my own mark in history. Not once did these women ever see themselves as inferior, and so badly, I wished every woman on Earth could learn from their example. They were strong, fearless, and committed.

So many ladies live for the here and now. I know because I used to be one of them. I lived for fun, seeking thrills and swaying with the wind instead of using my potential to harness that wind. That's probably my biggest regret, wasting my twenties on such trivial pursuits. I was always a formidable force. But I was playing by the rules of men that benefited men.

No more. From there on out, I was determined to progress women of all walks of life. I would lead by example as the Andalusian, the dark horse, trampling any man dumb enough to stand my way.

After that ceremony, everyone drank, danced, and enjoyed themselves in the ballroom of the palace. Even Scarlet and Mandee for once, acted like sisters to others, friendly and polite. It was probably one of the few times I saw a side of Scarlet she kept hidden away, a giggling inner child.

After an hour of all that, I retreated to a balcony overlooking the Adriatic as the moon shimmered in the waves. By then, I was getting restless and frustrated. I couldn't wait for my next mission. Socializing was all well and good, but I'd much rather put my hands to use.

Why? Because I knew what would happen. And sure enough, it did.

There on the balcony, I was struck by the thoughts of him. Marcus was still in my head. His opinions, his disapproval or rejection about the path I was on, it scathed in my chest like a flare from the sun itself.

They said killing him would absolve me of the past. But how long before that takes effect? I hoped the sooner the better because at that moment, leaning over the rail, the regret was unbearable. I remembered him staring up at me from the gutter as I shot him. Those eyes that conveyed his every single thought. It made me angry. I just couldn't shake it! So stupid! He was gone and I needed to stop giving a damn. But it was hard. I couldn't!

"So, you're the Andalusian."

I looked over and immediately stood up straight. It was Barbara Godwin, one of the Twelve Chairs, with Breanne Cunningham by her side.

Barbara smiled as she came near. "I've heard so much about you. It seems you've gone through quite the ordeal. I don't think we've ever gone to such lengths, such an elaborate production to help a protégé with her initiation. Hopefully, it conveys how much we value you, my dear."

"Yes ma'am! I'm extremely grateful."

She put a cold hand on my back as she joined me, shoulder to shoulder in looking out at sea. I glanced at Breanne for an instant. She stood back with a cold stare that didn't blink.

"Ever since the dawn of antiquity," Barbara began, "men have sought to control and possess us. We're taught that God made Adam first, and then he created Eve so Adam wouldn't be alone. To give her to him. What rubbish. What most Bibles don't have is that there's another woman, named Lilith. She was created at the same time as Adam. And while Adam and Eve sinned, Lilith did not. She remained a perfect woman all her life and only produced sin by procreating with the weak-minded, easily tempted man. Did you know that?"

"No ma'am."

"It's true. Look at it. Look at this world. God created the heavens and the earth. His worst creation has always been man. He delivered them from Egyptians by parting the Red Sea. He sheltered them, protected them from their enemies. Provided food and water and all he asked was that they obeyed his commandments. But no. Man gave into false worship. False gods out of animals and the Baals. And now…do you know whom they worship?"

"Who?"

"Themselves. That's why you have wars, avarice, corruption and endless injustices. But that's all right. Women are more than capable of taking the reins and enduring such hardships for the sake of the greater good. Our suffering, our sacrifice will lead to that proverbial paradise prophesized by so many. But it'll take every one of us to make that happen. Anna Marie, are you with us?"

I turned and squared my shoulders to the old woman who exuded such elegance, the class of a patrician. Despite wearing a dress that rode up, I got down on one knee and bowed, reciting: "The wheel will never be broken. We till the earth. We grow the seeds. We've come to collect on all man's deeds. To the martyr. Till the end."

I heard no response, just the rushing of waves. When I looked up, Barbara was staring at Breanne. Breanne was staring at me, still full of distrust. Then she beamed in what was obviously a fake smile as she came and embraced me in a hug. She squeezed tight. Then with her lips so close to my ears, she whispered something I'll never forget.

"If you ever jeopardize us like that again, I will open your neck with my teeth."

She kept smiling but I knew she was serious. I nodded and told her, "To the day I die, I am yours, Breanne."

She kissed me, wiped my tears, and chuckled for me to lighten up. After that, we rejoined the celebration in the ballroom. From that moment on, the past remained in the past.

Or so I thought…

The embodiment of pomposity, the pain in my side, the fly in my lashes, Gladys-fucking-Vandelay herself, dug up Marcus and brought him back from the dead. And yes, she did catch me in a bout of depression, but you know what, I'm not a machine. I'm still made of flesh and blood. As a Sword, I still slept other with men here and there, but they were disposable, like Kleenex.

None of them, none of my fellow Swords, not Breanne nor Barbara could ever fulfill what Marcus was to me.

So yes, from time to time, I thought of him. But it was rare. And it was Christmas for fuck's sake! I never expected Gladys or anyone else to be at the Villa. But that's just Gladys, nosy and all up in everyone's business.

No…I'm being too harsh on Gladys.

To be honest, I never thought Gladys would amount to anything the first time I saw her. Never even thought she'd make it through the first week. But they said she had rage and I saw it. For someone so small and dainty, I admit, I was a bit fascinated by her. Curious, anticipating, wondering what she was destined to do.

Never did I imagine she'd transform so much. From that timid little girl with a quiet affinity for guns, to a blazing inferno of relentless rebellion. She's so much younger than me but came to conclusions I should have reached long ago. And even though everything went to shit, I give her credit for repairing a broken part of my heart when she brought Marcus back to me. I wasn't prepared for it. Caught me completely by surprise…but what's a girl to do?

Like I said. My life begins every time he dies. This time…I'm free.

11. Gladys Vandelay - For the Living

"Honestly...I don't care about dead people. When you die, you're either conscious of nothing, or heaven or hell, or whatever you believe. Either way, you're not part of this world anymore. And in that sense, I envy them. The living have it worse. Especially the friends and family members who have lost their loved ones."

"Geez, Ellie. Sounds like you're saying it's better to not have been born at all."

"Nah, I wouldn't go so far as to say all that. Life is full of hardships and tragedies, yeah. But there's also triumph and success. Major wins like marriage, the birth of a child. Winning something you busted your ass for. Things like that make it all worthwhile. I just wish..."

"You wish for what?"

"I just wish I knew what it felt like to love someone and have them love me the same way. I never had that. I've never had someone who wasn't related to me tell me that they loved me on a romantic level. You see it on TV. Commercials, especially around the holidays. So much so that you'd think it's normal for everyone to be loved and have someone. But it's never happened for me. That's why love is messed up. Because it's not guaranteed that everyone will have it."

"Ah. Poor baby!"

"Haha! Yeah, Gladys, you laugh about it now. But once you hit thirty, it gives way to pause. Makes you wonder...All this time. Can you really describe what it feels like to be alive?"

Elliot...Ellie...El. He was my Paramour. Mine. All mine.

...

I opened my eyes to a gray ceiling fan with cracks in the wood. Everything looked old, as if the house was taken straight from a post-civil war documentary. The windows were milky and stained. The dresser looked like a device for splinters. My bed was twin size with a rusty iron headboard. Even my pillow was stuffed with real feathers. I could feel the stems pricking through the pillowcase, scratching my neck.

My bullet wounds were patched up. Someone had sewn me shut and dressed me in a faded pink nightgown. There was a table on the other side of the room with a pitcher and two tin cups. I was thirsty like you wouldn't believe, so I got up.

Anyone in the house wondering if I was awake didn't have to wonder long. I was so weak. My bones felt brittle. As soon as I tried to stand, I crumbled to the floor with a wooden crash that probably sounded much louder than it was. The problem was, I couldn't hear anyone else. I was on the second floor and sound carried.

I hugged the wall and hobbled to the table like an old woman. There was nothing in the pitcher. I expected water.

Timed perfectly with my groan was a howling wind that rustled through the last remaining leaves of a withering tree just outside my window. And through the branches, I saw the distant figure of Anna Marie all dressed in black. She was deep in the woods. Her long hair shrouded her face, but I knew it was her. I grabbed sheets from the bed, wrapped up, and left.

In the downstairs kitchen was a black family. A mother, a father, and three toddlers. They were all so quiet it was creepy. I could sense the feeling was mutual. They stared like I was a ghost wandering the halls. No one said anything, not even so much as a greeting.

Finally, I just shuffled over to their breakfast table and grabbed about four strips of bacon. "Thank you." I whispered before scurrying off. But of course, my bed sheets got caught on a splintered floorboard.

I tripped, scraping my knees and the children laughed. I whipped around to see which ones, but only caught the tail end of their mother snapping her fingers at them.

"Who are you people?" I asked.

"The owners of this house," the father said.

"I don't suppose you have a name?"

"Just call me, the Caretaker."

I squinted. "Are you the one who put me in this nightgown?"

The mother rolled her neck with spiked brows, a matrimonial warning, not worth ignoring. So, I threw up my hands and whispered, "Sorry."

"You should put on more clothes before you go out." she said.

"I don't have any clothes."

She rolled her eyes, "Stay there, ya hear."

…

I stepped out into frigid air with thick gray clouds looming overhead. The mother provided me with clean underwear, blue jeans that were two sizes too big, black traveling boots, a red flannel shirt and a brown jacket that felt like a tarp made of cattle hide.

Geographically…I assumed we were in upstate New York or possibly Pennsylvania. As I trudged through the woods against icy winds, I wondered how long I had been out. With each step, I could feel a sharp sting in my thigh. The wounds hadn't fully healed but I managed.

I found Anna in a clearing about a hundred yards from the house. So solemn, she was, bound in a black overcoat with her long hair tucked in the collar. I stepped lightly, like a kitten to milk left by a stranger.

Once by her side, I leaned forward to see her face. She kept her gaze to the ground. And there, I saw two graves. Stones outlined two patches of dark soil. She pointed, "My man. And yours. We lost them both on the same night. What are the odds?"

Guilt swelled in my chest. I had to ask, "Do you blame me? For what happened?"

"Tell me, Gladys. What exactly did you think would happen? That Marcus and I would make up and live happily ever after? Hmm?"

I mumbled, "But you told me that—"

I literally choked on my words as Anna grabbed me by my throat and pulled me close. I saw the pain in her eyes, the twitch in her cheeks.

"I'm sorry!" I whimpered.

"You're sorry?! Sorry won't bring them back, Gladys!"

"But I did bring him back!"

She let go and raised her fist like she was about to hit me. "You brought him back?!"

"Yes. You thought he was dead! And I brought him back to you! He wasn't dead."

"He is now, Gladys! And what, you think I should thank you? I'm not stupid, puta! You we're planning on using him, to get me to change sides and get your revenge. Well guess what. You got it. It's all over the news. You're famous. Gladys Vandelay, the spoiled little rich kid who killed her daddy! And her sister! And many others! They're calling you a spree killer. A terrorist!"

I shook my head with a clenched jaw. "Anna…we are terrorists."

"I'm not a fucking terrorist!" She shouted. "I was part of an organization that stood for something. And thanks to you, I betrayed them."

"You betrayed yourself! Marcus loved you and you betrayed him."

"Bitch, I will slit your fucking throat."

"I'm not afraid anymore, Anna! What's the point?!"

"DON'T CALL ME A TERRRIST!"

"ALRIGHT! Geez!"

We stood there for some time staring at the graves.

…

"I really am sorry about Marcus. I spoke with him a great deal. I can see why you liked him."

Anna sniffled. "What did he say?"

"He said he knew you had a tough exterior but you were soft underneath."

"Pfft! Everyone is soft underneath. He *would* say something stupid like that."

I smirked. "Elliot…my man. He warned us that things would go south. I mean, he really gave me and Marcus all kinds of crap about it. But your man, he said he just wanted to see you again. He didn't care. He wasn't going to convince you to change your ways or betray the Society. He just wanted to hold you one more time."

"Idiot," she said in a frustrated chuckle.

"Anna, they're all idiots. Men..."

We laughed. We cried. We honored their memories with laughter and tears and for better or worse, we said our goodbyes to the only men who could invoke such sentiment.

About an hour later, Anna and I started walking aimlessly through the woods by a narrow stream. She asked me where I had been for the past year. I asked her the same. Neither of us wanted to share. So, we didn't.

"I met the caretaker. Who are they?" I asked.

"Gladys, I have contacts all over the world. I have so many sleeper cells. The Society doesn't even know."

"Okay, so who are they?"

"Friends, Gladys. They can be trusted. Speaking of friends. Your man, Elliot. I saw him rappel down a building and fling himself through a window to save you. Where on earth did you find him?"

To be honest, I was reluctant. I never swore some oath of loyalty to the Paramours. I wasn't even sure if I owed them my allegiance.

"Anna…if you were anyone else and I told you that there's this secret organization of women hell-bent on taking over the world, it would sound crazy, right? But what if I told you that there's another secret organization, one who knows about the Swords and exists solely for the purpose of undermining them?"

Anna furrowed her brows. "You mean competing against us?"

"Well, not exactly. It's more like a response. They're called the Paramours. It's a brotherhood with some ladies sprinkled in. More or less, they're the loved ones left for dead by the Swords. The Paramours seek out these survivors and invite them to join their group. While the Swords work feverishly to overthrow the patriarchy, the Paramours work from the shadows sabotaging their plans."

"Bullshit."

"I know. Sounds far-fetched. But think about it, Anna. The Swords of St. Catherine have been around for how long? And it wasn't till the past forty years or so that they finally made any headway. Intersectionality, political correctness, Social Justice. Call it what you want. If it wasn't for our generation's complete disregard for religion, history, tradition. Worse, creating our own history, the Swords of St. Catherine would be nowhere near as powerful as they are today."

"Gladys, you're underestimating the Swords. Everything is going according to plan."

"Really? Because, I'd say the fact that the Paramours have managed to elude the Swords all this time is proof positive. Or are you going to tell me, the Society have always known and actually allowed them to fuck up their plans?"

"You really think these Paramours can stop us?"

"You keep saying 'us'."

"I'm still a Sword, Gladys. I swore an oath."

"And that oath is so sacred, is it?"

"It has been for centuries. Some of the most influential women have worn this ring. Joan of Arc. Queen Mary. Catherine the Great. I can go on and on. Thus, the wheel will never be broken. We till the earth. We grow the seeds. We've come to collect on all man's deeds. To the martyr. To the death."

It was sickening to hear her say that. I know she's in there, behind all the social engineering that prompted her to recite those words. But still…She needed to break free. I had to go deeper. And what I was about to tell her took courage like you wouldn't believe. Because, I knew…if Anna wanted to, she could have reached out snatched the life out of me at any moment.

"Anna…I think it's time you accept the truth. The Swords of St. Catherine are evil. If they were really so righteous, they'd be concentrating their efforts on the Middle East, in Myanmar, in parts of South America. And if you say it's only a matter of time before they do, I think I might slap you.

"You say they've been around for centuries. Well, that sounds like back before the United States was even a thing. And yet they've done nothing. Nothing! To stop the millennia of torture and abuse, of honor killings, of forced marriages, of women being herded and sold like cattle! It's a fucking joke!

"Even now, here in the states, women are trafficked and forced into the sex trade from Vegas to Vancouver. What about those women?! What about the women muling for the cartels?! With all the strength, skills, and resources, the Swords of St. Catherine should've abolished all of that! But no.

"They don't give two shits about women! They're elitists. Totalitarians. It's all about control. They only care about issues that propel them to the top of the society. What societies? ALL OF THEM! Anywhere there's a community by which the few can control the majority, there you will find the Swords of St. Catherine. Wicked little harpies who killed my father just to prove a point! Who will tell me that's not evil?"

Anna turned and snarled, "And what? You're a shining light in all this?"

"I know I'm rotten, Anna. But the Paramours...they're a bunch of wimps, sure. But they have honor. And virtue! They have this whole thing about not killing. It's absolutely insane, but still, I can't help but respect it. They're strong. To endure the pain and suffering of the past and not harbor such hate and resentment. Instead, they cling to...love."

Anna didn't respond. The sound of the trickling stream took over. The frosty breeze continued to rattle the branches.

"Anna, I have to ask." I said after some silence. "In my case. Why do you think they chose me as a prospect? It would make sense if they were after my father's company in some shadowy takeover. But they already had my sister, Clarice. They didn't need me. So why put me through the trials? Why train me? They must have known I would never kill my father. They had to. To suggest otherwise, would mean that they're intelligence is beyond piss-poor and I'm reluctant to land on that conclusion."

Anna's gaze kept to the stream. "The Paramours, are all the members made up of those who are supposed to be dead?"

"I'm not sure. Some are members who lost everything, surviving family members of the deceased. My man, Elliot. His mother killed his father when he was a baby. Some cunt named Jaida Fong. She's at the top of my hit list, actually."

At once, just by standing next to her, I could feel a jolt of electricity course through Anna's body as her eyes widened with shock. "You said Jaida Fong? The network executive?"

"Wait, you know her?"

"Gladys! Everyone knows her. She's one of the Twelve Chairs! Holy shit, this is bad. Elliot was her son? Please tell me you're joking."

"Well, I mean, that's what he told me. Why would he lie about that? What are the Twelve Chairs?"

Anna was wringing her fingers through her hair, looking around in a frantic state of paranoia. I'd never seen her like this. The panic was contagious.

"Anna! What's wrong?" I shouted.

With bated breath, she stressed, "Elliot was killed in the Upper East Side. There's camera everywhere. Gladys, I went back and got his body. You're all over TV. But there's no mention of me as your accomplice, which means the Society knows I was involved and probably paid to have that information withheld."

"But wait! You're assuming Jaida gives a damn. Elliot told me she bombed his apartment."

"But he wasn't killed, Gladys! Bombings are messy. Reckless. We used them to intimidate, coerce, create collateral damage. But when it comes to targets we want dead with a certainty…trust me. I've met Jaida. She's a cobra. If she wanted Elliot dead, he would've died a long time ago.

"The Swords of St. Catherine may hate men but we're still humans. You don't fuck with a mother's son without her explicit consent. The Twelve Chairs are the closest things to gods on earth. We might as well have killed Jesus Christ in their eyes. This is war. I'm telling you they will deploy every available resource to rectify this."

"I say good. Let 'em come! Jaida, Breanne, Scarlet and whoever else wants it."

"So stupid." She sighed.

"What do you suggest? We just lay down and take it? I'm not goin' out like that!"

"Shut up!" She whispered. "Listen!"

I got quiet and tilted my head to focus.

"Shots fired." I whispered.

At once, Anna and I raced through the woods for the house. We saw smoke rising above the tree line. At fifty yards out, we could see the second floor was on fire. A team of about ten soldiers, private contractors in black body armor had formed a perimeter and were fanning out.

The mother. I saw as she frantically ran from the house. She got about halfway across the yard before she was mowed down by a P90 submachine gun. It was horrible and sent chills down my arms.

"Daddy!!!"

The children! They were still alive. Something sparked in me and I emerged from the trees in a full sprint. Soldiers turned their guns at me as I went crashing through the dining room windows.

I hit the ground rolling whilst spotting three soldiers in my peripheral. Before they could figure out what happened, I slung off my cowhide jacket and used it like a whip to wrap it around a man's head. I yanked him into another's line of fire, grabbed the soldier's rifle and returned fire. The third soldier tried to shove me away, but I held onto his arm and used his momentum to run along walls and hurl him to the ground.

Another soldier ran in. I aimed the P90 and lit him up. The soldier I hurled to the ground got up and wrapped me up from behind. I could still hear the children crying. I attacked with my elbows like a trapped falcon. One of which, broke his nose, but he pulled my hair and dragged me to the floor.

"ARRRGG!!!" I shouted.

With all the strength I could muster, I picked this bulky soldier up by double hooking his legs and shouldering through a wall. Another soldier spotted us just as I rolled off and ran into the adjacent room. He followed but by now I had a submachine gun with no restraints.

I dropped the soldier with a triple tap and dashed into the hallway to finish off the son of a bitch who pulled my hair. As I raced up the stairs, a soldier fired off too soon and hit the wall just in front of me. Rookie mistake letting me know his location. I shot through the wall corner he was hiding behind. The high-velocity rounds penetrated like cutting through flour.

Another soldier kicked in the front door. It was down and to my rear. I glanced just in time to see someone else shooting him from behind. It was Anna. She was fighting outside.

"I'm telling you, I don't know!" the father screamed from behind a closed bedroom door.

Again, a soldier fired prematurely, spraying through the bedroom door and into the 2nd floor hallway like a coward. Clearly, this man didn't care about friendly fire.

As the soldier stopped to reload, I squatted and flattened my back against the wall in this dark, smoke-filled hallway. It was a warzone outside with Anna going to work. But inside, it was quiet for the moment. I waited. Solid as a statue, I waited.

Again, he fired a burst through the bedroom door. I fired once, aiming for the center of the flashes. Then, and as fast as I could, I hurried for the door and kicked it open, making sure I got my shooter. He was staggering back with a hip wound. I finished him off with a blast to the face. He went spilling out the window.

The father and his children were tied up on their knees.

"My wife! Where is she?" the father asked.

I didn't answer but focused on untying them.

As soon as I released him, he grabbed my shoulders. "MY WIFE! WHERE IS SHE?"

I shoved him off and hurried to untie the children. The father ran to the window. It was facing the front yard.

"Kesha NOOOO!" He screamed.

The three boys were crying. Scared. When they heard their father's scream, they shriveled further. Bad went to worse. I could hear the chopping blades of an Apache helicopter in route.

"We need to go!" I shouted.

The children huddled up and refused to move. I grabbed one by the wrist, but he pulled away. The father tackled and tried to choke me.

"You not taking my boys!" he shouted.

"We need to get out!" I stressed.

"YOU ARE NOT TAKING MY BOYS!"

I kneed him in the balls and kicked him off. My instincts were to shoot him, but the children...I needed to get them out of the house.

"Get up! GET UP!" I shouted.

The boys ran to their keening father. He curled them in his arms and refused to leave. I shot at the floor and ordered, "LET'S GO!"

Out of time. The Apache chopper was sixty yards out and directly in sight. I ran out of the room, entering a cloud of smoke and flames, and scurried down the stairs. I got outside and wasn't even six steps from the house before the whole place exploded. The Apache fired a missile at it...as expected.

I was launched probably twenty feet into the woods with thick bushes cushioning my landing. My ears were ringing and I'm pretty sure I was upside down when I saw more soldiers rappelling from the chopper.

Then…I saw a woman, a tall, blonde, woman with the sharp brown eyes of a hawk. Everyone else was dressed in soldierly fatigues, but this woman was dressed in beige hunting attire with brown boots laced up to her knees and a Marlin 336 lever-action hunting rifle. I'd seen her before. In Iraq.

The smoldering house looked like a tornado had ripped it from its foundation. My hearing was starting to come back. The men rallied around the woman, and I wasn't about to let them have fucking team meeting after slaughtering this innocent family. So, I opened fire, picking off at least four of them before the rest took cover.

The woman, however, didn't flinch. She calmly spun to her knees, raised her rifle and aimed her muzzle my way. A bullet zipped past my ear and hit the tree behind me. I didn't flinch either.

"Come on!" Anna said as she grabbed the shoulder of my flannel shirt.

I followed her through the fluctuating terrain of forest grounds. Just as I started to climb up a ridge, this sharp burning pain burst through my pelvis. I fell down the banks and came to a sliding halt with freezing water from the creek rushing over my legs.

Anna leaped down the creek to reach me. "You hit?"

"My stitches. I think they ripped."

"Damn it!" She whispered. "That woman is Sammy McPherson, based out of the Detroit. Gladys, she's one of the best trackers in the Society. A bounty hunter."

"Then we have to keep moving." I said, wiping the sweat from my forehead.

Anna shook her head. "Sammy's been hunting since before she could ride a bike. We ain't getting away and we're wasting energy. We have to make a stand."

Anna gave me her P90 and looked around before setting her sights on a barren pine tree with its roots protruding from the ridge. Then she looked at me and I nodded, taking off my red flannel shirt and muscling up to a stand.

Wearing just my white tank-top with water-soaked pants, I cringed through the pain and icy winds to climb the tree. The Andalusian tied her long hair back and brandished her field knife.

The plan was simple but risky. Anna would go on the prowl, combing through the trees like a tiger, stalking her prey one-by-one, slitting throats and piercing hearts. Meanwhile, I'd post up in the tree with my rifle at the steady. I wasn't about compromise my position on small fry like the men. My prize was Samantha "Sammy" McPherson. A Sword of St. Catherine and supposedly one of the best trackers the society had to offer.

My eyes scanned the foliage. The soldiers and their glaring muscular frames were easy to spot. I watched as Anna grab a man by his chin and turn it one way while sliding her knife the other way. It was nasty. She disappeared before his knees hit the ground.

Another soldier emerged from two juniper bushes. Anna plunged her knife through his heart and yanked him back into the bushes like a trap-door spider.

Another soldier lost his nerve and started shooting indiscriminately into the shrubs lining an outcrop. It was so noisy and constant. So, I felt confident about dropping him with a shot to the back of his head. At once, the echo ceased. I only hoped Sammy wasn't nearby. I only hoped she hadn't heard me.

"MCPHERSON!"

Anna's call came from the north, over my left shoulder. She was fast. Just two minutes earlier, she was about 200 yards in front of me to the east.

"Let's do this Sammy! It's just us now!" Anna shouted.

Just then, I heard a twig snap. To anyone else, it would have come like pencil drop. To me, it was like someone snapping their fingers right by my ears. I didn't have to turn my head to look. I knew I was in danger and reacted by hurling myself from the branch just in time to see it obliterate from a .35 round. I must have hit every branch on the fall down.

Samantha… She was good alright. She had approached from the stream, keeping low with the water to mask her steps. It wasn't until she reached the banking ridge that I heard her.

Sammy didn't say anything. She simply cranked the lever of her rifle and approached to aim at my head. Suddenly, a line of bullets burst into the ridge just over her. If it was me shooting, Sammy would've been dead. But Anna, for all her skill and prowess, wasn't the best shot while on the move. She came running from the other side of the creek.

Sammy aimed and fired, clipping Anna in the thigh. I heard it. Anna yelped in pain as the forward momentum sent her tumbling down the ridge and into the stream. Sammy reloaded, but by then, I had the P90 in my hands. She saw me out of the corner of her eye and reacted with lightning-quick reflexes. My shot merely grazed her temple, drawing blood, but not enough to kill or even knock her out. It only made her mad.

With this menacing snarl, Sammy aimed and fired, clipping my shoulder like a hot poker hammering into flesh. Anna tackled Sammy into the stream and the two proceeded to wrestle like grizzly bears jostling for territory, or in this case, the hunting rifle that Sammy refused to surrender.

Anna unleashed a relentless barrage of elbows and uppercuts, but Sammy managed to see an opening and smashed the barrel into Anna's face. She got on top and forced Anna underwater. Anna choked and gurgled, struggling to get air.

Sammy…this bitch was something else. As focused as she was on Anna, she detected me crawling for the P90. Our eyes met and I was frozen in legit terror. But in that brief lapse of diverted attention, she made the fatal mistake of letting up on Anna. Because Anna was a beast. She roared, erupting from the water with both hands on the rifle.

In a frightening burst of strength, Anna slung Sammy to the stream and started beating the crap out her. Sammy let go of the rifle in a vain attempt to stop Anna's pummeling. But as soon as she did, Anna grabbed the rifle and started jamming it into her face. And when Sammy lost consciousness, Anna aimed and shot her three times.

Then…Anna threw the rifle away, screaming with rage. It was amazing. I was literally star-struck as I sat there and watched the Andalusian reel in fury with clenched fists, biting down on her bottom lip as if to scream, "THE AUDACITY!"

After she calmed down and breathed the fired out of her lungs, I called out, "Anna! You know what we have to do."

"It'll never end." She grunted.

The adrenaline was wearing off. The pain, the freezing cold and exhaustion were beginning to settle in, but my resolve was absolute.

"The Swords of St. Catherine. The Paramours. We don't fit in with either. Yet, we have purpose. We have drive and we know what we have to do. The Paramours don't kill. But we do. So, we will. Starting with Breanne and going through the ranks, scouring the whole fucking earth to rid ourselves of this cancer."

———

200

Anna shook her head as she reverted back to a human. "Why bother? I lost Marcus. Your man is gone and you already got your revenge. If this is about getting rid of that so-called cancer, you can start with me."

I was starting to faze in and out consciousness but what I had to say was critical. With stiffness spreading down my legs and back, I cringed and shouted with whimpers.

"IT'S CALLED REDEMPTION, ANNA! I believe in the Paramours. Marcus and Elliot believed. Let's help them. Let's honor them by doing what they can't."

By then, I was done. My last memory of that place was the sight of juniper bushes scraping by as I was carried in her arms. I also remember the chopping blades of a helicopter. I remember my eyes opened at one point to see Anna in the cockpit. Then, I was out again.

Interlude

...

After some time, I woke up in a dark room. A strip of light flooded the floor from beneath the closed door. From that, my eyes adjusted and I was able to make out shapes and objects to discern I was in a hotel room with two queen size beds. Not a classy one, but one of those independently owned motels. We were at a high altitude. I could feel the barometric pressure in my bones.

I reached over to turn on a lamp. The dull, aching pain in my waist and shoulders still lingered, but at least they didn't feel like they were on fire anymore. I was starving. Could have devoured a whole cake by myself. In fact, I craved it.

I had no doubt Anna was taking care of me. My wounds were dressed and there were antibiotics on the nightstand. Apparently, I had an infection and she tended to that as well.

I supposed the most alarming thing about the room was the inventory of weapons leaning against the wall like brooms. Everything I needed to take over a small country was right there. I saw duffle bags full of ammunition, smaller gym bags packed with grenades and explosives. Two bulletproof vests were folded on the sofa, and a laptop workstation was set up at the desk. Anna had been busy. She was gone, I knew not where.

After taking all this in, I turned on the TV and couldn't believe it. So much time had passed. The news of my sister's assassination had run its course. And now…the former United States president was in jail. He had been impeached and awaited his day in court for the murder of his wife, the First Lady. This was huge with global ramifications.

This coupled with propaganda of Russians interfering with the last elections prompted the first re-election process in American history. On November 8th, a chief justice swore in the first female president of the United States of America.

My mind was blown. And yet, part of me was excited and glad. I was never a fan of the old president. Nor was I sympathetic about the Paramour's endeavors to clear his name, but clearly, they failed. I knew the Swords of St. Catherine were probably flying high on Cloud Nine. Triumphant and celebrating.

My own glee was kind of like a boxer who realized his main rival had won the championship with me being next in line for the title. Making it that much more glorious when I step in the ring.

The door opened and in walked Anna. She was dressed like a civilian, and by civilian, I mean exactly what one would expect from a Columbian hottie with a body like that. She had the hoop earrings and a purple satin cold-shoulder blouse.

"Oh! Finally!" She gushed.

"How long has it been?" I asked with a weak voice.

She smirked. "It'll come back."

I pointed to the TV and threw up my hands in astonishment.

"I know right. So much for your boys. If this is any indication of their competence, I'm not impressed."

For some reason, I was offended by her criticism.

She sat on the bed next to me and laid out food and drinks, saying nothing as she rummaged through the bag for straws and napkins. I just looked at her, examining her, trying to pick up any sign on what she's concluded. I saw her little armory, but I needed certainty. I think my eyes conveyed that.

"We could disappear where nobody could find us." She said. "I have enough money. We can get by. Or, we could do as you suggest. And become redeemers."

Then she stopped and focused on me.

"Here's the thing. If we become Redeemers, who will redeem us?" She asked. "We can sit and try to justify all the death and carnage but in our heart of hearts, we know. I know. We're just hypocrites."

"Anna, everybody is a hypocrite." I whispered, clearing my throat. "Parents are hypocrites to their children. Pastors to their parishioners. Politicians to their constituents. CEOs to their employees. We are all walking contradictions.

"The Swords of St. Catherine should not be allowed to exist. How many loved ones must they destroy before someone stands up and does something about it? You and I are just the beginning. We'll create a code, just like the Paramours. Never kill the innocent, not even to justify our own ambitions. Our enemy is the Society. Not just the Swords, but all societies lurking in the shadows to corrupt the natural order."

"And what if the existence of these secret societies are in league with that natural order? That one cannot do without the other?" She asked.

I smirked. "Then I guess you're right and we'll be the ultimate hypocrites. Anna, if you're still wrestling with your conscience, just ask yourself, has anything really changed in your resolve. From when you thought Marcus was dead till now that you know he's dead? When the storm inside clears up, let me know the answer to that."

She squinted. "You really read all those books they doled out, didn't you? FYI, no one else did. They just got the summaries from Google."

"I think you're making fun of me."

"Well, you talk a lot, Gladys. Sometimes, I think you just spit out a volley of logic. Hoping one or two points stick."

"Whatever. You get what I'm saying though, right? I made my case. Whatever you decide to do, I'll go along with it."

Anna got up and walked to the windows. She peeked through drapes and peered into the dead of the night. She was so pretty. A twinkle in her eye, just like Marcus said. For all the fights, and nasty bare-knuckle brawls she's been in, Anna's visage was still flawless. She turned to me and slumped against the wall with this hopeless expression.

"I want to make this clear. I don't care about ridding the earth of societies. People are free to do whatever the hell they want. But the Swords of St. Catherine…They killed my man. They'll kill anyone we get close to. And something about that just doesn't sit well with me. I don't care about redemption, I want justice. My justice. Not the world's. Not any society's...my own."

I smiled, "So, we attack?"

"Before I answer, just one final question. Are you afraid to die?"

I could feel my heartbeat, a surge of anxiety all of the sudden. I didn't know what she expected me to say. I didn't know what I needed to say to convince her to take on my crusade. So…I took a shot in the dark and chose honesty.

"Yes."

"Why?" she asked.

"Because it's not fair." I answered.

"What's not fair, Gladys?"

"That the wicked are able to prosper. That the wicked keep winning. I don't want to die knowing my enemies are still having a good time."

Anna nodded, "You don't know Breanne Cunningham. Jaida Fong is one thing, but Breanne…She scares the living daylights out of me. Her eyes alone petrify me worse than lightning in a storm."

"That's exactly why we need to…"

"Shut up, Gladys. Just shut the hell up. I'm not Elliot or whoever else you think you can manipulate. Alright? We're talking about taking on some of the most dangerous, cold-blooded killers I've ever seen. And as good as you think you are, Scarlet will eat you up for breakfast. So, I'm not just scared. Feels like the dumbest thing. Like, stepping into the cage with a bunch of grizzly bears with nothing but my bare hands."

I got out of bed and started for her, but she held up a hand prompting me to stop. I continued on.

"Anna, this gives us an advantage."

"Shut up." She whispered.

"We're fighting for our lives."

"Shut…up."

"No!"

And of course, true to Anna form, she reached out and grabbed my neck. She didn't squeeze hard, but with a creepy smile, she let me know that she could.

"Listen to me," I wheezed.

"You listen. Truth be told, I still haven't decided whether or not I blame you for getting Marcus killed. So, don't push it." She said before letting me go.

I stumbled back and sat on her bed.

"You still blame me for Marcus? Screw you! Only one of us here refused to kill their paramours and it wasn't me."

Anna smiled the creepiest smile. I saw her chest inflate and cave in with a sharp exhale as she approached, one hard step after the other, drawing a knife that she kept hidden along her waist.

I must have been like a rabbit on the prairie as a hawk swooped down. As quick as I could, I dashed for one of the pistols along the wall. But she pounced. With one hand, she palmed me to the floor while her blade hovered in the other.

"I'm sorry!" I whimpered. "Please don't kill me!"

"You shut the hell up talking about Marcus, comprende? COMPRENDE!"

"Yes! I…No. No. I'm sorry. I can't. You're going to have to just kill me!"

That's when I started laughing. I can't explain it. She started laughing too.

"Oh, I see!" She laughed. "You really are loco!"

"Maybe…" I laughed. "You're just gonna have to fucking kill me!"

And that was it. We laughed, both of us out or minds. I can't explain it to this day, but Anna and I simply understood each other. We understood the pain, the sad tragic comedy behind our grief. We became partners in crime. Both of us, bringing our own set of special skills.

And, I dunno. Something about what Anna said lit a fire in me that night. "As good as I think I am…" Whatever. I'm not just good, I'm the best! And the next time I see Scarlet I'm gonna prove it.

…

For the next three weeks, Anna and I moved from safe house to safe house, inching our way closer to the Pacific Northwest. After getting their puppet in the White House, we knew it was only a matter of time before they let their guard down for some victory dance. And if there was to be a celebration, it'd take place at the Villa, nestled deep in the mountains of British Columbia.

As expected, Anna confirmed this from one of her contacts. "Everyone's invited. They're gonna get down and party on Saturday night. Everyone's gonna get drunk. It'll be perfect." She said.

"You sound excited," I smirked.

"It's our best chance. Not just to hit them but to make a statement."

"So…I have your permission to go all out?"

"Go to town, Gladys."

"And you? Will you, 'go to town'?"

"Just remember. Breanne's the quarterback. Take her out of the game and the whole team crumbles."

12. Gladys Vandelay – Redemption

"I believe in the Paramours! Understand?"

His voice rings. I'll never forget that night. Triumph and tragedy. Shrouded in blood, fire, and broken walls.

Elliot...I believe in the Paramours too. I just don't have the patience. And I was a killer long before I met you. There's no going back from that.

My pilot, Anna Marie, cruised an Apache chopper at 200 mph on the way to go and kick the deadliest nest of hornets in the world. We came fully equipped with Hellfire missiles, 30mm cannons, Hydra rockets, M230 chain guns, and my personal favorite, a mounted M2 Browning .50 caliber machine gun. I installed it myself.

As the icy wind scraped against my face, I imagined those whores celebrating with champagne and vodka. It was a job well done. They managed to frame the president and get their puppet in office. And all it cost was the death of one of their own. Or was the First Lady really innocent, collateral damage in their never-ending war on men? Didn't matter.

It was just after sundown as the sky turned dark and powdered with stardust. The snowy slopes of British Columbia looked the same as when Breanne first brought me here way back when I was fifteen. Back when I was nothing but a kitten with no direction, no passion, just a vacuum of bottled up rage. Now, I had passion. I knew exactly where to direct all that rage.

"We're coming up. Five minutes out."

Hector Rodgers was an Army discharge clearly infatuated with Anna. He was on board for one purpose and one purpose only. To jam and hack the Villa's comms system. He had already picked up the signal and began masking our approach. I knew he wouldn't survive the onslaught. Anna insisted on bringing him along, but he didn't have our training, our experience.

As the glow from the perimeter lights got brighter and brighter, Anna and I exchanged a mutual glance. We were wearing gray Navy SEAL combat suits with short sleeves even though it was below freezing. Our pants had kneepads and ample pockets. Our bulletproof vests had built-in spine protectors and our boots were laced halfway up to our knees. We brought duffle bags full of goodies; bombs, guns, ammunition, all that.

Anna had a belt of field knives wrapped around her thighs. When I asked her why, considering firearms should primary, she wouldn't answer. She didn't say anything before liftoff. Just scary silent with this intense focus as if she was already getting shot at.

"Two minutes out. They're gonna see us from the towers." Hector warned.

"Show me the living room," I said as I crawled over to his computer monitors.

He hacked into their camera system and sure enough, an assembly of over forty Swords and associates were all having a ball. I saw creatures in cocktail dresses and casual wear. No diversity in their colors. Everyone was either in black or white. Everyone looked like they just got their hair done, their mani-pedis. And there she was. The center of the universe herself. Breanne Cunningham, one of the Armored Front. One of the Society's elite generals.

I returned and stationed myself behind the machine gun, inhaling that frosty air, visualizing the carnage. I was smiling. I shouldn't be, but I was. A bit wicked of me but still, I was so happy. I've waited so long.

"They spotted us, Canary. I'm about to light it up." Anna shouted, her voice coming through my earpiece.

"Wait!" I said.

"Yo, seriously? These bitches are scramblin'. Jumping over couches and shit. Damn! Who are these people?" Hector shouted.

"I said wait! Take us 'round the towers."

Anna swooped in at a low angle. The sentry guards started firing at us with their submachine guns. The crackle sounded like popcorn. My eyes were peeled. Maybe one or two taps hit the chopper, but not enough to warrant concern. They had stinger missiles and trained snipers in the towers that could've taken us out. So, we needed to hit them first.

There!

With both hands on the grips, I pressed the trigger and man…the .50 Cal tore through the towers as if the stones were made of sugar cubes. Three snipers spilled out of the first tower. I quickly aimed for the second, but they were good. A bullet struck the metal just inches from my face and we were over 150 yards out with a cloud of snowy rotor wash creating a veil. I smirked and returned fire, whittling the tower down to nothing.

Rockets screamed as Anna launched Hellfire and Hydras from the helicopter. The bombardment was spectacular, explosions galore, our declaration of war. Even Hector got on the controls and started shooting from the M230 chain gun. All the cars and limos parked in the driveway, that was Hector's handy work, riddling them like soda cans poked by pencils.

"Anna! The west wing!" I shouted.

She targeted the communications hub on the west wing while I blew out the floodlights. And of course, they had a backup generator that activated five seconds after the blackout. By then, there were bullets coming at us from all directions. Anna was shouting something, but I could barely hear her. My thumbs were squeezing the trigger so hard that they almost got jammed.

In less than a minute, we made the place look like it was caught in a California wildfire. Half of the roof had collapsed. Three out of four towers were destroyed. Bodies were strewn about and everyone was screaming.

BOOM!

The helicopter jerked up and down so violently that my head hit the ceiling. There was a hard tilt so all I saw was the dark sky. And once it started in a tailspin, I was ejected.

I spiraled out of control before my body crashed through a wooden table in the backyard. I felt this intense pain in my hip, and yet, a pistol was still in my hands. I remember chuckling. It was like involuntary muscles took over to aim and fire.

Soon, I was back on my feet, hobbling as I skirted the edge of the pool and picking off ladies who were foolishly blasting shotguns from long-range.

Almost as if "walking it off" course corrected the injuries from the fall, I picked up speed. The pellets that hit me were absorbed by the vest. I darted into the bushes and almost immediately popped back out to hit them with headshots.

"Oh! This bitch!"

A Sword whose name I can't remember came charging at me. She scooped me up by my legs and tackled me backwards into a set of lawn chairs. I rolled on top and put two slugs in her stomach, one in the face.

Whilst still mounted on the dead Sword, I switched from pistol to the ARX battle rifle. Striding low, I shot at anything remotely resembling human. Some were on fire and wounded from the explosions. I ended their pain.

The shattered patio doors were my point-of-entry into the main living room. Fire stretched along the walls, but the living room ceiling remained intact. I went in guns blazing. I saw girls in cardigans carrying vintage Colt revolvers. They were pissed.

I took two shots in the back before spinning to my knees and dropping the girl who was leaping across the pool table. A lamp crashed to my left. I glanced and lit up three Swords who were running my way.

As I raced down a hallway, there were explosions left and right. No one knew what was going on until I opened fire. Then…I saw a flash of black hair before someone shoulder-checked me over the walkway railing. I fell from the 2nd floor and it busted up my shoulder, dislocated. Out of pure rage and adrenaline, I popped it back in place just as Scarlet made her superhero landing.

She swung at me. I leaned back and recoiled so hard that I tumbled down a set of marble steps. My face was bleeding. She managed to land a cut below my right eye.

Scarlet was...a fucking demon. Not fazed in the slightest by the flames or the smoke filing the air. She approached, shaking her head, taunting with, "I knew I should've stomped you out the moment I first..."

She kicked at my ribcage, but I grabbed her leg and used her momentum to swing her down.

"Haha! Seriously?" She chuckled.

It was ridiculous. Through sheer will and superior strength, she stuffed my takedown attempt and shoved me against the wall before throwing a barrage of punches as if she was breaking me down in the corner of the ring.

I managed to side-step and swing my rifle like an ax, popping off shots whenever I had her in front of my muzzle. I kept missing. She slipped, bobbed and weaved better than most pros. Not to mention, I had to shoot at others who weren't about to let us have a one-on-one.

And as we struggled, I kept feeling this burning sting. There were spikes jutting from her knuckle rings. She scratched and punctured with each blow she landed.

"Come on! Where's all that rage!" she jeered.

I grinned. The rage was there. Even with blurry vision and the heat scathing my lungs, I wasn't going to run. Only one of us walks away. I'd have it no other way.

———

"BREACH BREACH!"

BANG

A stun grenade was detonated with a blinding flash and a bang that ruptured the eardrums. A team of soldiers stormed in, and oddly enough, they were men. The fucking hypocrites had a backup unit of soldiers living in an underground bunker not far from the Villa. This was new and unexpected.

The soldiers approached, clueless as to whether I was a friend or foe.

"SHOOT HER!" Scarlet screamed.

Shots rang out but not from them. Anna burst through the flames with her M16 and started gunning them down from behind. When she ran out of bullets, she pulled those field knives and started slicing hamstrings in a violent dance only she could perform. Krav Maga. It was magnificent. She was dropping two at a time, stomping out knees and stabbing necks.

"Fucking bitch!"

Scarlet tackled me again, but this time I shoved her off with my rifle and did my utmost to mow her down. She took off running behind pillars and I gave chase. I could hear Anna shouting my name, but I refused to take my eyes off the target again. Scarlet grabbed an idle pistol and returned fire. I rolled a grenade her way and she went diving into another room.

A bullet whizzed by my ear just as the grenade exploded. It came from my nine o'clock at a high angle. A Sword was up on a walkway with a KSG shotgun. I could barely see her so I knew she could barely see me. I kept moving. Small pops came from the plaster in a straight line just above my head.

I finally posted up behind one of those ugly marble pillars. Taking off my vest, I whipped it to the left. Sure enough, she fell for the decoy and shot at the vest. I peeked out to the right and shot her in the throat.

"AGH!" I groaned as a bullet scraped across my shoulder.

Scarlet...She came sprinting from the kitchen with her Glock. And as soon as she stepped into the hallway, Anna shouldered her into the wall and hip-tossed her to the ground. While they went at it, I checked my six and finished off the soldiers Anna merely wounded with lacerations.

Scarlet was a warrior. I'll give her that. Didn't think anyone could give Anna a run for her money in hand-to-hand combat, but there she was, in the flaming hot kitchen, throwing elbows and knees to the midsection.

Thankfully, Anna was stronger, taller, and more aggressive with a longer reach. Anna blasted her with a furious combination of hooks and uppercuts before sending her sliding across the floor with a back-heel kick to the chest.

Scarlet was drooling with fury as she popped up. She lunged in with that spiked fist. Anna trapped her arm, elbowed her jaw, and picked her up to slam her over the granite kitchen island. Scarlet did this windmill dance to get upright on the counter. And that's when I fired off a round that ripped through her knee.

She unleashed this hellacious scream as she fell on the counter, squirming and writhing like a wounded animal. I shot two more women who came into view while Anna walked over to pick up a butcher's knife. The last I saw was Anna carving into her neck while holding her in a headlock. Scarlet kicked skid marks into the counter with her one good leg until she was no more. I moved on.

Bodies were everywhere. As I moved through the corridor with the stock against my sore pulsating shoulder, I could feel my heart beating like a drum. Orange embers and floating sparks floated in the dark clouds of smoke. I couldn't distinguish between walls and open space. The terrifying sounds of collapse and splintering beams amplified my anxiety. And then...I coughed.

In a flash, a white hand emerged from the smoke and grabbed my neck. I swear it was something out of my worst nightmare. The back of my head hit the wall so hard that my eyes rolled. And out of the smoke came her face like a pale ghost with lifeless blue eyes. I tried raising my rifle, but she easily yanked it away and tossed it down the hall like a mother discarding a toy. Anna was right. Breanne Cunningham was terrifying.

"The Canary and the Andalusian. Two prized pupils. At least they'll say I can sure pick 'em. Only you two could possibly be such...a PAIN IN MY ASS!"

I kneed her in her chest, and she returned with an uppercut my kidneys that hit like a sledgehammer. I wanted to keel over from the pain, but she kept my neck pinned to the wall in that vice-like grip so all I could do was cough up spit and blood, choking on my own saliva.

"I'll tell you what." She said. "Even now with my house burning down all around me. I'm willing to forgive and forget if you two get down on your knees and swear an oath of loyalty to me. Here and now. To obey me with your lives."

"That's all everyone is to you. Aren't they? Just tools!"

Breanne looked down the hall to see someone who stood as tall as she. Scarlet's blood was spackled all over Anna. She let the butcher knife fall from her fingertips before bouncing her brows at Breanne as if to say, "you ready?"

With an emotionless smile, Breanne let me go and faced the Andalusian.

"Get out of here, Gladys. Find Hector and take off." Anna said.

As if Hector was still alive. Before I could respond, Anna and Breanne charged at each other like two lions on the pride. They locked up with handfuls of hair, grappling each other in monstrous bursts of brute strength.

These were the Swords of St. Catherine. I stood in awe of these bare-handed gladiators. Every punch was brutal. I could feel it just by watching. Their long hair whipped in violent jerks and feral grunts. It got to the point where Anna wrapped Breanne by her legs and speared her through a wall that collapsed in behind them.

I tore off a strip of cloth from around my midriff and used it to cover my face from the smoke. Then, squinting my eyes, I ran the other way. Had no idea where I was going. Nothing looked the same anymore. It was like a thick fog of volcanic ash. My only instinct was to follow the direction of the cold draft. It led me up and out onto the 3rd floor veranda of the observatory.

As expected, Hector was dead. His body was pinned under the helicopter. There were survivors crawling in the snow away from the Villa. I was tempted to pick them off one by one, but I didn't. I was trapped high on the 3rd floor veranda with fire closing in. It all seemed so…I don't want to say hopeless. But more so, pointless.

I could hear police sirens.

Then, I saw Anna crashing out onto the back patio deck like a brick thrown through a window. She went rolling across the rubber gripped flooring with Breanne leaping right behind her. Anna struggled to push herself up, but Breanne kicked into her ribcage. I saw the anguish over Anna's face as she let out the most agonizing scream I ever heard.

I still had my ARX battle rifle. I checked the clip. Three bullets left. Had no idea how I was gonna get down from the observatory. The fall would have killed me even if I aimed for the snow. But at least taking out Breanne would have been my parting gift.

With the fire warming my face like an open furnace, I stabled the stock of my rifle against my wounded shoulder. The drying blood served as a convenient cohesive. Turning on my infrared optics, I stared through the scope and aimed at the back of Breanne's head.

Anna unleashed one last burst of aggression, a cross-hook combo that followed with a kick to Breanne's body. The cross landed but Breanne blocked the left hook and before lifting Anna's entire body and slamming her to the floor. She quickly mounted and started raining down punches to Anna's face. And when she clasped both hands on Anna's neck, leaning her weight forward with murderous intent, I fired all three rounds. Breanne's face was no more.

Suddenly the ground beneath my feet jerked in an inverted angle. A satellite mounted on the roof crashed down and almost hit me if I hadn't moved. The access door from whence I came was engulfed in flames so hot that I was getting cooked. Cracks in the pavement webbed out across the walls, and the floor continued to sink in jerking successions.

Then, there was light. A blinding spotlight shined down on me as I looked up. It was another helicopter, dark with no markings on it. I heard the poofing discharge of something being fired...just before a harpoon penetrated my shoulder. My eyes went wide as the strike was unlike anything I had ever felt. I screamed as the harpoon yanked me into the sky with this excruciating pain that caused my legs to shake.

And from there...I blacked out. The last thing I remembered as my limp body banged through branches was the observatory crumbling into a cloud of fiery dust. The Villa was destroyed.

13. Gladys Vandelay – The Truth

The one who shot me with that harpoon and saved my life Jake Buchanan. The Paramours. Don't know how but they managed to find us. Or maybe they knew what we were up to and waited for us to unleash hell before swooping in to clean up.

Anna Marie...while I was brought back to Hollow Rock, their quaint little estate in Derbyshire England...Anna disappeared. Her body wasn't recovered in the rubble. I had no doubt she was alive but in the wind.

...

"And there you have it. That's the truth. That's everything that happened."

Two months after Anna and I went on a rampage that destroyed the Villa and annihilated scores of Swords, I found myself standing before the Paramours in the same auditorium where Elliot and I had heard Lincoln talking about the death of the First Lady. Now, an audience of over 3,000 was listening to my bloody tale. Their disapproval was self-evident.

I stood center stage addressing the Paramours' Senior Council. My body had recovered for the most part, but I still lacked strength in my left shoulder from the harpoon extraction. I was professionally dressed in corporate attire. Befitting, since it felt like I was on trial.

I could tell Col. Jake Buchanan was torn by the loss of Elliot. He knew Elliot had saved my life and that Marcus, in one way or another, saved Anna's. But still...I saw resentment in his gaze.

"Do understand," said Lord Dathan. "While this house does acknowledge the two of you have gone through a great ordeal. We cannot condone the wanton acts of death and destruction."

"Two renegades doing whatever the hell they please with little regard to the consequences," blurted an angry Benaiah.

"And where is the other one!" Alekzander said. "Or would you have us believe you have no idea."

"How many times are you going to ask me that?" I snapped. "I don't know."

Alekzander leaned into Lord Dathan to whisper exactly what the entire assembly soon began to grumble about.

"She killed Breanne Cunningham." I spoke up to say. "One of the Armored Front. She may have been a Sword, but I'd say she's proven she no longer holds any allegiance. Just read her letter. It details their structure, how they operate. She didn't have to do that."

"Be that as it may…" Jake said. "The two of you are killers. That's not the way of Paramours. You know this, Gladys. To the day you die, you will be hunted. Not just by the Swords of St. Catherine, but the CIA, FBI, Interpol. No amount of money, resources, or strategy could ever clear your name. Your best bet is to turn yourself in. Or…stay here forever. We can protect you as long as you…"

"No, thank you!" I had to stop him right there. "I can never be a Paramour, Jake. God knows I tried. I listened to Elliot and all his idealistic drivel. But I…I used to be good. Ten years ago, I never would've guessed that this is the kind of person I'd grow up to be. I used to be so sweet, kind, and innocent. I'd never hurt a fly and would sooner take a flu shot for someone if they were too afraid to take it themselves.

"The Swords of St. Catherine made me who I am. I may not have taken their stupid oath, but I made a promise to Anna. She's alive. I'm going to find her and dedicate my life to hunting down each and every one of the Armored Front, clawing and killing my way to the Living Martyr. This isn't about revenge or justice. It's about purpose. It's the only reason why I'm alive. And if I get killed, so what. That's the way it should be."

"Then you're no longer welcome here," Lord Dathan told me.

"You're breaking my heart," I said before heading for the exit.

…

"Gladys!"

I was halfway down the front steps of the main house heading for my car when I heard Jake's voice. I rolled my eyes. He's been lecturing me almost every other day for the past two months while I was in recovery.

I turned to him. He had his hands in his pockets with those aviator glasses on as if he was still in the military.

"What is it?"

Jake smirked. "And if I get killed, so what? What the hell is that all about?"

"What do you want from me? I said 'sorry' a thousand times."

"Save it. What I need from you is to get over your own shit."

"Excuse me?"

"Gladys...Elliot sacrificed himself to save you. The next time I hear you say some dumb shit like you don't care whether you live or die...I think I might just haul back and hit you like a man."

"Yeah, and you'd break your wrist."

"I'm serious, Gladys. I know life and death might not mean much to a Sword of St. Catherine, but you're not a Sword of St. Catherine. You're not a Paramour either but I'd like to think you have a little bit of Elliot imprinted in you."

"Come on..." I groaned. That's when he hugged me.

"Let me go," I whispered.

"Instead of focusing so much on death...all I'm asking is that you stay alive. Just try." He said before letting me go.

"You owe it to El. And Marcus. Shit, kid. You owe it to me." He said before lighting up a cigar.

"Listen..." He said, glancing over his shoulder. "What if I were to act as your handler. I throw you some bones, you throw me some bones. A liaison of sorts. At the very least, I can warn you when you're in danger and do what I can to back you up."

"Won't your buddies get mad? Never mind. Don't care." I said before continuing down the steps.

"Wait!"

"Come on. I don't have all day." I said, thinking about a lovely little rapist in the Middle East I've been dying to put down.

He sighed as he came down the stairs to catch up to me. "I'm taking a risk by telling you this. Anna Marie. You know she has a younger sister, right? We found her. Working at an aquarium in Tampa Florida. They're talking about bringing her in as a Paramour but, one of our contacts was killed last night while tailing her."

"You think Anna killed your contact?"

"No. I think...I think Anna's sister is in danger. The Society's either waiting for Anna to visit her. Or sooner or later they're gonna kidnap the sister and use her as bait. Maybe even kill her to make an example. Either way, the sister's in danger. You wanna talk about purpose, right? There's your purpose."

...The Perennial War of Paramours...